I'M NOT MUHAMMAD

An *Ordinary* Rendition

JASON TRASK

www.redwheelbarrowbooks.com

Similarities between the events depicted in this novel and 'real life' are intentional. While *I'm Not Muhammad* is a work of fiction, hundreds of 'extraordinary renditions' actually occurred during the Cheney/Bush era. In fact, they continue to this day under the Obama Administration. Despite those similarities, all of the characters in this novel are products of the author's imagination and bear no intentional resemblance to actual persons, living or dead.

Published in 2011 by

RED WHEELBARROW BOOKS
310 West 72nd Street, PH # 2
New York, NY 10023

Many of the passages quoted from the Koran are from the E.H. Palmer English Translation (1880), which is in the public domain. Others are the author's versions (i.e., reworkings of a number of other translations).

Acknowledgements:

Thanks to Amy Farranto, Gary Watkins, David Daniel, Tim Trask, Virginia Valdes, Phil Ferreira, Kevin Daley, Laurent Brondel, Jonathan Laurence, Carl Blanchard, Helen Bray, Byron Hoot, Daniel Trask, Emily Trask, Charles Hayes, Farhad Yusuf, Paola Biola, Michael Isbell, Phil Mace, Peter Wortsman, Kahlil Koromantee, Vanessa Greeley, and the Tamarack Writers—some for editorial advice, some for technical advice/help, others for their encouragement and common sense suggestions.

Thanks to my wife and family for taking patience to the extreme.

Special Thanks to Mark Jay Mirsky for twenty-five years of mentoring, friendship, and encouragement.

"Stiller?" I said. "My name's
not Stiller."

—Max Frisch

It's merely a case of the
chickens coming home to
roost.

—Malcolm X

It's not dark yet, but it's
getting there.

—Bob Dylan

Prologue

"I'm not Muhammad."

I repeated that phrase so many times that even now, though I am dead, it is with me. My rendition was difficult. Dying, on the other hand, came easy. And why wouldn't it. My wife was a course in dying. Every day she made me long for my death. Not in the beginning when she could heat my loins just with a look. But beginnings, like everything else, end.

Look at me—I'm getting ahead of myself, speaking of the end at the beginning. Like it or not, I am ahead of myself. As a dead man, my life is behind me. At this point it's simply a matter of looking back. There's no such thing as the future, or even the present. The only tense relevant for me anymore is the past. Other than that there's just timelessness.

Timelessness, by the way, is not what I'd pictured. I'd awaited infinite time stretching out before me. The fact is, with timelessness there's no time at all. There's not even an absence of time. There's only being. And being doesn't flow as time flows. Being simply is. Not that I expect you to understand this, living as you still are. But keep it in mind. One day it'll come in handy.

Chapter 1

If I'd known her mother had just died, I would have gone out to her when I heard her key in the door. Instead I finished performing *Ishaa*, the fifth and final prayer of the day. I climbed into bed and began reading. Ruth entered the bedroom and stood by the door, her eyes welling. She sighed. And with that thin voice that comes from trying not to cry, she said, "She's gone."

The thing that struck me was, despite her tears, she looked happier than I'd seen her in a while. She looked tired, but beautiful, her eyes magnified as they were by her tears, her face entirely relaxed. There was a confidence about her—she now dared to be vulnerable. All of this was the first clue that she'd betrayed me. But I didn't take it as such.

I told her I was sorry. I put down my book and got out of bed; I went over to her, hugged her. As the hug ended, that's when the second clue came. We were standing now in an open hug, holding each other's arms so that together they formed a kind of circle and we were looking directly into each other. Her tears spilled onto her cheeks as she said, "I have to tell you, Yusuf. Mom's death...I...I made peace with her. Just before she died, I made my peace."

I told her I was happy for her.

"I made my peace with everyone," she said.

I assumed that by "everyone" she meant her family. She watched my reaction as though I was a puzzle she had to solve. She continued: "Something happened to me tonight, Yusuf. I'd like to tell you about it. But will you promise you'll just listen and not judge me?" She was crying now.

"Of course," I said. "Of course I will."

"I..." She sighed as though to dump excess energy. "Tonight I was... I was born again."

My body understood her before I did. I know this because at that point my arms detached themselves from hers. But my mind didn't get it. The funny thing is, I'd been around her family for six years by now, to say nothing of the research I'd done about Christianity. I certainly understood the religious significance of that phrase. But I also understood Ruth well enough—thought I did—to know she couldn't have meant it like that.

While in her teens she had left the Evangelical Christianity of her childhood, thereby straining her relationship to her family. Then, when she converted to Islam and married me, the situation with them grew worse. Publicly they tried to accept her decision. But a sadness ran deep through her family, a sadness of loss that affected Ruth in ways I didn't understand.

What I did know was that when her mother's breast cancer metastasized, Ruth developed a sense of urgency to heal their relationship. It didn't occur to me that the only way she could do this would be by returning to the Christian fold.

I never found out the details of her conversion, because after that night Ruth and I never actually spoke again. But what I picture is *there's her mother lying on her deathbed. She has barely enough breath to maintain her life, but she spends some of this breath telling the rest of the family she would like to speak to Ruth alone.*

Everyone leaves the room, and her mother, with great difficulty, asks Ruth if she's ready to turn her life over to Jesus. It takes all of her strength to tell Ruth that Christ has assured her that she will live to see all of her children in Christ's hands and Ruth is now the only one for whom this isn't true. She says she has faith that now is the time. She asks Ruth if she's ready to make the commitment.

Ruth hesitates. She can't find a way to grant her mother's last request. But neither can she find a way to say no.

Her mother asks if she's going to make a liar of God. She says it with what you'd have to characterize as love.

Ruth is crying. She's weeping. She's practically pleading as she tells her mother that if she were to become a Christian, it would be the end of her marriage.

Her mother says, "If your only reason...for not becoming

*a Christian"—she pauses every few words and gulps in air—
"is that you're worried...how it will affect your marriage...,
then essentially you're saying...you believe Christ's way...to
be the true way..., but that you don't dare take it." Her words
are coming stronger now. She seems reanimated. "And if
that's the case...then you're saying that you don't have
faith...that God can intercede on your behalf...and that He
will work things out. Realize that God will do...what God
does best. He'll make your life perfect. Place yourself in His
hands. And place Yusuf in His hands. Don't forget that
God...has a plan for him as well."*

What ever it was that happened, in the end, her mother
had her way. Ruth said yes and I imagine she knelt beside her
mother's bed and wept and prayed that God forgive her sins,
including, I suspect, the "sin" of Islam.

As I stood there now, I watched her teary cheeks, her
runny nose, watched her wipe them on her sleeve. I was on
the verge of panic and I sought some sign of hope. She raised
her blue eyes bravely to me now. Surely there would be
shame if she meant it as it sounded. She couldn't have meant
it that way. I'd seen no evidence of dissolution of her faith in
Islam. Her devotion to Allah was without question. Nor had I
reason to question her relationship to me. Surely she knew
that leaving Islam would mean leaving me.

Evidently she saw my confusion. With a sigh, she made
her revelation complete. She said it nearly matter-of-factly, as
if that were the only way she could get it out. She said, "Yusuf... Tonight I accepted Christ as my personal savior."

Ruth's face was a mirror—it reminded me what was happening to mine—and she watched as my face morphed into a
kaleidoscope of negative emotions. I don't believe this went
on for more than ten seconds before she burst out crying in a
way I'd never heard her cry before—it was a wailing. I'm
certain we were feeling the same thing at that moment,
namely, that our marriage was over. I didn't feel the pull that
she was feeling, the pull between two irreconcilable worlds.
But I could see in the off-balanced way she now stood that
she was feeling it—the pull of Islam from me; the pull of

Christianity from the still warm ghost of her mother. In that moment, I could see it hit her that she could have all the faith in the world, but there was nothing that was going to make me side against Muhammad (peace be upon him). She held her hands out to me pleadingly, her head bent to one side, a look on her face that would have melted my heart had it not made me furious.

Her statement horrified me, appalled me, saddened me, and more. But accompanied as it was by her imploring, her crying, her outstretched arms, that's where the anger came in. I saw it all as evidence that she was taking advantage of my love for her. Which essentially is what her mother had done to her.

In my fury, I said only one thing to her, and I'm ashamed to say, I yelled it. It was somewhere between a question and a curse: I said—and you'll notice that I used a word that I never use. I said, "So now I'm married to a fucking infidel!"

I attempted to regain control of myself and I moved immediately from her, my arms folded across my chest. I hugged them tightly to me, afraid what they might do. I was actually shaking. I felt betrayed. She might as well have told me that she'd...well, that she'd had relations with another man. I honestly don't believe I would have been any more upset.

You American types—and I'm not sure what I mean by that, since I too am American. But whatever I mean, let me continue: you American types may be judging me for being overly possessive, for thinking I own my wife to the point that her internal decisions are my domain. I'd just like to point out, that when people become Christians, particularly the Evangelical sort, it affects far more than their internal world. Christianity becomes their life.

Now, obviously the same could be said of Islam. But there is a difference. Christians not only begin telling everyone how much Jesus has done for them, how much they love Jesus. They take it further: to prove that what they are saying is true, they place a permanent smile on their faces, a smile that passes for genuine to all except those who truly know them. Unless you've lived with one of these smiling devils, you've no idea how draining it can be. The fact is, I married one woman and got another. Ruth played no less a trick on me than Laban played on Jacob in that story from the Bible—a book, by the way, to which Muhammad (p.b.u.h.) appeals as an authority. Jacob agreed to work seven years for Laban, after which he would win Laban's beautiful daughter, Rachel. But at the end of those seven years, on the morning after the wedding, Jacob realized he'd been given Laban's plain daughter, Leah. And in that moment, he must have felt as I now did—duped.

The day Ruth had converted to Islam, how happy I had been. How perfect the world had seemed. I could now marry her. When we met, Ruth had already left the church of her childhood and essentially was living in the absence of God. In entering the Shelter of Islam, she was re-establishing a connection with the God of her Christian childhood. After all, Allah is the one God, the God of Abraham, the God of the Christians and of the Jews. At the time I felt it selfish of her family to be upset. I wondered why they didn't rejoice at their daughter's reconnection with their God. But now as I stood there listening to her speak of confessing her sins to Jesus, I understood her family's reaction.

One thing I will say for Ruth's family. Though they were sad when Ruth converted to Islam, though they were broken-hearted, they continued to have a relationship with her. I can't imagine what would have happened with my family if I had left Islam. In fact, just marrying an ex-Christian was enough to damage my position in my family. And this even though Ruth had converted to Islam and was as fluent in Arabic as I. The real problem was that she'd been brought up in the home of Christian missionaries who had actively sought to convert Muslims. For my family, nothing could atone for the sins of Ruth's parents.

In fact, my siblings claim our marriage is what killed Mother. They may be right. Two days before her stroke, when Ruth and I went to visit her, Mother held out her arms to me, and as she hugged me, she whispered in my ear, "How could you?" She sniffled a couple of times and then we got on fine until it was time to leave and much the same thing happened. That was the last time I saw her.

Though I did not marry outside the faith, my siblings will tell you that the pressure on Mother of watching her youngest child throw away the teachings of Muhammad (p.b.u.h.) was more than she could bear. The truth is, of all of her children, I'm the only one who took those teachings seriously. Of course, when it comes to playing "the game of Islam," that is, when it comes to making it *seem* as though one is entirely devout, there's no besting my siblings. They insist most vehemently, for instance, on the strictest observance of *halal* dietary practices. These days I'm far more strict about my diet than they ever were. But back then, there were occasions when I would settle for *haram* restaurants—though when I did so, I limited myself to vegetarian dishes, fish, or eggs. You should have seen my siblings react when I mentioned this one day. It didn't matter to them that I always insisted that my food be cooked in its own separate frying pan to ensure that it didn't mix with bacon grease. And it didn't matter to them that I left if the restaurant would not agree to my terms. What mattered to them was that one of their friends might see me, which could prove embarrassing to them.

Please bear in mind that I am not criticizing my family for being overly conservative in their interpretation of *halal* practices. I respect that sort of thing in sincere Muslims. What bothers me is that my siblings care more about appearances than in honoring Allah. When no one is looking, it's a rare day that they kneel all five times toward Mecca. Sure, they'll kneel when other Muslims are around. And they'll kneel when it's convenient. But if they're alone, and "something comes up," prayer times tend to pass by forgotten. Grudges are another matter—grudges they never forget. Following Mother's death, my brothers and sisters would not speak to me for several months. Only Father remained true to me.

By now I'm sure you've guessed that my family is "not from around here." I, on the other hand, am—well, if you believe my family. That's because I'm the only family member born on this continent—in Montreal, actually. We moved to the States when I was six.

I learned English and French while I was learning Arabic, which gave me an advantage over my siblings. Though their English is for the most part accent-free, to this day there is something unidiomatic about the way they phrase things. I noticed this when I was quite young, and I would imitate them when they were mean to me. This upset them because they were also being made fun of at school. They didn't need to hear it from their little brother.

No one ever made fun of my English. Despite that, the only time I ever feel truly American is around my family. As I said, they think of me as the American, a foreigner in their midst. What's odd is that in the things that matter, they're far more American than I. For instance, all they ever think about is money and they've never shown the least bit of interest in ideas. I'm American on the outside only. Not that anyone seems to notice. In fact, one of my fellow students in the graduate program I was in—and this is a guy who was working on his Ph.D. in philosophy—he once said to me, "You don't act like a Muslim." I didn't bother to ask him how Muslims act—to do so would have blown my cover.

More frequently I hear such comments as, "For a guy named Yusuf, you're like so American." I realize that statements of that sort are intended as compliments. But the subtext is, "Thank God you're not like the rest of your people." The fact is I *am* like the rest of my people. I just don't show it. And that's how it is for many of us whose parents arrived here from elsewhere. In public, we pass for Americans. But in our hearts, we're from some far-off land. In my case, Al-Ahwaz. It doesn't matter that I've never actually been there.

I've met only a few non-Arab Americans who have ever heard of the place. Even the CIA agent who abducted me had never heard of it. I've met a few more Americans who know it by its Persian name, the Khuzestan Province of Iran. "Iran?" others ask. "Iran? But Iranians aren't Arabs." In general that's true. In general, Iranians are Persians. But there are several million Arabs living in Iran, and most of them live in the province of Al-Ahwaz—or Khuzestan, if you insist.

It's in the southwestern portion of Iran and was once known as Arabistan. A few older Arabs still call it that, but most of us call it Al-Ahwaz or just Ahwaz. Arabic is no longer the official language there, not since the Iranians, thanks to help from the British, annexed the area in 1925. Then in the 1930s, the Iranians changed the name to Khuzestan.

We have proved a troublesome lot; they hoped to turn us into Persians, hoped to tame us by robbing our home of the name we had given it, and robbing us of our language. To this day, we are forbidden from teaching Arabic in our schools. We are forbidden from publishing newspapers in Arabic, forbidden from wearing certain articles of Arab clothing. Publicly the Persians have succeeded in squelching Arab culture in Ahwaz; privately, however, they haven't come close. We remain Arabs, speakers of Arabic. Like our ancestor Ishmael, an Arab man is a wild donkey of a man, untamed, unbowed, nomadic. The western perspective, of course, is that it is the Arab wife, obediently following in her husband's wake, who must pay for his bravado.

The reality is far more complicated than that and brings us to the heart of why I married an American woman. Okay, I will grant you, the situation is also more complicated than some Arabs would have you believe. A lot of them claim that the man walks ahead of his wife to protect her. But there are, after all, equal dangers from behind. Walking beside one's woman would be the best way to ensure her safety. Many westerners, on the other hand, would have you believe that an Arab man walks ahead of his wife because he believes himself better than she. Both sides are wrong. An Arab man walks ahead of his wife because he wants to show that he can trust her. Or more to the point, he wants to show that his wife is behind him, that she supports him.

What I noticed was that this public support that Arab men demand of their wives comes at a cost. By the time I was in college, I had come up with what I thought of as my own personal discovery, namely, the more a woman feels forced to support her husband in public, the less she will do so in private. I loved Mother as much as any son has ever loved his mother. But I did not want to be married to a woman so much in control as she. In public, she obeyed Father. In private, it was another matter. She knew exactly what to say to embed her nails directly into Father's ego, exactly what to say to get all of my siblings on board—and when necessary, his siblings too. Her siblings were always on board. And with a few exceptions, if it was something she wanted, it was something she got. She couldn't change Father's mind. But she could change his actions. And then she would stand behind him, and as he announced his plans, she would beam with pride.

I decided that public support was not as important to me as private support. It was private support I sought in marrying an American wife. But that is not what I got. At least my mother supported my father in public. In the end, my wife supported me nowhere. Well, nowhere except in death. To this day, I'm told, she continues to support me.

They say life is funny. I assure you, death is funnier still.

* * *

On my way to breakfast, a police car drove up beside me and stopped. The officer got out and asked who I was. My nervousness seemed apparent to me as I spoke my new name: "Muhammad...Muhammad." The way I said it—pausing between the first and last names—it sounded as if I'd said the first name twice.

He told me I needed to come with him down to the station to answer a few questions.

"Officer," I said. "Can I ask what this is about?"

"According to what they told me," he said, "it's just a formality."

"A formality?"

"Yeah. Most likely they have some news for you. Maybe someone's sick—something of that nature. If it was serious, they would'a told me."

His relaxed manner, notwithstanding, I was afraid to get into the car. But given that I'd recently taken on a fake identity, there was nothing I wanted less than inviting scrutiny, and nothing invited scrutiny like not complying. As I got into the car, I wondered if this had something to do with being Muslim. But that was just one of a million questions that were racing through my head.

He drove me down toward the water and pulled the car to a stop outside a warehouse. He beeped his horn and waited while a huge garage door opened. The inside looked as black as a tomb.

I was still new to Seattle, but I had trouble believing that this was a police station. Just as we began driving into the darkness, I had the sense that I was being kidnapped. I felt around for the handle and tried to open the door. It was locked, and when I tried to unlock it, I couldn't. The garage door was closing and I couldn't see a thing.

Out of the darkness, five or six flashlights approached. As they neared, I realized they weren't flashlights, but head lamps, the sort that miners and hikers wear. There was no way policemen would behave in this way, and this convinced me all the more that this was a kidnapping. And because I was so convinced of that fact, I misinterpreted much that happened to me during those early hours.

They opened my door and before they had even yanked me completely out of the car, they'd placed a hood over my head. My hands were cuffed in front of me. All of this happened so quickly that I had no time to react. I was screaming by now, but no one seemed bothered by it. A man on either side of me grabbed me by the arms and dragged me for what seemed like twenty-five or thirty feet. At that point, I heard a heavy metal door open and I was dragged up three or four stairs and into a large cold room that sounded empty. No one had said a word the entire time and they seemed unconcerned by my screams. They got me where they wanted me and I could feel and I could hear someone cutting my pants, belt, and shirt in long and confident strokes. But for my shoes and socks, I was now naked.

By this point I was convinced, as I said, that I was being kidnapped. Demanding my rights seemed futile. Through the hood I could see a flash and hear the click of a camera. Amid adrenaline-pumping fear, I was trying to piece together who my kidnappers might be. Someone must have discovered that I had a lot of money. Who knew I had money? And who would they ask for ransom? I worried that they would call Ruth and ask her. If that were to happen, it wouldn't end well. She thought I was dead.

Someone pulled my legs apart—I was still standing at this point—and someone pushed my head down and bent me over. I felt someone insert something into my anus. I'd had diarrhea all night long, and as they did this, I nearly had an accident. I was still screaming, and they continued to act as if they couldn't hear me. They didn't ask me to be quiet or react in any noticeable way. After that, they pulled me up by my arms so that I was standing again. I tried to put my feet back together, but the men who were holding my arms each had a foot on one of mine. I could feel them unfolding something between my legs and they were lifting it up toward my crotch. It felt soft and dry. It came up over and around my waist and was tightened there. I remember thinking it was a diaper. But why would they put a diaper on me? They took off my handcuffs long enough to put me into another set of clothes, a one piece jumpsuit that felt as if it was made of canvas.

So far, no one had hurt me or caused me any sort of pain. But I was extremely afraid and I was beginning to feel dazed.

After they'd cuffed my hands again, they cuffed my legs with what must have been regular handcuffs—I couldn't separate my feet by more than an inch. It was about then that I began feeling incredibly relaxed and I realized they had administered a tranquilizer through my anus. I had already been off balance because of the hood that was over my head. But now I had no sense of which direction was up. Men on either side of me grabbed my arms and more or less carried me a short distance. At that point someone picked up my legs until I was lying horizontally in space—completely in their power.

They lowered me into what I soon found out was a wooden box, a coffin of sorts. They didn't drop me or anything like that. In fact, they placed me down rather gently. I could feel them raise the handcuffs on my ankles as far up my shins as they could get them, and they removed my socks and shoes.

The panic was gone as the drug took over and I simply relaxed and let them do as they wanted. I remember hearing the lid being closed and at least three latches were fastened. I lay there in absolute darkness wondering whether this was real. Then I remember hearing a humming that sounded like the electric forklifts my father kept at our warehouse near Newark, and sure enough, a few seconds later, I could feel that I was being lifted into the air and driven a few yards and loaded onto a flat-bed truck. But I wouldn't figure that out for a few more minutes. It felt as if I was dreaming now and I had no unpleasant sensations. The only fear I felt was in my head. My body was completely at ease.

I remember lying there feeling as if I was surrounded by cotton batting, as if the entire world had somehow softened. The noises of the men working on my box seemed distant and I remember wondering what they were doing. A truck engine started, and I could tell that it was a diesel engine and I could feel it vibrating. I could feel that we moved a few feet and when we stopped, one of the brakes squeaked. There was a long screeching noise and then we drove again. I'd been in their custody for less than fifteen minutes and they had me completely in their control. Nor did I know who these people were or what they wanted from me. Not one of them had said a single word. I'd screamed, but I hadn't actually spoken. It hadn't even occurred to me to speak—the entire event was unspeakable.

It was October 27, 2001 and for the second time in six weeks, everything had just changed.

Chapter 2

Just as marrying Ruth may have killed Mother, losing Ruth to Christianity may have killed Father. He had uncharacteristically stood up to Mother regarding our marriage—and I suspect that behind the scenes this caused him a good deal of personal pain. When Mother complained about Ruth retaining her maiden name, Father reminded her that in Arab countries women usually keep their maiden names. When she complained that Ruth was older than I, Father reminded her that the Prophet (p.b.u.h.) had married a woman fifteen years his senior, whereas I was marrying a woman only two years mine. Father even stood up to Mother when Ruth decided to wait before having children. Then when Mother died, he eventually persuaded my siblings to accept me back. But when Ruth returned to Christianity, that was more than he could handle. I think at that point he began to suspect that Mother had been right, that in siding against her, he had contributed to her death.

He was the first person I called to tell of Ruth's conversion. In fact, the very next morning, after Ruth had left to grieve with her family over her mother's death, I called Father. It was the hardest call I've ever made, harder even than the one to Mother telling her that Ruth and I intended to marry.

Not long after Ruth buried her mother, I buried my father. And when that happened, my siblings buried me. My actual funeral didn't come until three years later. But as far as my siblings were concerned, I died when Father died, because in their eyes I had killed both of my parents. They even tried to keep me from my share of the inheritance. I reminded them, however, of the verse from the Koran: "Whoever alters a will after hearing it shall be accountable for his crime. God hears all and knows all." I doubt if they even understood the verse, but they fear the Koran. Of course their reason for fearing it is so that they don't have to think about it, and thus they pretend to themselves that they have the greatest respect for it. At any rate, out of fear they allowed me my entire share, and that, I must say, has made for a comfortable death.

I did not insist on a divorce from Ruth. After all, Muhammad (p.b.u.h.) is quoted in the *Hadith* as saying, "Of all which is permitted, divorce is most hated in God's sight." And Ruth made no attempt to divorce me. In her church, the Church of the Nazarene, divorce is frowned upon. Of course the church also reminds its members of the New Testament verse, "Be ye not unequally yoked," another way of saying don't be married to non-Christians. Together, those two ideas create a kind of schism. In fact, we knew of a Nazarene woman—and like my wife, she too was a clergyman's daughter—who, rather than bring shame upon her family by getting a divorce, enlisted the services of her new lover, and together they killed the man whom she had promised to love and to honor until death them did part. In a sense she kept her vows. After my wife's and my de facto split, that story sometimes drifted through my head. And though I wished at times that my wife would commit a similar act, I knew that luck of that sort would never be visited upon me.

Though our marriage was fractured, we continued to live in the same house. I didn't speak to her unless something needed to be said or unless we were in the presence of others who didn't know. For instance, we didn't tell our neighbors, though it wouldn't surprise me to learn that they knew. If Fred, our next door neighbor, showed up at our house for some reason, Ruth and I would sit together and talk to him and during those conversations we behaved as a couple. But as soon as he left, it was back to silence.

I told no one about what had happened between us. By this time I no longer had a relationship with my family and I am not in the habit of sharing personal information of that sort with non-family members. And as far as I've been able to tell, Ruth told no one but her family. It was a secret we shared.

Now, the funny thing about a secret is that when you share it with someone, it draws you closer. And oddly, our secret had that effect on us. But it's also true that when you feel close to someone and are too proud to admit it, at that point your closeness becomes reconstituted into something mysterious, something unnamable.

We felt close, but we didn't speak unless it was necessary, and usually it wasn't. The bulk of our talking concerned household logistics, but even those conversations we kept to a minimum. Actually, I shouldn't say "we." I should say "I." She would have spoken and in the beginning she did. But she gave in when she saw that if she continued trying to get through, I would merely leave the house for several days.

When we passed each other on our way to the bathroom or kitchen, I wouldn't even look at her, wouldn't so much as grunt. It was as if she didn't exist. And there we were the only two in the house. And yes, I now realize how stupid I was—even at the time I had a sense of it.

We lived separate existences. We paid for our cell phones separately. We did our banking separately. I considered it possible when our split first occurred that she would seek a divorce. So when my father died, I hid my inheritance in an offshore account. I'm sure she suspected I had inherited something—my father had a lot of money. But she never asked about it. For one thing, she knew I wouldn't answer her.

We also kept a joint account to which we both contributed each month and from which she paid the joint bills. We paid for our own food separately just as we cooked separately and ate in separate parts of the house. In the beginning, she tried to cook for me. I, of course, refused to touch the food she had prepared, though I knew that she continued to cook *halal*—she left the wrappers lying around for me to see. I would go to the kitchen, find a plate of food that was far better than anything I could have prepared, food that had most certainly been prepared with love. How—or why for that

matter—I mustered the will power to refuse it I'll never
know. Actually, I think I do know—and this is one of the few
things I'm proud of with regard to my treatment of her. I
didn't want her to demean herself by cooking for me. There
was definitely stubbornness on my part, but there was more:
in not accepting what she had cooked for me, I was looking
out for her in my own way. I didn't want to take advantage of
her; I didn't want to use her. I would ignore the meal she had
prepared and fix myself something that, when I was lucky,
tasted half as good as what she had left for me. I'll say this
for myself. Even at my lowest, I usually looked out for her. I
just didn't want her to know it.

She continued to leave these plates for me for close to a
year—always at dinnertime. Often they were accompanied by
desserts. And not just any desserts. She had learned to bake
pie when she was twelve and she was forced by her parents to
return to the States to live with her grandmother. These were
the sorts of pies that fortunate people taste three, maybe four
times in their lifetimes, pies with crusts which were not only
flakey and tender, but impregnated with the taste and the
smell of butter. These desserts too, I turned down, or at least I
pretended to. The fact is, I would sometimes shave a sliver
off the piece of pie she had cut for me, and I would supple-
ment it by shaving a slightly larger sliver off the rest of the
pie, still in the pan. I would do this with care that may have
equaled that which she put into baking the pie. I suspected
she knew what I was up to when she began leaving a sharp
knife out, which I always washed and dried and placed exactly as I had found it. This dance I found strangely exciting.

At the very beginning of our split, we would frequently
show up in the kitchen at the same time. When that would
happen, I would leave until I could hear that she had finished.
Then I would wander out and get myself something to eat.

It was easy in the morning. She always ate before I did
because she left for work by six. I, on the other hand, was
writing my dissertation—at least I was supposed to be—and I
spent most of my day at home at the computer. So generally
I'd get up after she left, and get myself breakfast. Lunch was

not a problem because she was at work. Dinner was where complications arose. But after several weeks, I had figured out her schedule to the point that I could avoid her altogether. After dinner, she'd wait until she heard me bring my plates to the kitchen to bring hers out. It was our time to be together. Fifteen seconds of quality time—some times twenty. We wouldn't say a word, but it was still our time.

Actually, I'm exaggerating—I can feel myself trying to hide the following admission. The fact is, strange as it may seem, Ruth and I continued to share a bed. I don't know if it's strange, but as I'm describing it, it certainly sounds strange to me. At the time, it honestly didn't. During our actual marriage, we had always slept in the same bed. Even when we had fights, we always slept in the same bed. And that's how it was the night she betrayed me. That night it didn't occur to me to leave or to sleep in another part of the house. A week or so later, I remember asking myself why I didn't just find a different place to sleep. I could have easily moved to the upstairs bedroom that had been set aside for the baby that we'd intended one day to make. We had a fold-out couch up there and I would have been perfectly comfortable. Or why didn't I just move out? As I said, I had plenty of money. I could have easily afforded a house or condo of my own. For that matter she could have afforded one as well, what with the job she had. Her reasons for not leaving I understand better than my own. She was a Christian and felt she had made a vow to me that she intended to keep. But none of that applied to me. For Muslims, though divorce is frowned upon, it is definitely permitted. The rules for getting a divorce are as easy for a Muslim as for anyone. But I never considered getting a divorce. I guess the truth is, I feared that Ruth would try to get one and that she would leave me and meet someone else. My behavior would suggest that I didn't want her myself, but that's not what I felt in my heart.

There were some interesting problems with sleeping in the same bed. If our legs happened to touch in the night, most of the time I would move mine away. She always left hers put. This gave her the territorial advantage. Sometimes I would find myself crowded on the edge of the bed and I would say, "You're on my side." She always moved. I suspected she was pleased to hear my voice, but that's probably my ego talking.

I knew that she was trying to "win me back," trying to "win me to the Lord." Both of those were phrases I'd overheard her use to her sisters on the phone. That made me hold back even more. For the most part. But there were times during which I would wake in the night and I would hear her breathing beside me, would feel the warmth of her body just inches from mine. And I would be overcome with the knowledge that she would receive me if I made even the slightest move in her direction. On some of those nights I would be so aroused that I would feel I couldn't stand it. I would picture myself reaching out to touch her back or her shoulder and I would picture her responding with love.

In truth, this happened fairly often. Actually, it happened in cycles. Most of the time I was able to resist. But there were times when I would lose my resolve and my hand, on its own, would reach out and touch her leg or begin rubbing her back and she would roll toward me and we would love each other like we did the night we were married.

In the morning I would wake up entirely ashamed of my weakness. She would smile and say "Good morning" to me, and I would act tired and simply grunt in return—which was more than I wanted to do. She would come over and hug me and I would half-heartedly respond, all the while furiously churning my mind to keep from developing an erection. I couldn't simply push her away after she'd saved me in the night from my despair. But neither did I want her to know the effect she had on me. Later she would leave for work and I would ask Allah to forgive my weakness. When she would return home that night, I would have resumed my silent stance. I would feel terribly guilty. But somehow I could not humble myself and accept her back. Ruth would simply smile her Christian smile of forbearance.

The funny thing is, when I met her, she was as far from forbearance as it gets. Even during her Muslim phase, the patience she demonstrated didn't rise to the level of forbearance, or stoop to it, if you will. Forbearance was her mother. Her mother was Mrs. Forbearance, or so she would have you believe. In her mother, it always seemed put on, superimposed. And to a degree that became true of Ruth. Maybe if she had just come home and screamed at me and told me I was full of shit—which is what she would have done back in the day—maybe then things would have gotten back on track.

In her day she was the most independent woman I have ever known. And that's why I fell in love with her. I always felt as if she was the woman who could keep me honest. The woman who would make me want to be my best. But somehow she had migrated into a woman who practiced forbearance. It was a tragedy. Scream at me, Woman. Tell me what you think. Tell me what you need. Instead, she just suppressed everything. And here she was, the woman who as a teenager had left the fold and had let her parents know there would be no turning back. How could forbearance have happened to her?

At any rate, nearly every time we made love, it usually happened two nights in a row, even though, hours before, I would have resolved that it would never happen again. But there I would find myself, the very next night, awake in the wee hours. I'd be lying there, tempted, but I'd be convinced that this time I would resist the temptation. But there goes my hand, all on its own, and we're off and running. It never happened three nights in a row. Nor did it happen again within a week or even a month. I could always control myself for another two or three months, at which point the cycle would begin anew.

* * *

After we'd been driving for a few minutes, I believe I fell asleep. I don't know how long it was before I woke up, but when I did, I had a headache. After that, I remember lying there, still feeling relaxed and seeing blackness, smelling the wood of the box, hearing the whine of the tires and the engine and occasional horns. Once I heard a siren. But my predominant sense was of a head ache and of my body bouncing up and down and landing against the wood.

Lying there I had a sense that something was missing. It seemed as if something very close to me had vanished. What was it? After that a warmth spread through my heart and I remembered Allah, remembered that Allah was in control of this universe, remembered that there was not a single incident that He did not see, not a single incident that happened that He did not allow to happen. I was in Allah's hands. If Allah Himself had placed me in that box, I would have nothing to fear. And since Allah had seen that I had been placed in that box, and since Allah knew what was in the hearts of the men who had placed me there, and since He knew that I was one of His own, and since Allah could have prevented it if He had wanted, I knew I had nothing to fear. I could feel the fear slowly drift away and I felt as if I was lying on the foundation of all Being and that nothing bad could happen to me. Even in death I would be protected.

A passage from the Koran came back to me: "There is no God but Allah, the Ever-living, the Self-subsistent. Slumber overtakes Him not, nor sleep. All that which is in the heavens and in the earth belongs to Him. Who is it who intercedes with Him save by His permission? He knows what is before them and what is behind them, and they comprehend nothing outside His knowledge but what He pleases. He reigns over the heavens and the earth, and it tires him not to guard them both, for He is the Most High, the Great."

I felt comforted though I lay there in darkness in the hands of infidels I did not know. I did not have to know them. Allah knew them, and I knew Allah. I was safe and I felt courage in my breast.

Up until now, we had stopped a number of times—I assume at stop signs and red lights. But after we drove around a long corner, I could tell by the whine of the tires that we sped up significantly and I realized we were on a highway. A few minutes later we slowed down and went around another long corner and once again I could hear a lot of cars and horns. After a few minutes of this, we turned and drove off by our-selves before coming to a stop. For the first time, I heard voices, though I could not hear what anyone was saying.

Apparently they had no forklifts on this end. I heard the men climb up onto the bed of the truck and I could feel them lift the box I was in. Instead of maintaining the box's hori-zontal attitude, they lowered one end first—the wrong end. I was in effect standing on my head. I didn't have enough room to protect my head with my arms, and all of my weight pressed onto my right ear. I heard someone laugh and say, "I think his head's down there."

"Ooops," said another. More laughter.

One of the men jumped down and I could feel my head being raised until my body was close to horizontal and then someone took the other end of the box and they lowered both ends simultaneously until I was lying flat on the ground. At that point, a discussion began. There must have been air holes in the box, because I was able to follow parts of what they were saying.

"So are we shipping him in the box? Is that how they do it?"

"Search me. Like I said, this is all new to me."

"I don't see how we can keep him in the box," said a third voice. "There's no way that box will fit through the door. And we can't put him in the luggage compartment—it's probably not even pressurized."

"I don't know—it might be. But Peirce should be here soon. He's the man with the plan."

After that, I assumed they had wandered off. I heard foot-steps fade and then nothing. I must have fallen asleep again until I heard a shout from a distance and someone close to the box answered. I didn't know what they were talking about so none of it made sense to me. All I know is that a couple min-utes later, a car drove up and someone got out and stepped over to the box.

"No problems?" someone asked.

"Nope. It went pretty well."

"Okay, then. I guess we'll have to take him over behind

that wall."

I could hear the other men approaching now.

One of them said, "Hey, let me have one of those. I left mine in my car."

I suspected they were smoking. For a second, I felt an emptiness and a hunger for a cigarette, but then I remembered that I had Allah and my longing went away. I realized that the only way I could get through this was to keep my mind on Allah. It provided a kind of inoculation that I could not afford to be without.

"What's the plan?" one of the men asked.

"We've got to get him over behind that wall. After the plane arrives, we'll take him out of the box. I spoke to the pilot and he says he can taxi right up to the wall. He's flown out of here before and he's the one who suggested the wall."

"So he'll be flying inside the plane?"

"Sure. We don't want him dying on us. You know how I hate paperwork."

They all laughed.

Chapter 3

Until we married, we were both in grad school. She had been working on her MBA at NYU; I, on my Ph.D. at CUNY. Just before our wedding, she completed her degree and returned to Morgan Stanley where she had been an analyst between college and business school.

I found it difficult to believe that someone like Ruth would study business. She struck you more as the artistic type, or possibly the crusader type. I could imagine her as a lawyer working for the ACLU. Or as a sociologist working for an agency to help the poor. But the more I got to know her, the more her business degree made a kind of sense.

She had this unbelievable love of America, this belief that America, through capitalism, had the potential to create and distribute wealth around the world, wealth that could be spread to every village, to every human being. She claimed she'd seen it happen a number of times, had seen people's lives change, had seen entire villages go from hand-to-mouth existence to a healthy existence, had seen an influx of money end hunger, poverty, disease, and that this was the promise that America held for the world. It didn't take much money to make a huge difference, she claimed. A new well in the center of a village with a working pump could mean the difference between life and death for the people and their animals. She'd talk like this anywhere, in front of anyone and even the most jaded New Yorkers would refrain from rolling their eyes. Her optimism was contagious.

She was the daughter of Nazarene missionaries. She was born in Tanzania. She grew up in a small town just east of Mount Kilimanjaro. As a small child, she spent her days outside playing with Tanzanian kids, and like them, for the most part, she'd be dressed just in her panties. In the middle of playing, if she felt the urge to pee, she would step to the side, pull down her panties and pee. Then she would resume play just as the other kids did. She was a wild child, and that element came across to me when I first met her, in spite of her religious upbringing and her western education. We had only been dating a month, in fact, when we walked over to the Columbia campus after a party on the Upper West Side. We were sitting on the steps by the statue of Alma Mater. It was about two in the morning, and she'd had several beers—this was before she converted to Islam. Matter-of-factly she said she had to pee. "You dare me to pee right here?" she said.

I told her I did. She had on a dress. She hitched it up a bit, pulled her panties aside—but she managed to do this in a completely modest manner—and she peed right there beside me. We watched the golden stream run down the steps and we laughed our heads off. It was at that moment that I realized I was in love with her. I'd never met a freer spirit. And yet mixed with it, there was a very proper young lady. No matter what I tried—and I admit that even though I was committed to Islam, there were a number of times that I did try—there was no convincing her to sleep with me before the night of our wedding. She moved in many directions at the same time. But after her backslide to Christianity, she moved in only one.

When she was six, her parents moved to Sudan where her wild-child nature continued to flourish. But as she grew older, her parents worried about her and when she turned nine, they sent her away to a boarding school attended by the children of Europeans and Americans. She rebelled there and during her first year she was kicked out for refusing to wear shoes to class. After that, her parents home-schooled her, but when she was twelve, her mother caught her making out with a fourteen-year-old Sudanese boy. Within a week, she was on a plane to America to stay with her grandmother. She didn't rejoin her family until they relocated to Thailand later that year. By that time, she was already completely fluent in Swahili and Arabic. In Thailand she learned two more languages, Thai and Khmer. Her father ran a church school for Cambodian Refugees. By the time she was eighteen, she had developed native fluency in seven languages, five of which were associated with the developing world. This, of course, is why Morgan Stanley was so anxious to hire her for their Emerging

Markets Index.

While she would be at work in the World Trade Center, I would be at home supposedly writing my dissertation about the influence that Averroes, the medieval Muslim philosopher, had on Christianity, not only through his resurrection of Aristotle, but also through his direct impact on Aquinas. It had been going slowly, and I spent much of my time on elaborate projects that spared me from my dissertation.

At one point, I realized I needed a new desk. I shopped extensively for the perfect one. Soon I realized that the only way to get the desk I had in mind would be to build it. This of course, required that I design it. Before I could do so, I needed to learn about the types of joints available to me— dovetail, hidden biscuit, lap and dado. This project cost me three months all together. Then there was the time I realized that my car needed a new clutch. Though my knowledge of cars was limited, and though I had enough money to buy a brand new car, or for that matter, enough to buy a garage and hire a full-time mechanic, I decided it was important that I change the clutch myself.

There's a reason that people with Ph.D.'s have such global knowledge. The act of avoiding one's dissertation is an education in itself.

* * *

After a while, someone turned on a radio and I could hear it fairly well. They had it tuned to KZOK, Seattle's classic rock station, and I remember hearing that song by the Doobie Brothers, "Takin' It to the Streets," the first song that Ruth and I ever danced to (or I should say, that's the way I remember it). It got me thinking about her and thinking about how I should have just gone home after Ruth's and my near-death experience, how I should have thanked Allah that He had brought Ruth and me back together again. I decided now that I'd been a fool. I decided now that I'd followed not the will of Allah but the will of Yusuf.

I lay there in the box crying as I thought about the pain I

had put Ruth through. And now I was feeling that pain as well. I cried about how cold I had been to her following her return to Christianity. I cried about how much she had loved me, how much she had stood by me. I cried about how much she had continued to love Allah, and even though she loved Him as a Christian did, now as I lay there, that difference seemed unimportant to me. I knew that Islam was the best path to Allah. But what was wrong with her taking a second-best path? As long as it was a path to the one God, what difference did it make? Was that not what the Prophet (p.b.u.h.) had taught when he spoke of the People of the Book? Was not the second best path to Allah better than no path at all? Allah was Allah regardless of how one tried to reach Him.

I cried at the thought that I might never see her again, and I vowed to myself and I vowed to Allah that if I ever got home again, if it were His will I would return to her and confess my love for her and beg her to forgive me.

The drugs, no doubt, vivified my imagination. I lay there between waking and sleeping, picturing so vividly how it would be when and if I saw her again that I grew confused when I heard a plane take off on a nearby runway. After that, I must have fallen asleep. All I know for sure is that at a certain point I realized the men were standing around the box and I didn't recall hearing them walk over to it.

It was thoroughly black inside the box, and I wondered if there might be a crack in it somewhere through which I could see a little light. By now, I had forgotten that I had the hood over my head and I began moving my head around as much as I could in search of the slightest morsel of light. At some point as I stretched my neck around, the hood rubbed against my face and I realized the futility of my search.

I can't tell you how confused I was and how my mind was racing to figure out what was going on. Then the men picked up the box and moved it—I guessed over by the wall. When they did so, I thought this would mean that they'd be taking me out of the box soon, but they just put me down and we waited some more. Another hour must have passed before I heard a plane approaching. The men moved me again and I could hear that the plane was very close. Its engines powered down and I heard the latches of my box open. I had expected to be able to see, but once again I remembered that my mask kept me one further remove from reality.

I could feel someone removing the cuff from my right leg and putting it onto the left leg so that now both cuffs were on my left leg. I guessed rightly that this was to enable me to walk. Two men lifted me by the tops of my arms and up over the sides of the box and let me down until my feet made contact with the tarmac. The ground felt hard and cool on my bare feet and my body felt heavy—I was glad the men were holding me up.

They walked me over to a short flight of stairs and when we came to the top of it, one of them pushed my head down, apparently so I wouldn't bang my head. Then one of them walked ahead of me and one behind me, still holding my arms so that I had to walk sideways down what I assumed was the narrow aisle of the plane and they sat me in a seat.

The seat was unbelievably comfortable. I felt as if I'd stumbled onto a private luxury jet, which I would later find that I had. The seat was wide and deep and it felt as if it was covered in supple leather. One of my captors now unbuckled one of the cuffs on my left leg and rebuckled it onto my right leg. Then he buckled my seatbelt and I could hear that he seated himself across the aisle from me.

You may be wondering why I still hadn't said anything to them. On the one hand I felt this stubborn Arab portion of myself that didn't want to give them the pleasure of hearing me speak, didn't want to give them the pleasure of knowing that I was afraid. By speaking it seemed to me that I would be acknowledging that they had power over me. But in addition, there was a completely different part of myself that was afraid that if I spoke, things would go worse for me. All I know for sure was that both sides of me, or perhaps more accurately, two sides of me, were against the notion of speaking, so up until now I hadn't said a word.

But once again, I felt the presence of Allah spreading across my chest and I felt that He was with me and that I had no reason to be afraid. It was at that moment that I said to the man sitting across from me, "What's this all about? Why are you taking me?"

I heard someone snort and someone else said, "What did he just say?"

I answered the question myself: "What I said was, 'What's this all about? Why are you taking me?'"

"Why?"

"Yes, why?"

"That's a good question."

"I thought so," I said. I could hear an unmistakable strength in my tone.

There was some laughter, and I remember thinking they were trying to deny my strength—that it made everything easier to deny it—and then they seemed to go back to their own conversation.

I pressed on. "What did I do?" I was still under the assumption that I was being kidnapped, but I wanted them to believe that I thought they were the police. My thinking was that if I acted like I knew they were kidnappers, it would be tantamount to admitting that I had a lot of money.

"What did you do?" asked the man. "I was hoping you'd tell us. So, yeah. What did you do?"

"I don't know what I did," I said.

"Well, if you don't, who does?" one of them asked with a tone of mock concern.

Two of the others were laughing. I couldn't tell how many there were in all. Three? Four? Five?

"Who do you think I am?" I asked.

"Man, is this guy good or what? He already knows our questions."

"I think he might be one of those gifted and talented types—what do you think?"

"I didn't do anything," I said. "This is some sort of mistake."

"We made a mistake?" he asked. "Hey, guys. D'you hear that? We made a mistake. He didn't do it."

Their laughter had an odd slant to it. I took this to mean

that they knew that I was trying to lead them away from the fact that I had money.

And when one of them said, "I assure you, the mistake was yours," an odd ironic quality in his voice made me even more confident that my hypothesis was correct—they were kidnappers.

"I promise you," I said. "I'm really serious. I don't know who you think I am, but I promise you, I didn't do whatever it is you think I did." I decided I'd do my best to confuse them.

"What do you think we think you did?"

"I don't know."

"If that's the case, how can you be sure you didn't do it?"

"Because I didn't do anything that's against the law or anything like that."

"What makes you think we're the law?"

After that, there was no longer any question for me. I was being held for ransom—I was convinced.

"I don't know," I said. "I can't imagine who else you would be."

"Sounds to me like you have a guilty conscience if you think the law is after you."

"Well, are you the mafia?" I asked.

"The mafia? What would the mafia want with you?"

"I don't know. I can't figure out what anyone would want with me."

"You mean no body likes you? You poor thing."

More laughter. Another one said, "Do yourself a favor and don't concern yourself with who we are. Concern yourself with who you are."

Something about the way he said this made me question the kidnapping scenario. Maybe this was about my fake passport. Could it be that these guys were customs guys? I remembered again that I was supposed to have memorized all of the information regarding my country of origin, etc., that had come with my fake social security card and passport. I hadn't done that. I'd intended to look at it before traveling to Seattle, but then upon arriving, I told myself that I would do so before I flew again. So maybe this had something to do with my supposed country of origin. Maybe they were going to return me there."

"Are you guys customs agents?"

"Customs agents? What makes you think we're customs agents?"

"Yeah, are you a Mexican?" someone said to laughter.

Trying to sound Mexican, another one said, "He don't sound like no wetback."

"I think I know what this is about," I said.

"He thinks he knows what this is about."

"Well, good. So what's it about?"

"It's about a passport."

"A passport?"

"Yes."

"What about a passport?"

"A fake passport."

"Are you saying you have a fake passport?"

"Yes," I said.

"You could go to jail for that sort of thing," said one of the men. It was followed by laughter.

At about this time, the plane's jets started and after some initial racing of the engines, we taxied toward the runway and soon we took off.

The door to the pilot's compartment must have been open because I could hear them speaking on their radios.

After we were in the air I simply sat there in silence and listened to my captors as they played a game of cards. I was constantly on the verge of falling into despair. But I would remember that Allah was with me and was watching over me and I would relax and feel completely at home. Finally, I felt with my hands, both hands, handcuffed as they were, for the button to recline my seat and I pushed the button and leaned back.

As they continued their game, I lay there listening to them and after a while I fell asleep. I don't know how long I was out, but it didn't seem like more than a few minutes. When I woke up, I had to pee.

"Hey, can I use the bathroom?" I asked.

"No," came the answer.

"I've got to go really bad," I said.

"So, go then. No need for the bathroom."

"Yeah," said another. "Just go in your diaper."

I had no desire to entertain them further. I found the button again, and put my seat in the upright position. Changing my position helped me not have to go as badly. This worked fairly well for close to an hour. The men were ending their game and they seemed restless to me, but it could have been projection on my part.

By now I had determined that there were four men accompanying me. One of them had walked toward the back of the plane and two of the others were across the aisle, not saying much. I wasn't sure where the fourth man was. The only surprising thing that happened during this time was when the man at the back of the plane came forward, he put his hand on my shoulder as he walked past. He didn't say anything, but I realized it was his way of comforting me. At least one of them had a conscience, and that made a difference.

By now I had to go to the bathroom so badly that I knew I couldn't hold out any longer. Every moment required concentration to keep it from just happening on its own. My penis seemed to have shrunk to half of its normal size and there was a sting at the base of it that completely enveloped my consciousness. I finally accepted that I had no idea where I was being taken, or how long I would be. Eventually I would have to go. The sooner I went, the sooner the pain would cease. I relaxed the iron grip I had on my bladder, and when I did, I felt extremely happy. Going in my pants felt surprisingly familiar, exactly as I had expected it would. The only difference was that I had dreaded that the initial warmth would turn cold. But trapped as it was in my diaper, it stayed warm and was not uncomfortable. What was uncomfortable was trying to hold in the diarrhea I'd been suffering from since the previous night.

Chapter 4

By 2001, our marriage had been over for three years. One Tuesday morning at about seven thirty, I sat at my computer to check my email. We still had a dial-up modem in those days and I had my finger on the "enter" key. If I had hit it one second sooner, I would no doubt still be among the living, miserable as ever. Hitting that key would have prevented Ruth's call from coming through. As it was, I paused and the phone rang. I didn't answer it. I listened as Ruth left a message pleading that I pick up the phone, that she had left her cell phone at home and couldn't return for it because of a meeting. She said that as soon as the meeting was over, she had to call a client. There was a lot riding on this call, and the only place she had the number was in her cell phone. Could I please pick up the phone and talk to her.

I listened as she spoke to me, and I felt sympathy for her situation. As it happened, the previous night had been night one of our periodic two-night ritual, and despite myself, I found myself looking forward to tonight in bed. Part of me was announcing loudly to the rest of me that this time it would be different, that tonight, I would find the means to withstand the temptation. But most of me knew I was just talking.

I continued to listen as she asked if I would find her cell phone and call her back. She said she hated to bother me, but she didn't know what else to do. All she needed was for me to find the number and read it to her over the phone. She thanked me and hung up.

I found her phone in the upstairs bathroom. All I knew for sure was that I didn't want to call her. I was wishing I'd answered the phone when it first rang, before I'd heard her voice on the answering machine. Answering the phone after hearing her voice was more cooperative than I cared to appear. And calling her back was not something I wanted to subject myself to either. No, rather than call her, I decided I would take the phone to her office and simply drop it off with Flo, her secretary. Later when she thanked me, I would tell her I'd been on my way to Adham's anyway, Adham, the owner of a Muslim bookstore near the Trade Center. It was true, I had ordered a book from him, and there was a chance it had arrived. The main thing was, I didn't want her to think I'd gone out of my way for her.

As I thought about this, I looked at my watch. It was seven thirty, which meant Windows on the World had just opened. I decided to bring my laptop along and have breakfast there. They served a great breakfast and I felt that the exhilarating view might be the trick I needed to gear me up for my dissertation.

At about eight oh five, I arrived at the south tower where Morgan Stanley rented twenty-one floors. I took the express elevator up to the 78th floor, from where I took the local down to the 72nd floor. I walked the maze to the portion of the floor that housed the Emerging Nations Index.

I walked toward Flo, careful to stay to the right side of the corridor so that Ruth wouldn't see me through her office door. I held out Ruth's cell phone. "Hey, Flo," I said. "Could you please see that Ruth gets this?"

"Here she is now," Flo said. "You can give it to her yourself." Ruth was just leaving her boss's office, staring at a folder as she walked past me. I hoped she wouldn't see me, but Flo called out, "Ruth, Honey. Look who's here."

Ruth looked up absently. She saw me and smiled. I held out her cell phone.

"Oh, thanks so much," she said. She seemed surprised and so overly grateful that it made me feel terrible. Just for a moment I saw how mean I had been to her. Now, as I tell you the rest of this, please remember that I've been looking at this moment from the vantage point of death. Along with death comes clarity. Don't forget, there's no movement in death, and when movement ceases, blurring ceases; clarity reigns.

At any rate, as soon as I acknowledged my feelings, that is, as soon as I acknowledged my own meanness, it was more than I wanted to own. Immediately I switched the focus and decided that Ruth was being completely false. I did this, I now see, because recognizing my meanness left me no option but to change. And I was not prepared to change. I therefore had to change what I was seeing. In less than a second, I decided that Ruth's professional demeanor and her Christian thing worked hand in hand—they were both false. I wished she'd forsake them both.

She came over and hugged me and she took the phone and thanked me again.

"Actually," I said, "when you called I was just leaving for Adham's." She recognized my yawn as an announcement that I hadn't gone out of my way for her.

"Well thanks for bringing it," she said cautiously. "That was sweet." She was trying to draw me out, I decided, trying to sound my emotional state.

We stood there awkwardly. At that point, I decided she was trying to make Flo think we were still a couple.

"So what are your plans today," she asked. Making small talk together was work for us, out of practice as we were.

"I don't know." I felt a bit reticent, but for the most part I played along. "I was thinking of doing breakfast over at Windows on the World," I said. "I haven't been there for a while. After that, I'll head over to Adham's."

"Great. Wish I could join you," she said. "But I've got a meeting. I guess I told you." She looked at her watch. "In fact, I've got to head to it now. So I'll see you tonight." She placed her hands on my waist and stood on her tiptoes and I suffered her to kiss me. She was clearly taking advantage of the moment. She kissed me, a real kiss—an on the lips kiss—and she pushed herself up against me. She lingered there a moment too long, and I could feel an erection sprouting. From the way she smiled at me, I suspect she may have felt it too.

"See you tonight," she said and she actually winked at me. I couldn't help but smile at her freshness and she saw me—and I don't mean she saw me smile. She saw *me*, and I could tell she knew she was making headway.

The fact is, I truly loved her. I still do. I can complain about her all I want, but it means nothing. I can imagine people thinking, "If you loved her, why didn't you take her back?" Actually, I imagine westerners thinking it. An Arab man would ask no such question. She betrayed me—end of story.

Anyway, I left and waited several minutes for the elevator. People were heading into work now and I had simply to wait there and pace the lobby. As I waited, I rethought my day, thought about my dissertation, how I'd been working on it now for over five years, and was really no further along than when I'd started. I had to get this thing done. I knew what the problem was. I had no pressure on me. One of the people in the program grew up without money whatsoever. In order to attend graduate school, he had to take out loans that he would one day have to repay. He was the first person in our class to get his Ph.D. For those of us with money, there was no such external pressure and all of us were floundering. As I stood awaiting the elevator, I realized for the fiftieth time that if I were ever to complete the thing, I had to force myself. And if I were to force myself, it had to begin now. Windows on the World was just another ploy to keep me from completing my goal. Forget that. I would stop by Adham's, see about that book, and then I would head home. No more procrastinating.

* * *

The middle of the flight is a blur to me. I slept quite a bit. I was hungry and thirsty, but it was clear that if they wouldn't let me go to the bathroom, they weren't going to worry about feeding me. I pretended to sleep more than I actually did, hoping that someone would say something that would clue me in to what was going on. But they were more careful than that. They talked about nothing but sports and people they all seemed to know; they left me nothing to go on.

At some point in there, I realized that the cord that had been tied around my neck to keep the hood in place had loosened or come undone. By working my chin, I was able to lift the bottom of it just enough so that some light could enter. Seeing the light felt good to me. I was happier to see it than I had been about seeing anything in a long time. I was even able to see the top of my jumpsuit that I could now see was orange.

Later, just as I was beginning to fall into a really good sleep, I could hear the plane's jet engines slowing down and we began to bank as though we were entering a traffic pattern. We flew in this way for no more than five minutes and then the plane landed.

I assumed the flight was over, and I expected that I would soon be taken off the plane. This made me happy, as I had to go to the bathroom again. But this time, it wasn't pee I was worried about.

I heard a door open and I heard someone walking toward us—I assumed he was the pilot or co-pilot—and he told the others that we'd be there for between an hour and a half and two hours.

I don't know whether the pilot left the plane or not, but two of the card players said they'd be back in forty-five minutes. The other two sat around talking about all sorts of things. One of them was smoking a cigarette. I listened to their conversation for a while, but it was so irrelevant to my situation, that I soon tuned it out. Then I realized that one of them had just spoken to me.

"What?" I said.

He said, "We're not supposed to give you food, but would you like some water?"

I said I would and I thanked him. I wondered if he was the man who'd put his hand on my shoulder. I'd hoped he would take off my mask while I drank, but he inserted a plastic straw up under my mask and told me I would have to drink through that.

After I had finished, I asked him why I had to keep the mask on and he said that it was for security reasons.

"Where are you taking me?" I asked him.

He didn't say anything and the other man answered a few seconds later that I'd find out in a while.

"I'm sorry," said the man closest to me, "but we're not supposed to give you information like that. Like I said, it's a security issue."

"I wish you knew me," I said. "I'm not a security threat to anyone."

"Well, that's not how the government sees it," he said.

I suspect that the other guy signaled him by the way he stepped away. At any rate, it seemed clear to me that he'd already said more than he was supposed to, and I felt as if he had done it on purpose so that I'd have a sense at least of who they were.

Even though he had only given me two pieces of information, I had enough to understand my situation. I was dealing with the government; they considered me a security threat. That was all I needed. They thought I was a terrorist. Looking back on it now, it seems so obvious. I have difficulty explaining how it's possible that I didn't realize it from the start. All I know is that it wasn't until this moment that I comprehended my situation.

As I mentioned, I had clung to the kidnapping scenario that I'd first decided upon even after the evidence spoke against it. For one thing, though I'd never had as much faith in this country as Ruth had, I didn't believe it possible that the United States government would treat its citizens as I was being treated. This was the sort of story one associated with the ravings of a homeless schizophrenic on the streets of New York. I hadn't done a thing, yet look what they were doing to me. And without a trial. It felt as if something had slipped out of place in the country. This behavior was exactly the opposite of the way that America thought of itself and portrayed itself. As I sat there in a diaper and cuffs, I had to rethink myself. And rethinking myself was connected directly to rethinking America. America was going through a crisis of identity far worse than my own. Something had come to the fore in this country that was canceling out everything the country had previously stood for and I felt like I had no idea where I was. If Ruth were to see this, I kept thinking, it would destroy her faith in America. Though I missed her, I was glad she wasn't here.

Chapter 5

As I left the lobby of the World Trade Center, I remember looking at my watch—8:32. I walked over to John Street and pushed on the door to Adham's. It was locked. I looked at books in the window display for a couple of minutes and considered waiting until the store opened at 9:00. In the end I decided against it.

Just as I crossed Broadway on John Street, walking toward the Trade Center, the first plane struck the north tower. I didn't actually see it, being east of the building as I was, but I heard the plane approaching and heard it crash. I looked up just in time to see flames belching from the side of the building.

For the first minute or two after the crash I felt incredibly calm. All I could think about was how grateful I was to Allah that the plane had hit the north tower rather than the south tower where Ruth was. The second thought was, if I had gone up to Windows on the World, I might have died. I later found out that everyone who was in Windows at the time of the crash died.

Very soon my body began trembling upon realizing the enormity of this thing, and I could feel adrenaline flowing as I realized how close to death Ruth and I had come. I breathed a prayer of thanks to Allah. I felt confused about where I should go and what I should do. It was like I was looking for a script of what to do and there wasn't one.

I finally ran up Broadway and joined a fairly large group of people who had gathered on Park Place. We stood there together, our eyes angled up at the flames. Within minutes the sirens from police and fire trucks and ambulances began shrieking. Many in the group I stood with began crying when we saw a person jump to his death. There was nothing we could do and we felt completely helpless. We were sharing something that made us feel intimately connected and within minutes it felt as if we in the group were old friends. None of us were joking, which in New York is rare. We groaned together, said "Oh, no" as one each time we saw a body fall.

We speculated about the crash that most of us assumed was an accident. We were speaking in hushed tones. Then a man joined us who suggested that it was a terrorist attack. None of us argued with him, but I didn't hear anyone agree with him either. A little after nine, we heard a plane that sounded extremely low, its engines roaring the way they do at take off. We stood scanning the bits of visible sky. Some of us saw it for just an instant and then we all heard it crash into the south tower, the tower Ruth was in. Though the plane had hit from the south side and we were on the north side, a giant plume of fire flared out in our direction. A chunk of debris landed several hundred yards from us. We now realized the guy was right—it *was* a terrorist attack.

Again I prayed, this time asking that Allah would protect Ruth from the flames and the smoke. By that point, everything negative I'd felt about Ruth had vanished. In that moment, she was my wife. Frantically I counted the floors and realized it was going to be close. I didn't know for sure where floor one ended and floor two began because of those cathedral style windows near the bottom. And I supposed that the thirteenth floor was not counted. Either way, it didn't look as though she was on the affected floors. She was on the 72nd floor and, by my calculations, the plane had crashed some where around the 80th floor. As it turned out, the crash initially affected floors 78 through 85. But I didn't know any of that for sure. And I didn't know what the south side of the building was looking like.

All I could think about was Ruth. I wondered if I could get into the building and find her. No one seemed in charge and going in seemed like a good idea.

I said goodbye to people in the group I'd been standing with and wished them luck for their friends in the towers. I headed over toward Church Street, intending to head south on it. Fire trucks and policemen were arriving in huge numbers.

The sound of sirens and the horns of fire trucks were constant now and they added to the confusion I felt. I actually got lost on my way over there, though I had visited Ruth down there many times. Not only that, I had friends who lived around there and I knew the area fairly well.

By the time I found Church Street, cops were turning people away. I walked over to Broadway and tried to walk toward the south tower on Liberty Street, but again, I couldn't get through.

Ruth's office was on the southeastern corner of the south tower. She didn't have a window in her office, but she was close to a window. At Maiden Lane and Broadway I stood watching with another large group of people. In this group as well, several others had unaccounted for loved ones up there. I remembered my cell phone now and turned it on. I tried calling Ruth's cell phone as well as her work number. I couldn't get through. A recording told me to try my call later.

As I stood with this group, there was talk of Muslim involvement—I assumed it myself. A woman tried to remember Osama bin Laden's name. "What is his name, that tall, skinny terrorist with the beard?" I knew his name—anyone who read the papers with any frequency was certainly aware of him. But I had the feeling that if I were to come out with it, the crowd would notice that, come to think of it, I looked Middle Eastern as well. At that point, I believe I was being paranoid. No one in the crowd even looked at me askance, though I look as Middle Eastern as anyone. The next day, that's when things began to change for real. From then on, paranoia became appropriate.

There was a strange feeling as more and more people joined us. All of the normal routines had ended. People from all over the south of Manhattan had left their jobs.

I've stood in other New York crowds gaping at tragedies. This gathering had none of the normal circus atmosphere, none of the dark sarcastic humor. It was certainly nothing like the crowd of people I'd come upon on East 42nd Street a decade earlier. As I'd gotten closer, I could see that the crowd centered upon a bloody sheet that was clearly covering something, something so small that I assumed it to be the body of a small child. After several inquiries, I learned that the sheet was covering the severed leg of a man who had jumped from the top of a high building. The rest of his body had come to a stop on an overhang ten or twelve stories above, but his leg had cleared the overhang and had kept falling minus the body. As we had stood around this leg, there had been more than a hint of laughter in the air. Jokes were forming. I heard someone whisper, "Once a body's in motion, the leg stays in motion." But now as we stood looking up at the smoking towers, the atmosphere was completely different. There was not a hint of laughter. Everyone was serious and silent. A couple of Stuyvesant High School kids had sneaked away from school and were standing with us. They too were taking it seriously.

I was wondering about Ruth and whether she'd be able to get out alive. I suspected that she would not be standing around up there in her office. She'd be trying to come down the stairs. I couldn't imagine that the elevators were working. I decided to head north a bit to see if I could spot her among the people leaving the towers.

The problem was, they weren't leaving through the normal exits. They were being channeled down to the underground mall and up an escalator by the Borders bookstore. People were streaming onto Church Street with soot on their faces. Many of them were being helped by others, some coughing uncontrollably, others weeping, limping. By this time I'd realized that going into the building was not only impossible, but that it would interfere with the rescue operation.

I talked to a man who had obviously been inside. His suit was drenched and he had a cut on his face and dark streaks under his nose where he'd breathed in smoke. I asked him what it was like in there. I remember I had to ask him twice because just then a fire truck blasted its horn not far from us.

He said there was no power and the staircase was dark and crowded and completely full of smoke. I asked him what floor he had been on and he said the eightieth floor of the south tower. I was relieved. If he had escaped from the eightieth floor, Ruth had a very good chance of escaping from the seventy-second.

A woman joined us, anxious for news. She handed the man a tissue for the cut on his face. He seemed anxious to talk, as though he needed to unload what had just happened. He told us that after the first plane had struck the north tower, he and everyone in his department had boarded an elevator to leave the building, though they worked in the south tower. When they were mid-way down, an announcement had come over the intercoms saying that the accident had occurred in the north tower and that employees of the south tower had no reason for concern. They should all return to their areas.

He told us that when the elevator arrived on the ground floor, a number of his co-workers had remained in the elevator to return to work. He said that he had wanted nothing but to get out of the building. He shook his head and said he hoped his co-workers made it out. I wished him luck and worked my way closer. I quizzed a couple more people who had been in the building. One young Hispanic woman in a skirt had blood spattered all over her legs. She seemed to be walking okay, but she was crying uncontrollably. I asked her if she needed help. She looked up at me as if I were some sort of savior and held up her hands in supplication. Without even thinking I hugged her. She nearly collapsed in my arms and it felt as if she would fall if I let go. After a minute or so of her sobbing, she told me that the body of a man who had jumped from the building had landed not three feet from her. His body had hit the concrete with such force that the spray of his blood, when it had hit her bare legs, had actually stung. Before he had jumped he had taken off his shirt and tied it over his head and she was thankful to him for that—she didn't think she could have stood looking at his face. She kept saying she wished she could forget the sound of his body hitting the ground. "That sound," she kept saying. "That sound," and she was weeping.

She asked if I had a cell phone that she could use and I told her I did. I pulled it from my belt and as I handed it to her, I saw I had missed a call, apparently because of the noise. After the woman tried unsuccessfully to make her call, I checked the phone again and saw that the message was from Ruth. She had made the call following the second crash before I'd turned on my phone. The cell phone service was still working at this point but every possible line in the area was in use. She'd gotten through by sheer luck. I couldn't even get through to retrieve Ruth's message. I tried calling her again. I tried her father. Though I was unsuccessful, the fact that she had called me convinced me that Ruth had survived both crashes.

It isn't as though I left my station near the Trade Center because of some premonition that the building was about to fall. I had no idea that such a thing was even possible. I left because I was convinced that Ruth was alive. The fact that I'd received the message from her, the fact that the man on the eightieth floor had gotten out while she was only on the seventy-second floor: certainly she was out of there. I was sure of it. I didn't for a minute suspect that she would have returned to work when the announcement came over the south tower intercom. She had always worried about how dangerous the Trade Center was. She had a conversation with a woman who had been in the building in 1993 during the first bombing. After that, Ruth had twice attempted to transfer to the Morgan Stanley offices up on 50th Street and 6th Avenue, the building where she had worked as an analyst before going for her MBA. Everyone assured her the Trade Center was safe, but she was not one to put faith in technology. As I considered it from that perspective, I decided she was probably the first person from her area of the building to breathe fresh air.

I ended up walking east on Fulton Street searching for a pay phone from which to call home to leave a message so that Ruth would know I was safe. Tons of people were still just standing on street corners looking up at the towers, but by now some had started to leave the area. I walked along with a group of fifty or more.

When we got a little past Broadway, above the commotion of ambulances, fire trucks, car horns and people's screams and yells, a new sound was added, a roaring like that of a thousand foot wave about to roll over us at the beach. I turned and saw that the south tower was collapsing in on it- self, but slowly, as in slow motion, dropping and roaring so loudly that the sirens and horns and screams of onlookers were completely drowned out and the ground was shaking as violently as if some crazed god were on the loose. I'm told it took less than ten seconds to fall. But as I stood there watch- ing, it felt more like ten minutes. When it had landed, the building was replaced by a billowing cloud of dust and smoke that climbed and spread until it was clear that it was about to overtake the southern tip of Manhattan.

I stood there convinced that I'd just witnessed the deaths of thousands of Allah's creations. I prayed to Him that He have mercy on the many who were suffering, the many whose very lives were being pressed from their bodies at that very moment.

It took a few seconds to realize that this vast cloud of dust and smoke was traveling toward me, a cloud thicker than anyone has ever seen—so thick it looked solid, this cement colored cloud—so thick and so heavy, I felt it had the power to crush. I stood paralyzed until I noticed that everyone around me was running to escape this beast. I turned and ran up Fulton Street as fast as I could. An overweight black woman was right beside me. She had taken off her shoes and I was very impressed with the speed she was making. She looked amused at herself, as though she could imagine what she looked like, but she was also serious about getting away, just as we all were.

Earlier as I had been talking with the Hispanic woman who had nearly been hit by the falling body, a thought had darted through the periphery of my consciousness. But as I'd been drawn in by the details of her story, the thought had just sort of faded. Now that the tower had fallen, however, the thought was more true than ever, the thought that at the end of the day, a lot of people would be unaccounted for. A lot of people's bodies would never be found, and many bodies that were found, would be damaged beyond recognition. That's as far as I took the thought at this point, but the thought stayed with me, as though it had more to tell me.

I looked back to check the cloud's progress and saw that a few steps behind me a woman had fallen. I went back and grabbed her arm. She had scraped the palms of her hands and had a cut on her nose. The cloud was less than a hundred feet behind us now. I grabbed her and tucked my arm beneath hers and began running. As we passed a bodega, I dragged her inside and shut the door just as the cloud passed us. Some of the filthy, choking, smokey dust entered through the cracks around the door. It had an acrid smell, a mix of burning plastic, of dust, of kerosene, and a smell I didn't recognize until later as the smell of burning flesh.

This cloud did not just blow past and then disappear. For fifteen minutes or more we couldn't even see from the door of the bodega across the sidewalk to the street. Roman, who ran the store, was incredibly nice to us, though neither of us had ever seen him before. He offered us free bottled water and he applied hydrogen peroxide and bandages to Jennifer's hands and nose, Jennifer, the woman I'd helped inside.

A few minutes later, though the air was still thick with dust, we could see across the street. The sidewalk and streets, people's cars, everything was covered with a thick layer of ash that was over an inch thick. People walking past looked as if they'd been covered with gray chalk dust. Many were hacking and coughing. I saw one man repeatedly pumping an inhaler into his lungs.

Soon after that, I thanked Roman, Jennifer thanked me, and I left. I hugged them both and felt as if they were my friends, though we'd only spent fifteen minutes together. Already, a feeling had formed out of nowhere that we were all in this together.

As I got outside, I pulled out my cell phone to see about calling home. By this point I no longer had service, so I continued my hunt for a payphone. I walked east on Fulton Street to Nassau Street where I spotted a bank of pay phones. A line of people was waiting to use the three phones. Though the cloud was not as thick as it had been, there was still a lot of smoke and dust in the air. I got on line and as I waited, I listened to everyone as they told their stories about being in or next to the towers, having friends or relatives in the towers, and they were hell-bent on getting messages through.

I remember noticing something as I waited. No one I know admits that what I'm saying is true, but I know what I saw and felt: there was a certain mythology in the air, not only of a sadness, but of a repressed excitement at being part of this major tragedy. I assure you, it was there, at least during those first several hours. Later, as the enormity of the situation sank in, that feeling wore off and our feelings became more pure. Until the 9/11 tourists showed up.

The line moved quickly, but it was during this short wait that my idea reemerged about how a lot of bodies would be damaged beyond recognition. It was then that I saw this as the moment I'd been waiting for. This was my path to freedom, my path out of a marriage that was slowly killing me and killing my wife. In one flash, I realized I now had the chance to begin a new life, choose a new name. Ruth would think I'd gone to Windows on the World and when she didn't hear from me, she would assume I had died in the crash. She would not have to live with the guilt of a divorce, yet she would be rid of me. And I would be rid of her. And it would have ended on a fairly upbeat note—I had taken her phone to her and we had kissed goodbye. We had parted with a kiss. To say nothing of the fact that we had made love the night before.

Though I was thinking this way, I doubted I would actually go through with it. I stayed in the line, assuming I was simply fantasizing. Finally it was my turn to call. I lifted the receiver, put money into the slot, and as I began to dial our number, I realized that all I cared about was finding out if Ruth was all right. I called, and instead of leaving a message, I dialed our code and retrieved our messages. Sure enough, there was one from Ruth asking if I was all right. She said she got out about twenty minutes before the tower collapsed and she hoped I was out as well. She asked that I please call her father and let him know I was okay. She didn't use the answering machine as I had just done to check for messages because she was a technophobe to the point that she had pride in it. She said she'd keep checking with her father to find out if I had gotten through. She said she loved me and hoped I was safe. I hung up.

I felt an incredible rush of relief. My wife was alive. I could die in peace.

* * *

The other two men returned to the plane and took the place of the two who had been watching me. They didn't say anything to me. They sat there talking about an asshole waiter at the restaurant where they'd eaten. The one guy kept saying that the waiter was probably gay and the other guy kept agreeing. It sounded like they were looking at magazines as they spoke and after a while, they quit speaking and were quiet.

I wanted to get to know them a little bit. It seemed like getting them as close as possible made sense.

"So where are we?" I asked.

"In an airplane," one of them said.

The other one laughed.

"Where's the airplane?" I said. I felt I was demonstrating good humor.

"At an airport."

"Which one?"

"Ah, we're at the first stop," the man said.

"So why can't you tell me where we are. Are you afraid that I'm going to do something if I find out? What can I do? I can't move, I can't eat, I can't go to the bathroom, I can't do anything. How am I going to hurt you?"

"I don't believe you are."

"Exactly. So why is it that you can't tell me what's going on?"

"It's a state secret and you don't have a clearance."

"Why is it a state secret? I've done nothing against the

state."

At this point I heard the other guy whisper something about information.

After that I kept pestering them, but I couldn't get them to answer me and the two of them simply sat there ignoring me no matter what I said. Finally, one of them came over to me and stood close to me and said, "Listen to me. Do you want to be gagged? Because I'm this close to gagging you. Either you gag yourself, or I'll gag you. You got that?"

After that I said nothing. I put my seat back as far as I could and I tried to sleep. Instead I felt restless and I wondered how long it had been since I'd been taken. I could tell it had been a long time because I was extremely hungry. I hadn't even eaten that morning—they'd taken me before I'd arrived at the restaurant. I thought about how I had to go to the bathroom. I was able to pee into my diaper again, but I had to do so even more carefully this time. My stomach was paining me. The diarrhea wanted out.

Chapter 6

During those few seconds on the phone, it's difficult to believe how much information surged through my head. Questions formed such as if I were to "die," where would I live, what would become of Ruth, what would I do for money, what would I do with my life. These questions were accompanied by detailed answers, and all of this occurred during the time it took for the phone to ring and our answering machine to pick up.

I had enough money to last me a lifetime, and much of it, as I said, was money about which Ruth knew nothing. Neither my family nor acquaintances knew of my offshore account. By the time my father had died, my siblings weren't speaking to me and I wasn't speaking to Ruth.

The lawyer handling my father's estate had asked for routing and account numbers so that he could wire my inheritance to me. I had asked that he give me the money in a check. My original plan had been to establish a new account in a completely different institution from Morgan Stanley which handled Ruth's and my money. I knew nothing about money. Until I met Ruth, my father's accountant had handled my financial affairs. Later Ruth had turned my assets over to a colleague at Morgan Stanley where we got favorable treatment because she was an employee. But when my father died, I wanted to hide my inheritance from Ruth. So when I dropped by a bank to see about setting up a savings account, it was news to me that I had to give them my social security number.

I made some phone calls and found out about the Cayman Islands where I could set up a completely anonymous account by creating a "corporation." I would be given two accounts, a savings account and a checking account. I would receive not only checks, but a credit card and a debit card that would enable me to access my accounts, withdraw funds, and switch money from one account to the other. And all of it would be virtually untraceable, even if Ruth got a divorce lawyer to poke into my financial affairs.

I flew down to the Caymans and set up my account. In terms of the corporation I set up—I called it the first thing that came to my mind, "Muhammad's Books." For a long time I'd had a fantasy of one day owning a Muslim book store. My dissertation had been eating away at me since I'd finished my course work. It was the last thing I thought of before going to sleep at night and the first thing I thought of in the morning. I loved the material I was working with, the writings of Averroes, of Aristotle, and even Aquinas. But forcing them through the grid required for a dissertation sucked all of the life out of those works. What I really wanted was to forget my dissertation and set up a bookstore. But I didn't have the courage given my relationship to my siblings. They already scoffed at me as it was, and not completing my doctorate was a blow my ego would not abide. And even though it was unlikely that they were keeping track of my progress, it was at least in part because of them that I had continued.

At first the Cayman account was a source of relief to me. As time went on, however, it became a source of frustration. I kept feeling I should invest the money rather than let it sit in a savings account where it was collecting a minimum of interest. It called to mind the parable of the talents told by the prophet Issa, wherein the master entrusts each of his three servants with a certain amount of money. Two of the servants invest the money and double it, while the third, the lazy servant—and for Aquinas, this lazy servant was actually a coward—buries his share so he won't lose it. Before today, I had thought of myself as that lazy servant, allowing my inheritance to rot in a savings account. But as I stood there now with the phone in my hands, contemplating whether or not to be, I realized that my laziness had made it possible for me to live though I was dead.

Things were going to work out. I had my inheritance and I could access it as needed without anyone knowing. Not only that, Ruth would be fine. She would inherit the money in my personal account as well as my trust fund. In addition, the dividends that I had been receiving as part owner of my father's company would now go to her. And then there was the five hundred thousand dollar life insurance policy I had set up. Even if she lost her one hundred fifty thousand dollar a year job plus bonuses, she would be set. There was no reason to worry about her.

Many times after setting up my offshore account, I realized it had been overkill. There was no way Ruth would have gone after my money in a venomous way if she had filed for divorce. But again, standing there on the phone, I was glad I'd been so paranoid. It now seemed to me to be the work of Allah.

All of that was a huge relief. But the biggest relief came when I realized I would not be able to finish my Ph.D. without risking that Ruth would find out. And now my siblings would think I was dead, so I didn't have to worry about their judgment.

My dissertation, a source of torment, was now gone. I wanted to embark on something new. I would move to Seattle where I had traveled a few years back to visit a scholar of Arabic poetry who lived there. I liked the city all right, but more than anything, Seattle was a place that in no way interested Ruth. She found the rain depressing. In Seattle I would not have to worry about running into her. Moreover, other than the scholar, there was no one in the city I knew, and he was quite old and not someone I was likely to run into on the street. But to be safe, I would grow a beard and instead of contact lenses, I would return to wearing glasses. I wished I had my glasses with me now, in fact. I thought about returning for them, but if I did, I might be seen by a neighbor.

All of this zoomed through my head as I stood there on the phone. The only question I couldn't answer satisfactorily was how would I get to Seattle. I obviously couldn't take my car. And I couldn't rent or lease or buy a car because all of that required identification and they kept records. If I flew, even though I could pay with my anonymous card, they would make me show an i.d. and there would be a record that I had traveled. I wondered how long it would take me to establish a new identity. I only knew I'd figure something out.

My head was spinning. I felt incredibly light and a kind of joy traveled through me that I hadn't felt since Ruth had betrayed me. In death I would be absolutely free.

* * *

The other two guys returned a few minutes before our flight resumed. Once we were in the air, I slept for several hours. I woke up when a pain passed through my bowels that felt as if I'd been run through with a sword. I realized that I wasn't going to be able to hold it in any longer. I sat there for a couple of minutes trying to figure out the best way to take care of this problem. I didn't want to evacuate my bowels and then sit in it, but I realized I had no option. I then decided that if I could undo my seatbelt and shift around in my seat so that I was basically kneeling and facing the back, if things worked as they should, the product would be carried by gravity toward the front of my diaper and I would not have to sit in as much of it.

Before doing that, however, I decided to ask once again if they would let me go to the bathroom.

"Gentlemen. Could you please take me to the bathroom? I guarantee you, this is not going to be a pretty scene if you don't let me go."

"Go in your diaper like a good boy," one of them said.

I waited another two or three minutes and gently I undid my seatbelt and began to turn around in my seat. "Hey, get your seatbelt back on," one of them barked.

Two of them rushed to me and they twisted me around

with such force that I simply let go and voided my bowels. There was the signature explosion of diarrhea and the two men now seemed to understand my plight. One of them groaned and the other one laughed.

"We've got a live one."

They buckled me back in.

The hood I was wearing came down over the collar of my jump suit. All of the newly released smells worked their way up my jumpsuit and into my hood and I gagged and nearly threw up.

Quite soon I realized that though I had done my job, the diaper had not done its. I could feel things drooling out the sides of it.

The smell was now spreading to the others and there was some laughter as words like "ripe" were thrown about. One of them said, "I believe we have the right man. He possesses a weapons-grade biological agent."

I don't think I've ever been more uncomfortable. Finally I said, "Is there any way you could find the courage in yourselves to help me out and usher me to the bathroom. You wouldn't treat a dog this way."

There was some mumbling and joking, but it dissipated quickly, and I realized they knew it was true. One of them said quite sincerely, "I'm sorry, sir, but we are not authorized to do that. You're going to have to deal with it."

I realized that nothing was going to happen and I sat there and tried to think of other things. I tucked my hood under my chin so that the smell would escape into the air instead of into my hood. A few minutes later, when I heard the four of them talking, I was able to unzip my jumpsuit a few inches so that the zipper was at about my mid-chest. This helped vent a good deal of the smell.

I felt so disgusting that I couldn't stand it. Quite soon it felt as if I had acid eating into my buttocks and even my scrotum. I leaned back in my chair to spread the weight of my body over the entire length of my back rather than having it all bearing down on my buttocks. This made my situation slightly more bearable. I lay there trying to sleep remembering a similar set of feelings I'd had when I was five. I'd been at a friend's birthday party. The party was downstairs and the bathroom was upstairs and I was afraid to go up there by myself. I'd asked my friend if we could go up and play in his room, but his mother nixed the idea. After that, it had happened—seemingly on its own—and I remembered going into the living room by myself and crying. My friend's mother came in and spotted me and asked me what was wrong.

I remembered completely breaking down and just as I was going to tell her, she must have smelled it. She asked me, "Did you have an accident?"

I told her I had. She took me upstairs and helped me clean up and she let me borrow some of her son's pants. I returned downstairs and no one else at the party ever found out.

Chapter 7

My father had operated a successful import business that included a chain of five large stores, one in midtown Manhattan, and another in Newark. There were two others in Jersey malls and one in White Plains. Primarily he imported and sold high quality, hand-made oriental rugs. And because I was his only child who did not go into his business, he left me more cash than he left my siblings. His reasoning was that they would profit more from their association with the store than I would. This was embarrassing to me for a number of reasons, not the least of which was that I was the youngest child, the only one to have been born into comfortable circumstances. I was considered spoiled by my older siblings. All of them could remember the days before we'd had money. They'd tell stories about the good old days back in Ahwaz when people had looked down on our family. By the time I was born, we were on our way to becoming wealthy, and by the time we moved to America, we had arrived. The fact that I chose to pursue an academic path rather than go into the family business, as far as my siblings were concerned, that said it all. Not only was I an ingrate. I was living in a world of ideas while they lived in the real world. The fact that my father left more cash to me than to them did not go over well at all.

Father told me of his intentions before he died. Actually, he told us all. He sat us down a year or so after Mother's death to discuss his will. The meeting was difficult for me. His timing was bad. My siblings had just begun speaking to me again. They had barely accepted me back as it was. And that was the moment he chose to explain his will. Later I asked him about his timing and he said that he'd wanted to make clear to everyone that he was behind me one hundred percent. He wanted them to know that if they abandoned me, they were abandoning the family. Now that my mother was dead, he said, it was more important than ever that we all draw close.

* * *

Right after we landed, I heard one of the men ask what time it was local time. "Three thirty," came the response. I wondered how this could be. I realized I didn't know what day it was and I had no clue where we were. I suspected that it couldn't be the same day we had departed. I wondered if it was a.m. or p.m. and I tried to figure out what time it must be in Seattle.

A man came over and unbuckled one of the cuffs on my leg and rebuckled it onto my other leg so that I could walk. He made a gagging sound that I assumed referenced my smell. It may have been genuine, but I doubt it. At any rate, as he did this, I heard two of his buddies laugh.

By the time they stood me up, my bottom felt like it had been eaten through, so long had I been sitting in my own filth. They ushered me off the plane, and with every step, I could feel leakage at the sides of the diaper, some of it spattering onto my bare feet.

When we stepped off the plane, the first thing I noticed was that it was unimaginably hot. As we walked, my bare feet were burning on the tarmac. I heard two people speaking in Egyptian Arabic. Egyptian Arabic is *sui generis*. I had an Egyptian friend in college and I was very familiar not only with the Egyptian accent, but syntax as well. It was unmistakable. But surely they hadn't taken me to Egypt. I assumed I was simply hearing two Egyptians speak. Maybe we were in New York or some other cosmopolitan area.

I was put into a van and driven down a street that was so busy that I realized at once that it couldn't be 3:30 a.m. The driver had a strong Arabic accent when he spoke English, but from it, I could not make out where he was from.

I asked him in Arabic what time it was, hoping thereby to hear his accent.

Immediately one of my captors told the driver, "Say nothing to him. What did he say to you?"

The man said, "He ask me, 'What time it is?'"

No one said anything after that. I wondered if they knew what I was up to.

We hadn't driven for fifteen minutes when one of them began complaining about the way I smelled. The driver of the van thought this was extremely funny and soon he too was complaining.

"Damn," he said. "He smell like shit. Very badly smelling man."

After a few minutes, they had to dispense with the air conditioning and open all of the windows. At a stop sign or light, I heard a child in an adjacent car ask his mother where they were going and I realized from this little exchange that we were in fact in Egypt.

I said aloud, "Why are we in Egypt?"

"What makes you think we're in Egypt?" asked one of the men.

"I can hear it in the Arabic that's spoken here."

They were quiet and I realized they weren't going to argue the point.

Chapter 8

I was just hanging up the phone when the north tower fell. I saw, heard, smelled, tasted, felt nothing but the falling building. It took up every bit of perceptual bandwidth I had. After it had collapsed, I looked around and everyone was standing still and frightened as if they'd just witnessed the death of God. As horrific as it had been to watch the first building fall, the second building struck me much harder. It now seemed that we were vulnerable. When the first building fell, it seemed like an accident—a lucky shot. But this time, it felt as if the terrorists had known what they were doing.

As soon as the building had landed, a lone woman screamed and though we could barely hear her over the fire engines and ambulances, it was followed by a chorus of exclamation. But most people just stood there watching, many with tears streaming down their faces.

The cloud of dust and smoke sent up was worse than the first one had been, but long before it got to me, I ran around the corner to Fulton and returned to Roman's Bodega. He had just gotten inside himself, having gone out when he heard the tower falling. He was standing there with the door open inviting passers-by in. But after taking a final look to check on the cloud's progress, he closed and locked the door and both of us leaned against it. This time less of the smoke and dust got in.

I waited a few minutes for the air to clear but after fifteen minutes or so I grew impatient. The visibility was still low when I asked Roman if he would let me out. He told me I was crazy, but he agreed to let me out a side door that led to an alley. I moved back onto Fulton and toward the wreckage. The smell was overwhelmingly acrid and disgusting and I went through repeated bouts of choking. But that did nothing to stop me from moving toward the wreckage.

I was able to get fairly close, because by now most people, including the police, had either moved away from the area or had taken cover. I realized why. I felt as if I was choking to death, coughing every few seconds, but continuing on just the same. I saw firemen in air tanks standing around waiting for the air to clear, but there were only a few of them. At one point, I saw a cameraman from a news team walking around and he too was coughing. I ducked behind a clump of wreckage until he passed to keep from appearing on the six o'clock news.

The place was truly eerie. I one time saw a production of Samuel Beckett's *Endgame*, and the feelings engendered by the set were similar to the ones I felt as I waded toward the collapsed towers through what was now several inches of ash. Everything on the streets was covered by it, buildings, fire trucks, ambulances, cars—as well as the wrecked versions of each—fire hydrants, fire hoses, even a corpse that I saw of a man or woman who had been hit by a chunk of falling concrete.

The ashes on the ground and those that were still falling made everything unrecognizable so that I lost all sense of direction. Distributed among the bits of falling ash were thousands of intact, eight and a half by eleven inch sheets of paper, falling from the sky like giant snow flakes—memos, agreements, vouchers and briefs, all of which had been important to someone at some point.

As I grew closer to the pile left by the towers, I saw pieces of the outside metal face of the buildings sticking out of the ground, one of which looked like a giant hand. Everything in the area had been crushed except for an occasional item—often something that seemed incredibly flimsy. I remember seeing a stoplight attached to a pole that hung out over the street. It looked as if it could have been brought down by a strong wind or a drunk driver. But somehow it had survived while around it millions of tons of debris had fallen.

I removed my cell phone from my pocket and hurled it toward the pile of smoking rubble. I hoped searchers would find it and connect it to me. Certainly I couldn't use it again without jeopardizing my status as dead man. In that moment I realized how fortunate it was that none of my cell phone calls had gone through. Otherwise, the life insurance company could have potentially deduced that I was alive following the collapse of both buildings. Even if I had only succeeded in checking my voice mail, they could have found out. Given Ruth's relationship to technology, I doubted that she would have thought of such a thing, but it's even possible that she would have checked my cell phone bill to see when I'd made my last call.

I was so excited now at the prospect of a new life that I removed my wallet, intending to heave it as well. But just before doing so, I checked through it to see if there was anything I might need. Luckily I spotted the credit and debit cards associated with my Cayman account. I returned my wallet to my pocket, realizing I should proceed with caution.

I walked north now, trying to determine what my next move should be. I needed to find a hotel room. I realized it would mean showing an i.d. when I signed in, which could create problems later. I wondered how I could get a fake i.d. of some sort.

Everyone seemed to be moving northward now. I was walking with a group of strangers. I've heard it said that all landlines south of 14th Street were dead by now, but I came upon a set of working phone booths on Houston Street. I got in line and called information. I asked the operator if he could help me find the address of a passport photo place near the base of Manhattan. He listed several, and when he gave me the name of one on Allen Street, just north of Delancey, I asked for the exact address. That's a very iffy neighborhood, and I felt I might have a starting point.

My internal and outer worlds were both in extreme turmoil. I had just decided to play dead. And though the thought of this carried with it a certain freedom, I was also plagued with guilt and dread and doubt. But in addition to all of that, I had just witnessed a crime that was beyond my imagination, the falling of an icon that was part of my earliest memories. My mind kept jumping back and forth among these various facts and it would no sooner light on the one than it would remember the others. And then as I walked toward Allen Street, I'd have brief moments of seeing outside myself and I'd realize that the entire city was in shock.

Throngs of people walked toward the Williamsburg Bridge, many of whom wore ash-covered coats and hair. The traffic was crazy—horns blowing, people shouting, sirens blaring. Yet, in spite of the chaos, there was a sense of calm and of community in the air that is usually missing from New York. And strangely, mixed with the calm, there was adrenaline. People were walking in groups and speaking, people who didn't necessarily know each other. A number of people were limping—some because of injuries, and others because they had lost or discarded their shoes. People were supporting each other as they hobbled along. There was a sense of seriousness that I'd never seen in the city, and the most surprising part was that it seemed like everything had changed forever.

At one point along the way, I stopped at a corner store to buy some lip balm because my lips were so chapped. The ash in the air felt as if it had sucked the moisture right out of me.

I had never seen New York when it wasn't business as usual, but today, it truly wasn't. Three women were standing near the front of the store talking to the clerk about rumors they'd heard and what they had seen and about the smoke and smell that filled the air. They all looked extremely concerned.

When I stood by the cash register waiting to be served, the clerk looked up at me and told me that I could use the employees' rest room if I wanted. Apparently I looked confused. She said, "For the ashes, sir. You have ashes all over you."

I saw in the restroom mirror that I had ashes on the top of my head, on my forehead and eyebrows, as well as tiny flares of dust just under each nostril. In addition, my shoulders were covered with it. I got myself cleaned up and as I passed the clerk at the front of the store, I thanked her. By now I had used the lip balm and placed it in my pocket. It was not until I had walked a block or so that I remembered I had not paid. I returned and paid her. As we laughed about it, I noted that it was the first laughter I had seen since the initial attack.

When I arrived at the passport photo place, the sign read "PASSPORT RENEWALS – ONE DAY SERVICE." It was a small, run down affair on the ground floor of a two-story building. I don't think it was more than three hundred square feet in all, though there was a door to a room in the back.

The front door was locked though a small sign claimed the office was open from ten until five. I looked at my watch. Ten past one. I cupped my hands on the glass to peer inside. A woman was sitting behind the counter and seemed to be filling out a form. When I knocked, she looked at me and waved me away as if I were a fly. I held up a twenty-dollar bill and knocked again. She came over and stood by the door but didn't open it. She bobbed her chin in a short quick movement, but so slightly as to be barely perceptible, and she accompanied this gesture with dead eyes—New York speak for "What? You can't see I'm busy?"

I looked at her closely through the glass and was pleased to see something dissolute about the way she held her jaw. She looked about fifty-five and had the solid build of someone who could deliver a good punch. Her bleached blond hair was teased and she wore too much make up. She held her eyes half closed against the smoke of the cigarette she held between her teeth. Clearly she had seen it all. She looked like she'd just stepped off the set of a B movie. I was convinced I'd come to the right place.

"Do you do passports for name changes," I yelled through the door window.

"Yes. But we're closed," she yelled back.

"Listen. I'll make it worth your while. I need this done soon." I pulled out my billfold and found three more twenties and a ten. "Just open up and talk to me, please."

She opened the door. "What, you think cause you're cute I'll open?" She was nearly smiling. She had a kind of sexual appeal that overrode her weight and age.

"Listen, I've changed my name, and I need a new passport," I told her. "I'm American and I need a new passport. I don't have my old one with me." She just looked at me as if I still hadn't spoken. I continued, disconcerted. "I used to work in the Trade Center and I had my passport in my desk. I actually just changed my name two weeks ago—you know?" I stopped. She was giving me nothing. I couldn't tell if she believed me or not. I spoke on. "I had the new passport and…you know. And all of it was lost in the Trade Center. I don't know what I'm going to do. But if you could get me a new one by…well tomorrow would be ideal. If you could do that, I'd pay you…I don't know. Five hundred dollars. A thousand. I really need…"

"Mister, if I understand you correctly, what you're asking for is totally illegal. Do you honestly think that I could get you a passport with no documentation?" What struck me was that she didn't seem as horrified as she was trying to sound.

"Well, I don't want to do anything illegal," I said, "if that's what you're thinking."

She grinned. It was clear she saw through me. I worked at not smiling back.

"But the thing is," I continued, "everything I'm telling you is true, you know? I'm an American and it just so happens that I lost all my paperwork, you understand? So it's not like I'm asking for anything that's fake or anything. This is totally legit."

She looked at me for a long time. "Come in," she said. "I don't expect you work for the Feds. Their excuses are way better than yours. Not only that, they're all tied up today." That was the closest she ever came to mentioning the Trade Center, which was odd, because that's all everyone else was talking about.

She closed the door and locked it. "Listen to me. If you'd really lost your passport, you'd just have to apply for a new one, whether you'd just changed your name or not. You know? Your passport would be on record at the agency. Capiche?"

She looked at me to see how I'd react. She was smiling. When I joined her, she laughed. "Aha," she said. "So it's like that."

"Well…" I said.

"He says, 'Well,'" she said. She sighed. "Listen. I can get you a passport. But I'm telling you; it's going to cost you. Five large to be precise. And don't be asking questions. I'll just tell you that we get them through someone who handles witness protection passports. I guarantee you that what you get will be an authentic US passport. It won't be doctored in any way. It's the real mccoy. It will be in the system just like it is for any other passport. But there's no way I can have it by tomorrow. And you have to pay me at least three of the five thousand in advance. And I just want to tell you one other thing that you may not have considered. If you go through the normal channels, you can get a legit passport without giving them your social—it's just that they charge you an extra five hundred which goes to the IRS. But the people I'm dealing with don't play that way because they don't want to draw attention. They want a legitimate social. Otherwise, it gets too dangerous. So if you're going to do this, you're going to need a new social, and a new social is an extra five k. And again, I guarantee you that this will not just be a card. It'll be a number that's in the system and it will check out. They'll give you a history that will make sense. And it will be linked in with your passport. If you want it, I'll need another three in advance, which with the passport will be six in advance."

"I don't have that kind of cash on me," I said. "I do have a credit card that would handle it."

"What, are you kidding? Plastic for this sort of thing?"

"Well how about a check?"

"Good one," she said. She began unlocking the door for me to leave.

"I'm telling you," I said. The thing will clear. My only way of accessing my money is through an ATM, and I can't find an ATM that will give me more than three hundred dollars a day. The money is not a problem. I promise you. What about this? We wait for the check to clear. How about that?"

"Listen, clearing is only part of the problem. I don't want our name appearing on some sort of statement that's going to end up at the IRS or any other part of the Feds."

"No, this is a totally untraceable offshore account. If you understood my situation, you'd realize that I've got no interest in having this appear on any kind of statement. I... Let me just say, none of this will appear on any statement."

She smiled. "Where's the account?"

"The Caymans."

"What sort of name is it under?"

"A completely untraceable corporate name, Muhammad's Books. Believe me, it will be fine."

"If you have time to wait for it to clear, I guess I can go with that," she said.

"How about this? While we're waiting for the check, could you get things rolling, you know, just sort of order the passport and social security number and I won't be able to pick them up until the check clears?"

"That's not how we work. Nothing gets done until we're holding sixty percent of the cash."

"I kind of need this stuff in a hurry," I said.

"Okay, so the sooner you give me the check, the sooner it'll happen."

"Okay, so here's the problem. My check book's in my safe deposit box."

"How soon can you have it here?"

"About an hour or so."

"I just noticed your watch," she said. "What kind of watch is that?"

"It's a Breitling," I said.

"Yeah? Well, if you want to hurry things up, I guess I'd consider taking the watch as collateral."

"I can't do that," I said.

"I guess it depends on what you want."

"Would I get it back?"

"Of course you'll get it back," she said. "As soon as I get the cash. I just don't want to be left holding the bag is all. I don't make the passports—I just deliver them. It's going to cost me three thousand for the passport and three thousand for the social. So give me the watch—let me see it; hold it up. That's a nice watch. Is it real?"

"Of course it's real."

"You let me hold onto it until the check clears and I'll get things moving right now. Otherwise, we have to wait till the check clears. I give you my word on it; nothing will happen to the watch."

"Listen, the watch cost my father over $10,000, okay. But it's worth a thousand times more than that to me, you know? He died so the watch is irreplaceable. I can't let you have it."

"No problem. But you'll understand that we can't begin processing your items until I get the six grand. If you're okay with that, so am I."

I looked at my watch. I would have never bought a fancy watch like this on my own. My father was a different story. He'd left Ahwaz with nothing and he was proud of what he had achieved. He wanted people to know that he was some-body, wanted people to know that his children were some-body. At first the watch had embarrassed me, but over the years, especially since my father's death, I had grown fond of it. I couldn't just leave it with this woman. I had no idea who she was. The only thing I knew about her was that she had no qualms about breaking the law. If she took my watch and never gave it back to me, what could I do about it? She knew I was in a desperate situation or I wouldn't be doing what I was doing. It was unlikely I'd be going to the cops. Of course, it was also true that she could run off with my six thousand dollars and there would be nothing I could do about it. But the money I could replace. The watch, I could not.

"I'll be back soon," I told her.

She looked skeptical and handed me her card.

* * *

They opened the van doors and helped me out. With one man on either side of me, they walked me into a building, down a short flight of stairs and through several sets of doors. From the way our footsteps echoed, I decided we were walk-ing down a corridor and because we walked for so long, it was clear that we were in a very large building.

I was ushered into a room that seemed to be an office of some sort. We were taken into an inner room and one of my captors spoke with a man. I assumed he was Egyptian since he spoke English with an Arab accent. He seemed to hold a position of some importance. One of the Americans kept calling the Arab Amun and Amun called the American Mr. Peirce.

Amun kept referring to "the prisoner." I could hear someone open what sounded like a briefcase and Peirce said something to the effect of, "These are the pertinent papers. I believe you've already been given an overview of his case."

They talked a few more minutes, and just before it seemed like the Americans were getting ready to leave, Amun spoke to me. "I take it you are not comfortable," he said in English. "In very short time, you will be out of clothes and taking shower." I noticed laughter among some of the Americans, but I decided they were simply laughing about how filthy I was.

I thanked Amun, who to me sounded completely sincere. I decided that my hell had ended and that things were about to get better.

Peirce told Amun that he would be in touch to check on our progress. He said he would be in and out of the country, but that for the next couple of days he could be reached at the Cairo Marriott. He gave Amun his number.

I could hear that the Americans were still standing there. Amun asked if there was anything else. Peirce said there was not, but that they wanted to wait until there was someone to take the prisoner to his cell.

"Oh," said Amun. "There's no reason for concern. I'm more than capable of dealing with the prisoner."

Everyone laughed, and I wondered if he was holding a weapon of some sort. The Americans now left and Amun told me in Arabic—and now I knew he was Egyptian—he told me that two steps to my left was a chair and he welcomed me to sit in it. He sounded so polite.

I sat and he got on the phone and asked his secretary to summon two escorts. After that we sat in silence for two or three minutes. I could hear him thumbing through paper work, and occasionally I could hear his pen moving across paper. I was rethinking him now that I'd heard him claim he was more than capable of dealing with the prisoner. There was something ominous about his way of speaking, polite though it was.

There was a knock. In Arabic Amun said, "Enter."

I heard the door open and he said, "Take the prisoner to interrogation room number one, and give him the shower. I will be in presently."

Silently they came up behind me and grabbed me by the arms—one on either side of me. They walked me back through the office and down the corridor. We walked down two flights of stairs. With each flight we descended, the air felt cooler. They then took me down another long corridor, up a short steep ramp and through a door. As soon as I was inside this room, one of them grabbed my arms and the other cut my jumpsuit off and my diaper as well. My hood they kept in place. There was no laughter about the smell the way there would have been from the Americans. I was standing there naked and I felt insecure. After that, they walked away from me, and I heard a squeaky valve turning and heard water running. At that moment, a giant stream of ice-cold water hit me and though I tried to move out of its way, it followed me and I had no choice but to bear it. The water was hitting me with such force that I realized it must be a fire hose—a thick and powerful stream of water so cold that I didn't think I could stand it.

It reminded me of a trip I'd taken with my parents to Maine as a kid. We'd gone to a beach near Pemaquid Point. My older siblings all began swimming, but I stood on the beach, afraid of the cold water. Finally, Farhad, my oldest brother, picked me up and carried me out into the water over my head and, ignoring my screams, he threw me in. First of all, I couldn't swim. At first that didn't concern me as much as the temperature of the water. It was bone-chillingly cold and I couldn't imagine that anyone could be so cruel. But then I began coughing and going under and I tried as hard as I could to find the bottom with my foot. I was trying to stand on the tip-toe of one foot and I was stretching my body to give me as much height as possible so that I could touch the ground and have my nose above water. Farhad saw my struggle. He swam over to me and grabbed me under my arms and sidestroked me toward shore. After we got to the point where we could wade, I kept trying to hit him, and he was laughing, and I would try again and he kept putting his hand on my forehead. And because his arm was longer than mine, I couldn't even touch him. Everyone in my family was laughing about this and I was crying and feeling extremely upset that they all found this so funny. And now all of that experience came back to me as I stood there barely able to stand against the violence of this cold stream of water.

That memory left me feeling small until I remembered that Allah was with me, that He saw all that was happening and condoned it. He knew what I was going through and He knew I could stand it. It gave me the strength I needed, and I transformed this experience into a genuine shower and realized that this was my chance to clean myself, to rid myself of the filth that clung to my body. I turned around so that all parts of my body were exposed to the water. Though my hands were cuffed together, they were cuffed in front of me. I used them to scrub the parts of my body that I could reach. The water continued to feel extremely cold to me, but now it felt like water from a crystal cold spring that was able to wash away my sins. I felt cold but exhilarated and I was reminded again of how much Allah could affect my attitude and therefore my experience.

The men shut off the hose and told me to stand where I was. I stood there, freezing. Outside it may have been hot, but in this basement, I was extremely cold, particularly after my shower. I began shivering and I felt like a little kid. But again, I remembered Allah, and my attitude about my shivering changed—it now seemed natural to me that I would shiver after what I had just been through and considering the temperature in the room.

I heard a door open, and I heard someone walk slowly toward me. I assumed it was Amun, but not until he spoke was I certain. He waited until he was less than a foot from me before saying to me in Arabic, "You are now mine." He said it softly, so that it had a romantic flare.

I was feeling very connected to myself through Allah, and I did not react. I said nothing, and since he could not see my face, it occurred to me that I had an advantage of sorts.

He continued, "The job that I have before me today is to let you understand that you are mine."

Again, I said nothing, nor did I move. I simply stood there and I felt surprisingly relaxed. I suspected that I was making him nervous. I was certain that other prisoners would have reacted in some visible way. Some would have insulted him. Some would have pleaded. Some would have tried to make a deal with him. Some would have moved about nervously. Some would have cried. Some may have even laughed. But I did nothing. I simply stood with my body facing him.

I could hear a slight change in his voice, just a note of concern as he spoke: "We know about you," he said. "We know what you have done. We know what you intended to do. We know of your connections. The only question is are you going to admit to these things and give us the details? Or are you going to be stupid like the last prisoner who came before me? Are you going to make it necessary for me to use force? I am prepared to use force. In fact, I have no problem with force. That is why I was hired for this job. I am very good at force. Force is my specialty."

Arab grandiosity is certainly something with which I have more than a passing familiarity. But even I was surprised to encounter it in a torture chamber. My hood prevented me from seeing Amun during his little speech, so I have no idea of the stance he adopted. But my picture is of him standing there with his fingers inserted Napoleon style between the buttons of his shirt:

"And, by the way, not only is force *my* specialty. The fact is, force is at the very essence of civilization. This is obviously true when it comes to reshaping the physical world: bulldozers move tons of gravel and stones in a single pass; lathes reshape steel. But civilization also applies force in a far more abstract manner: consider, for instance, the amount of force contained on a single sheet of paper on which our laws are written—a flimsy sheet of paper, yet behind it lies the full power of the state to control the individual. Which, of course, brings us back to you.

"During the next few days, weeks, and months, should it come to pass that you refuse to cooperate with me, you will see that I am an enormously civilized man. And if you do not believe it, you will come to regret it. Does your understanding meet with mine?"

I did not answer him and within a couple of seconds I saw that he was right—I regretted it. Without warning he hit me on the side of my face with something other than his hand. It felt like a flexible pipe. In a few minutes, I would find out that it was a two foot length of electrical cable about two inches in diameter, a cable made up of many smaller cables all bundled together and insulated from each other and surrounded by a thick coat of plasticized rubber.

It nearly knocked me out and I reeled. Unable to find my balance, I fell to the ground. Amun came over to me now and told me to stand up. "Remove your mask," he said.

I did as he asked, my hands still cuffed. Though the light in the windowless room was dim to say the least, it seemed so bright that I could barely see. In fact, I had to cover my eyes with my hands for half a minute or so to even make out Amun's face.

He was about five foot seven and he was squarely built. His head gave the impression of a giant fist. It was the face of a bulldog. Picture the Arab equivalent of Winston Churchill and you'll realize that he was not in the habit of being crossed. He wore a look of pure hatred and he put his face right up to mine, hoping, I suspect, that I would try to hit him. "You are mine. And the sooner you understand that, the sooner all of this will be behind us."

Still I felt the reassurance of Allah within and I felt certain that my expression did not change. I said nothing, and let him wonder where I had hid my fear. With Allah in my heart, I truly felt no hatred for this man, and I could see that this confused him.

Try though he might to hide it, I could see a moment of

weakness in his mouth just before he hit me again with the cable. This time, I turned and it struck me in the back across my shoulders. I could see him observing my eyes closely to see if I'd received the full weight of the blow.

I looked confidently into his eyes, but it was not a challenging look. This is what worried him, I told myself. If it had been a challenging look, he would have relaxed because he would have understood it as anger. But this look was outside his control.

He swung his cable again, this time even harder than before. Instinctively I lifted my arms to protect myself. The cable slammed into my left forearm and it felt as if it nearly snapped it in two. If it had hit my head, I think it might have killed me. Now I could tell from the look in his eyes, that I was in trouble.

"If you want to live, you will never try such a thing again. Do you understand?"

"Yes," I said. I felt that it was the only way of making it through the next minute.

He turned away from me now. I assumed he would turn and hit me again. But he didn't. Instead, he walked a few feet to a small stand on which he placed his cable. He picked up a blue pack of cigarettes that were lying there and put one into his mouth. He lit it and smoked. I watched him.

"Would you like a cigarette?" he asked me.

I assumed he would not give me one. But it seemed like if I said no, he would be disappointed at not being able to withhold something from me. I did not want to disappoint him. The side of my face was numb. My shoulders ached. My arm felt like someone had swung at it with a machete.

"Yes," I said.

He walked toward me and held out his blue pack of filterless cigarettes to me. Where one hand went, the other followed. I raised them both and took a cigarette and put it into my mouth. He held out his lighter and lit it for me.

I inhaled as deeply as I inhaled cigarettes in the States. I coughed for several seconds and looked at Amun with tears in my eyes, nearly choking. He surprised me by not laughing at me. After that, I inhaled his cigarettes with care—they were as strong as bad cigars.

During the entire five or six minutes it took us to smoke our cigarettes, he stood about four feet from me, facing his body directly at me so that it felt as if his body was focused on mine like a magnifying glass. He simply stood there, and except when he smoked, his arms were relaxed at his sides. He watched me the entire time. I was completely naked; nevertheless, I tried to keep my body from turning away from him. My feet, however, without my consent, kept shifting me ever so slightly to my right, at which point he would reposition himself to maintain the focus.

He was definitely trying to intimidate me, but he was using the intimidation as a tool to learn who I was. In fact, at one point as we smoked, he moved his hand rather quickly up to his mouth and I believe I flinched. But all of this was so subtle that I can't say for sure if that's what he even intended.

He was watching all of this and I realized that he had been through this little ritual before with other prisoners. The way I held myself, the angle at which I inclined my head, the way I inhaled and exhaled the smoke, the way I kept moving my feet, all of these were peep holes through the façade that was Yusuf Alsawari.

I wondered if Amun had learned his methods as part of his training or if he had discovered all of this on his own. As he watched me, I began to watch myself. I became intensely aware of my body during this time, and this watching felt foreign to me. There came a moment when something shifted, and for the first time in my life I became aware in some way, other than with my mind, that I had an actual body. That's how deeply I had been locked in my head. The change in the way I felt was dramatic. Amun did not change his expression,hol but I wondered if he had noticed. He just kept watching.

After that he surprised me. He looked at his cigarette and then back at me. "Life is essentially sad," he said. "There's nothing we can do about it. That's just how it is." He took an extraordinarily deep drag from his cigarette and then, speaking with smoke breath, he said, "Most people never realize this…" He paused and blew out the rest of the smoke: "but I'm hoping you will. It will make all of this go much faster."

It seemed to me that he was being utterly sincere and that in his own way, he was apologizing for what had been and was about to be. But I'll admit—I was merely groping to make sense of him.

He held out his hand for my cigarette butt. I handed it to him and thanked him. He walked back over to the stand and squashed our butts in an ash tray. He put down his pack of cigarettes and picked up his cable. He walked back over to me, and stood before me. "I need your help," he told me. "I need you to tell me about your connection to al-Qaeda."

"But I swear to you," I said. "I have no connection to al-Qaeda. This is a terrible mistake. They must think I'm someone else."

For an instant, as I stood there looking into his eyes, I was convinced that he believed me. Clearly he had heard the unmanufactured sincerity in my voice. And I'm certain that I saw a slight bit of fear in his eyes. But in less than a second, whatever portal I'd looked through closed, and a resolute twist appeared at his jaw as he swung his cable at me and he hit me across the back.

I groaned, and not merely reflexively. I wanted him to know that he was having the intended effect. My original stance of not showing any reaction had quickly changed. By this point, we were definitely engaged in a dialogue.

"I am telling you the truth," I said. "I don't know why they are doing this to me."

I was consciously trying to make him feel that he was not the originator of the pain.

"Who do they think you are?"

"I don't know."

"Who are you?"

"I'm Yusuf Alsawari."

As he went to hit me again, I raised my hands instinctively and he hit them instead of my head. Immediately I said, "I'm sorry. That was a reflex."

"You had better shut off your reflexes," he said. He walked over toward his stand and pulled a stool from behind it, a backless metal affair with loops welded onto the sides. He carried it over toward me and told me to sit in it. He pulled out a key and undid the cuff on my right arm. He then inserted it through the loop on the left side of the chair. Then he undid the cuffs that were both on my left leg and cuffed my right arm to the loop on the other side of the stool.

"That's better," he said, and he hit me again across the back of my head with his cable.

It felt to me that he was going against what he was feeling. And at that point, he proved it, at least to me, by hitting me again, this time much harder. It felt to me as if he was working hard to overcome something in himself that he considered a weakness, but to my way of thinking was a human connection between two people. But just the same, rather than hitting me in the head again, he hit me across the back of my shoulders.

"Now, I forget. Where were we," he said.

"You asked me my name."

"That's right. Thank you. What is your name?"

"My name is Yusuf."

Again he hit me, this time across my shins. My left shin took the brunt of it. I winced, and this was not any sort of act or attempt to please him. It was a reaction. My shins have always been the most sensitive spot on my body.

"What is your name?"

"I promise you. I promise you before Allah that my name is Yusuf."

He hit me across the shins again. Apparently he had found the spot he'd been looking for.

"You know," he said, "I thought that you were a man I could trust." He walked closer to me as he spoke. "I had thought we could get this over in a hurry." He picked up the hood I had let fall to the ground when I'd removed it. He placed it over my head again and I realized that he was using it not to keep me from seeing him, but to keep him from seeing me. As he tied it, he said, "But now I see that I was wrong. Now I see that you have fooled me. That you are not the sort of man I can trust. In fact, you are a liar. And I speak quite truthfully when I tell you that I cannot abide liars. Liars and thieves—these are two people I do not like. And you are a liar. Are you also a thief?"

"I'm not a thief and I'm not a liar. I promise you that I am not lying."

"You promise me that you are not lying. What good does it do for a liar to promise that he is not lying? Do you not see that once you are a liar, nothing from your mouth can ever be trusted?"

Just before the cable hit the side of my face, I heard it speeding through the air. It hit me with such force that it knocked me off balance and I actually tipped over along with the stool. I was on my side with much of the weight of my body pressing the stool onto my hand and arm. I could not use my arms to help myself up and Amun did nothing to help me. In fact, he came over and hit the chair with his cable. The loud noise scared me so much that I jumped.

I didn't know if it was all right for me to shift around to my knees and try to get up, or whether it made more sense to simply lie there. I tried to rearrange my legs so that there wasn't as much weight on my arm and hand.

"I will ask you again. What is your name?"

"Yusuf. It's the…"

Before I could say "truth," he had hit my left shin again.

"I'm sorry," he said. "I must have heard you incorrectly. What did you say your name is?"

I didn't answer him. He hit my left shin again.

"I still didn't hear you. Again. What is your name?"

I don't know what he was doing now, but from the way he spoke, I pictured him leaning forward. Frustrated at the pain and that I couldn't put my hands over my shin, I said, "Please don't hit me again. I need to explain…"

He hit me in the same spot on my left shin.

"I need to explain to you what happened."

"Very good," he said. "But don't bother with lies. I am a man who does not countenance lies."

"I don't like lies either, I swear. I promise you, I will not lie to you. I swear on my life, I will never lie to you. I swear that I have not lied to you."

Again the cable slammed into my left shin.

"Are you a Muslim?" I asked him.

"I am."

"I am too. And I swear to you on the Holy Koran and on the name of The Prophet (peace be upon him), I swear to you that I have not lied to you, and…"

Once again he struck me with the cable, but this time on the side of my head. I remember hearing his voice and not being able to hold together the sentence that he spoke, and then I heard him shouting at me, "Muhammad."

I came to with my head resting on the floor and realized I had been knocked out. I lifted my head now and I told him, "You can hit me until you kill me, but I promise you, I am not Muhammad."

"Why do they tell me you are Muhammad? Why do your papers say you are Muhammad?"

"My papers say I am Muhammad, but I promise you—I am not Muhammad."

"Why do you carry papers that lie? Who but a liar would carry papers that lie?"

He hit me again, this time across both of my shins. The left one felt like it had a nerve as big as a highway that fed directly into my brain and was delivering pain at an unbelievably efficient rate.

"My wife became a Christian, and I was afraid she would divorce me and try to take all of my money. So I got a secret bank account and I used a fake name."

He hit me on my left shin again.

"You have no wife."

"I do have a wife."

"They say you have no wife."

"They are wrong. I'm married under a name I suspect they don't know about."

"You say you are not lying. So this I propose. You tell me your real name. I will speak to them and they will find out if you are right. I promise you, if you are lying, the next time you are here, you will pay. Do you understand this?"

"I understand."

"So that name?"

"Yusuf bin Ismail bin Ibrahim Alsawari."

"Okay, then. We'll see what they say."

I heard him walk away. From the direction he was walking in, I suspected he was headed back toward the stand. I heard what sounded like the cable coming to rest on the stand. After that, he walked back over to me and just stood there. Through the hood, I could smell a cigarette. I was fairly certain that he would not offer me one, and I was right. I heard him type numbers into what sounded like a cell phone. He waited then for a couple of seconds and said he was finished with the prisoner.

I heard a door open and footsteps approached. Then there was a man on either side of me and nearly simultaneously they undid my handcuffs. They stood me up and one of them removed my hood. The other handed me a clean jumpsuit.

I put it on and they marched me out of the room and down a hall to a cell so small that I couldn't stand straight in it, but I could straighten out in it when I lay down.

The cell's walls were cement and the door was of heavy, rusted steel. In the middle of the door was a smaller door that could be opened from the outside. This smaller door was big enough to look through and to pass a small tray through.

There was no light in the cell, but as I was entering it, enough light shown through the open door to see a bucket sitting in the back right corner. What can only be described as a nest ran along most of the left wall, a nest comprised of folded rags that had been doubled and redoubled to mute the stone floor enough to make sleeping possible.

When I saw all of this, I was filled with horror. The bucket had stains around the top where its contents had been emptied. The cell looked as if it had never been cleaned. How many prisoners had lain on this nest, and had worked to make it more comfortable? I wondered if any had done so with an eye toward the next tenant. If so, any love that had been woven into the nest was overcome by the smell. The entire cell smelled like an animal stall. Once during a summer vacation as a kid, I remember visiting a farm in New Jersey that had just laid down a thick layer of chicken manure over a field. And while this cell did not smell the same as that manure, it smelled with the same intensity.

The door closed behind me and all was darkness except for three short cracks of light: one of them ran along the entire top edge of the door; several feet below it ran a ten inch crack parallel to the first—this one from the little door intended for trays; and then perpendicular to those two ran a two foot sliver of light along the right side of the larger door. I could never forget those three line segments of light, their relationship to each other. The shorter horizontal was perfectly centered under the longer one. The two-foot vertical began a little above the lower of the two horizontals and dropped from there. I'd spend hours each day examining those three slivers of light. They were my only sun, my only connection to the outer world. Even that first day, as the door closed, I noticed that their relationship to one another gave them the appearance of a hieroglyph, the meaning of which could only be hopelessness.

I turned now and holding my hands out in front of me, I moved toward the left wall, toward the nest and when I felt it with my foot, I sat on it. It was about an inch thick in some places and not even a quarter inch in others. I lay on it to check its comfort, and I was amazed at its lumpiness. I couldn't imagine that I would ever be able to sleep on it. My bare feet, however, were on the cold, bare floor, and when I put them onto the nest, they felt much warmer. I realized that the lumps had been consciously done to protect one's body, not only from the hardness of the floor, but from the cold as well. We were at least two stories underground, and the sun had no jurisdiction down here. As a result, the place was permanently cold. Within a few minutes of sitting there, I realized that the cold was going to be my main problem. In time, the smell faded into the background, but the cold remained.

Chapter 9

I hailed a cab that was returning from Williamsburg. As I opened the door, I saw and heard two F-16s fly overheard. This was my first glimpse of a sight that would become commonplace during the next few days.

I told the driver to take me to my bank on Madison between East 38th and 39th. That's where I had my safe deposit box in which I kept all of the paperwork I wanted to hide from Ruth—basically, everything having to do with my Cayman account.

I was glad we didn't have to go any further because it was difficult to get around. It was mainly pedestrians who were holding things up, walking in the streets with no apparent concern for cars. Despite all of that, we were there in thirty minutes. I asked the driver to wait for me for the return trip. He made me pay and said he'd wait for five minutes.

I had opened the safe deposit account after my father's death, so Ruth knew nothing about it. I had been able to open it without a social security number and I had transposed my middle two names to throw off any sort of search that a divorce lawyer might make. That may not sound like much of a disguise, but it's something that very few Arabs would ever think of doing. An Arab's middle names tell who his father and grandfather are, so transposing those names changes those two facts. If you know anything about Arab pride, you understand why I assumed that this rendered the transaction untraceable. So whereas my entire name is Yusuf bin Ismail bin Ibrahim Alsawari which means Yusuf, son of Ismail, son of Ibrahim, I changed it to Yusuf bin Ibrahim bin Ismail Alsawari.

When I'd first opened my safe deposit box, I'd considered keeping money in it—maybe fifty or a hundred thousand dollars. It was strictly forbidden, of course, but I didn't see how anyone would find out. I didn't go through with it; I now wished I had.

I signed in and learned immediately that I was lucky to have made it in—the bank had decided to close early. "Because of everything that's happened today," is how the bank manager put it.

"It's terrible, ha?" I said.

"I can't believe it," he said. "I just can't believe it. It's horrifying. It's just…" He shook his head.

He put his key in the lock and I put in mine and opened the box. He left me alone in the room. I had done what I could to make sure Ruth knew nothing about this safe deposit box. For instance, I had been keeping all of the paperwork regarding the box in the box. I had asked the bank to give me receipts at the time of each transaction. I only had to pay rent on the box once a year. The first two times I had remembered to go in and pay it well in advance of them sending it home. But this last time I had forgotten. It arrived while I was out. Ruth had seen the unopened envelope, I am certain, because she had laid it on my desk. Whether she noticed the name of the bank, I had no idea. When it happened, I had not been particularly worried about it, because divorce had begun to seem unlikely to me. Regardless, of whether she had noticed it or not, I would need to close this safe deposit box account because I was moving to the west coast. I needed to ensure that everything was all taken care of lest they send additional paperwork that Ruth would intercept. She could potentially find out I'd closed the box on the day of my apparent death and deduce something was up. I needed to make sure that didn't happen.

I found the checkbook and put it into my jacket pocket. The extra checks and all of the other paperwork I put into my computer bag. After emptying the box, I found the clerk and told him that I wanted to close the account and take care of all of the paperwork. I told him I'd moved and that I didn't want any mail going to my former house. "Separation issue," I told him. "I can't get into it." I rolled my eyes. He nodded and smiled. He asked if I had my second key with me. In that moment I went into panic mode, and because of the way he reassured me, I'm fairly certain he noticed. The thing is, I wasn't worried that I'd lost the key. I was worried that I had not.

When I'd first opened the box, they'd told me that if I lost both keys, it would mean that the bank would have to drill out the lock and install a new one. They said it could take a while and cost me several hundred dollars. At the time the possibility of losing the key didn't worry me. What worried me was that Ruth would find one of the keys. For that reason, I always carried both of them with me. But after a while, I no longer suspected that she wanted a divorce. With that concern out of the way, my new concern became keeping the two keys in separate locations so I wouldn't lose them both. I'd decided it was safe to leave the spare key at home locked in my desk drawer. In fact, lately I hadn't even been locking it.

But now, my former concern reasserted itself—I didn't want her to find that key. Now that she thought I was dead, she would certainly go through my personal effects, and she would certainly find that key where it lay in my desk drawer. I couldn't remember if the drawer was locked or not. But it didn't matter. Either way, Ruth would eventually get into that drawer. And when she did, she would find the key, and that would lead her to this bank. Or would it? As I stood there now, I took a look at the key in my hand. The name of the bank was not on it. It all depended on whether she had noticed the name of the bank the day the bill had arrived. I also wondered if I'd ever thrown that bill away. That too might be lying around on my desk and it could lead her here. She had to know that I'd inherited a lot of money, so I could imagine that she'd be curious. She might very well be contacting the bank, especially if she found the key. The key might jog her memory. If I wanted to protect her from knowing that I was still alive—and I did—I had to sneak home and snag that key. And possibly that bill.

I told the man, "I guess I lost it."

"Not to worry," he said. "You still have the one key, so the replacement fee will only be thirty-five dollars."

He took me to a woman who handled the paperwork. She told me one final statement would be sent to my home, that it was standard practice, that it would be going out in a little over a week, and that she could not stop it. She suggested I get a mailbox and then give her the mailbox address if I didn't want it sent to my home. I told her that's what I would do.

My taxi had left. As I was waiting for another one, I remembered the card that the passport woman had given me. I could simply use her address as my forwarding address. I didn't care if I ever got the letter about the box or not. I just didn't want Ruth to get it. Not only that, getting a post office box would require a home address, which would put me right back where I started.

I went back into the bank and told the lady the address of the passport place, and asked her to send it in care of Sheila Picard—that was the passport woman's name. After that, I had to wait a good fifteen minutes for another cab and I headed back down to Allen Street.

This driver was not as skilled as my first driver had been at getting around, and this time the trip took longer. I did not arrive back at the passport office until close to four. I had to knock on the door for about ten minutes to get Sheila to respond. She was in the back room and when she came out, she was wiping her nose. She handed me a form for my passport. It looked like a legitimate passport application. In addition, she gave me a second sheet that didn't look as though it had been put out by the government. Basically, it was a chance for me to tell who ever was creating my social security card as much as possible about myself so that they could create a fictional past that would correspond in some way to my ethnic background. They didn't want the background information that they put in for me to contradict who I was, i.e., it wouldn't work to say that I, an Arab, was from Sweden, etc. Moreover, they didn't want it to appear as if I had been cre-

ated *ex nihilo*. Who ever was providing my social security
number intended to provide me with a past. Sheila reminded
me that they would be linking my passport and my social security number and that they would provide me with a sheet
that told of my fictional past so that I would know the key
events of my life. She told me it was essential that I memorize the information to prevent any sort of mess-ups in the future.

The part I hadn't anticipated was choosing a new name. I
hadn't given any thought to the matter. For a few seconds, I
considered going with an American sounding name, but decided against it. I am proud of my Arab roots and didn't want
to deny them. I had no idea what was about to happen in this
country, no idea of the degree to which anti-Arab sentiment
would sweep this land. And not just this land, but the entire
non-Muslim world.

The first name that came into my head was Muhammad
Muhammad. As a boy living in Montreal I'd had a friend by
that name, and I now decided to make it my name. Not only
that, it tied in with my idea for a bookstore, Muhammad's
Books. The next day I would realize it was a bad choice. But
it would be six weeks before I'd realize just how bad.

I gave her a check for six thousand dollars and suggested
that it would take three business days to clear. She said,
"Well, since today's Tuesday, that means it won't clear until
Friday, and if that's the case, you won't see your passport until Monday, maybe Tuesday."

After that she took my picture. She retook it a number of
times because she didn't want me to look angry in any way.
"These guys don't want to call attention to themselves.
They've told me they won't do passports for criminals because it could expose their entire operation. So I hope you're
not a criminal. You're not a terrorist, are you?" She smiled as
she said this.

"No, I'm not a terrorist. I've been working on my Ph.D.
in philosophy."

"Oh, I thought you were working in the World Trade
Center." She said it with a trace of humor behind her disbe-

lief.

"Yeah, and where's the contradiction? Haven't you heard of students working before?"

"And yet you seem to have no shortage of money."

"You want to know the truth? My wife worked in the Trade Center, and she had my passport at her office."

"Aha," she said. "So now he has a wife. I see how it is."

All the while she was shooting my picture and was obviously just having a good time with me.

She finally found a picture she could live with, one that she thought would pass muster with her passport people. Just before I left, I asked her if it would be possible to give her a second check for which she would give me cash when it cleared.

"For a fee," she said. "It's all about the fee." She smiled.

"Okay, what would be the fee for ten thousand dollars?"

"Four thousand."

"Come on," I said. "You can do better than that. You're already making a ton of money off me."

"So what do you suggest?" she said.

"How about one thousand?"

"One thousand? Now you're kidding me. How about fifteen hundred? I can do it for that."

"So if I give you a check for twenty three thousand, you'll give me twenty grand."

"That's right. But don't forget, I'm going to need the rest of the money for the passport and social in cash. Otherwise, you'll have to wait for that check to clear too."

"So should I make this check out for twenty-seven thousand?"

"Works for me."

I wrote the check and as I was leaving, I realized I was a complete fool. I'd just given her a total of thirty-three thousand dollars, and I had no reason to trust her whatsoever. But what else could I do? I decided to make my peace with it.

* * *

I'd been lying there practicing, if you will, for how I was going to sleep. I had tried lying with my head toward the back wall. It felt as if many prisoners had slept with their heads that way, and so I could feel the form of the human body—no particular body, but the average of many bodies—and the rags seemed thin in all the wrong places. I considered that sleeping with my head toward the door might be more comfortable, even though it felt wrong psychologically. It then occurred to me that I could turn the nest around and still sleep with my head toward the back. As I was doing this, the thing came apart and I felt lost. In the darkness, I had a tough time figuring out how to get it back together again, but after a while I had it about as good as it had been. After that, I never tried to change it again.

At about this point, I heard some loud noises. It sounded like someone was pounding on the doors of the neighboring cells. Soon the pounding was on my door, and light appeared through the little door and I realized that someone was passing a tray of food to me. I went over to it and took it. The door closed and on my way back to the nest in the darkness, I banged my head on the low ceiling and lost my balance. I stumbled and dropped the bowl. I guessed that I hadn't eaten for at least two days, probably more like two and a half. But I'm still not sure if that's accurate. I have no idea how long it took me to get there.

All I know about the supper was that when it was handed to me, it had all been in a bowl. It was a soup of some kind. But I never did get to eat it as soup. I felt around the floor and the nest for clumps of food. I remember that I found a bunch of a vegetable that tasted like chard. I later learned that it was amaranth leaves. It was in much of the food that we ate while I was there, and it tasted fairly good to me. Ruth had often added chard to soups, and this stuff had a similar taste.

The bowl didn't break, and I was glad of that. I feared they would think that I'd willfully broken it and that they wouldn't feed me for a while. An hour or so later, the man returned and clanged on the doors. I heard the little doors opening and trays being handled. Occasionally, I would hear a remark or two exchanged, but never loud enough to decipher.

I didn't want to miss going to the window and have him think I was ungrateful for the food. So I made sure to be there and I handed him my bowl on my tray. He asked where the spoon was, and I apologized and told him I'd dropped it. I promised him I would find it before breakfast the next day.

That evening, I said *Ishaa*, though I truly didn't know if I had the time correct. I merely knew that I needed union with Allah. I had no water to perform *wudu* so I decided that I would perform *Tayammum*, or dry ablution. In the place of water, I used dust from the floor. As I prayed, I felt cleansed and connected to Allah. Afterwards, I spent a few minutes feeling around with my hand for the spoon. Finally, over by the bucket, I found it.

In the night I woke up at one point unable to sleep and I thought of Allah and I pitied myself and asked Him why He would allow this to happen to me. At that moment the realization returned to me that Allah was aware of everything in the universe and that there was nothing that He did not oversee. I felt as if I was being warmed by the sun, and I realized I had no choice but to have faith in Him. I had no idea what time it was, but I decided that it might be about the time for *Fajr*, the morning prayers. After my prayers, with no idea what time it was, I lay down. Within half an hour, I could hear the man from the kitchen coming round with breakfast.

As soon as he opened my tray door, I handed him my spoon. He took it and handed me a clean one along with a bowl of hot cereal. I thanked him. He said, "Good. Normally I don't receive a thank you so soon."

Chapter 10

The second hotel I stopped at was the Douglass on West Fifty-Sixth Street. I told the man at the desk that I'd lost my passport as I was escaping from the Trade Center and that it was the only identification I had. He told me he was happy I'd made it out alive and he gave me a room. He asked me simply to write my name. I went with my new name, Muhammad Muhammad.

Rushing around, I hadn't noticed how wound up I was. But as I lay on my bed I became aware that my entire body was vibrating from everything that had happened. There's only one way to describe what I was feeling: I had the temporal equivalent of claustrophobia—it seemed as if I didn't have any time. So many thoughts and feelings were pressing for my attention that I felt paralyzed and my mind was racing. I'd just start to think about how I had left Ruth and how I would never see her again when it would occur to me that I'd seen the World Trade Center destroyed, had seen people jump to their deaths. Not only that, I was dead and I had a new name. That would get me thinking about how I would soon be leaving New York. My mind kept whirling around from one issue to the next and I felt completely overwhelmed.

I was exhausted. But before going to sleep, I turned on the news. I saw several videos of the planes flying into the Trade Center. A reporter referred to the men in the planes as cowards. At the time I agreed with his assessment, but now I see it differently. Even if you disagree with the actions of those men, even if you find their actions despicable, the fact is, they were willing to give up their lives for a cause they believed in. How does someone like that meet the definition of coward?

At any rate, when I saw the image of the plane hitting the south tower, I actually began to cry. I don't know how many times they showed those scenes, the planes flying in and the towers folding. But they affected me in a way that I found totally surprising. Every time I saw them, I prayed to Allah to relieve all of the suffering that had occurred and was possibly still occurring beneath the wreckage.

And watching all of that suffering changed the way I felt about leaving Ruth. What I longed for most was to grab a cab and head back to Williamsburg. I pictured how happy she would be to see me, pictured how we would hug each other and weep with joy. I realized in that moment that if I were to do that, we would end up back together the way we were before she returned to Christianity. Several times I picked up the phone just to call her so I could hear her voice. I pictured her at home crying and praying that I was all right. I pictured how swollen and red her eyes were by this time. And how cold her mouth always felt when she cried and I kissed her. She loved me in a way no one had ever loved me, and that's how I loved her. Looking back on it now, I can't believe I was able to leave her as I did.

The only way I was able to resist calling her was by reading the copy of the Koran that I had on my laptop. I searched for the verse about setting your wife free rather than keeping her as a way of punishing her. Though I couldn't find it, I felt that this was the right path to take, that I was following the will of Allah. Ruth would mourn my loss for a while, but in the end her life would be easier and she would be happier. She would be able to move on instead of feeling trapped by a marriage that was not about to budge. She would be free to remarry and have kids, which is what she had been getting ready to do just before she returned to Christianity. Now she could marry a Christian. The thought of it pained me. I kept trying to believe I thought this was the better way, but it did nothing to stop my tears.

Then later that evening, President Bush came on to address the nation. There was an excruciating moment—it probably lasted for only five or ten seconds—during which we could see him, but he didn't seem to know that we could. He stood there with his eyes wide open, looking as afraid as anyone I've ever seen. He looked as if it had finally hit him that the country needed a Roosevelt or a Lincoln, but all we had was a Bush. As I lay there watching, I felt bad for him. I felt even worse for the country.

* * *

I had no sense of time; there were no windows and no light except the unchanging cracks of light around the door and the food tray slot. But I suspect it was two hours later that I heard an outer door open. Two sets of footsteps approached my cell. The key turned and when the door opened, I was unable to open my eyes against the light.

I held my hands in front of my eyes attempting to see the darkness in the shape of a man. He yelled at me to stand up and approach him. I wasted no time complying, bending over as I walked to avoid bumping my head on the low ceiling. Once I had reached the corridor, he told me to put my hands on the wall and another man handcuffed them together. After that, I tripped along beside them as they walked me down the hall. I was still having difficulty seeing because of the brightness. When my eyes finally adjusted, I realized that the two men were Amun's assistants.

This time they took me into a different room. This room was smaller and it contained instruments unfamiliar to me. One of them was a table, the top of which was built on a slant. First they blindfolded me. I was encouraged by the fact that they did not cover my entire face with a hood.

They laid me on the table so that my head was lower than my feet. They undid my handcuffs, stretched out my arms and handcuffed my wrists to rings on the sides of the table. I don't know what they used to manacle my legs in place, but it involved chains of some kind. They then fitted a broad strap across the table so that my chest was completely secured in place. All the while I was becoming more and more frightened of what lay in store for me. I kept thinking they were going to beat me, but they just stood there waiting. After that I heard someone open the door and come walking toward me. In that moment I could feel the warmth—the physical warmth—of a face directly in front of my own.

Amun spoke at a very low volume. He couldn't have been more than an inch away from my face. "You lied to me," he said.

"I did not lie to you," I said. "I promise you. I did not lie."

"You lied to me and I told you that if you lied to me, you would pay. Today, you will see that I do not lie."

"I did not lie to you. Please believe me." It was through hearing the sound of my pleading that I realized the extent of my fear.

Amun now moved away. One of the men standing on my right side, ordered me to open my mouth.

As I considered whether to comply, Amun spoke: "You will definitely open your mouth," he said. "The only question is, will you do so voluntarily?"

I opened it and the man told me to open it wider, as wide as it would go. I did this and he stuffed an incredibly hard object into the right side of my mouth. Whatever it was, it was made out of metal and shaped like a "V" so that it fit between my upper and lower teeth and kept my mouth pried open. Apparently it was attached to a handle with which he could keep it in place without sticking his fingers into my mouth. This made it possible for the other assistant to insert what felt like a towel down my throat. He too kept his fingers clear of my mouth. He used a wooden object that may have been the handle of a wooden spoon—I could not tell. I only know that he poked the towel so far down that I was gagging and I felt as if I was going to vomit. I was overcome with a total fear that I was going to die. My gag reflex continued for nearly a minute. It wasn't until I remembered that my only hope lay in Allah that I finally relaxed. At that moment, I stopped gagging and instantly I could breathe better, but only through my nose—I could not pass air through my mouth, so far had the towel been rammed down my throat.

I concentrated on keeping my mind on Allah and I relaxed onto the table so that my entire back made contact with it and I felt assured that everything was working according to Allah's plans.

That was before they began pouring water on my face, before I felt the water being absorbed by the towel and running down my throat directly into my windpipe. The towel had forced my epiglottis open, so I had no defense against the water. I coughed, but the cough could not exit through my mouth because the towel made that impossible. The cough forced the water that had drained into my throat out through my nose. This caused a burning sensation that went from the back of my throat up into my nose as if tender little flaps of skin were being torn by the violence of the water that was under pressure from my cough.

Breathing in through my nose did no good because by now the flow of the water had been increased to the point that it found its way into my nostrils as well as my throat. Because my head was lower than my lungs, it began to feel like my head was filling up. At the time, I didn't understand what was happening, but as I think it back over, I imagine that my sinuses were filling up before my lungs could. At any rate, soon enough the water began traveling up—because remember, my head was lower than my lungs—traveling up my windpipe toward my lungs. I was coughing non-stop by now and I was convinced that Amun intended to kill me.

I've heard so-called experts describe waterboarding as an interrogation technique in which a cloth is placed over the subject's face and water is poured onto the cloth. I have trouble believing that such a method would be effective. The truth is I can't say, because I have no experience of that method. What I can say is that Amun's method *was* effective—it achieved the desired effect almost immediately. Within seconds I was drowning. This was not as the experts deemed it, "simulated drowning." This was the real thing.

I had always been moved by a passage in the writings of Averroes in which he recommends that when a person dies, he should do everything in his power to make his final thought be of Allah, that by so doing, the person will be led to Him in death. This notion had registered with me at a very deep level. Up until now, every portion of my body had been in an upheaval, fighting desperately for a way to stay alive. Every muscle had been working with that one aim in mind. I'd been thrashing about on the table within the limits of my restraints. This of course only increased my need for air and the more I breathed, the closer I came to drowning. But when I recalled Averroes' advice, there followed a moment of the deepest acceptance of Allah's will.

I'm sure that a skeptic would say that I had begun to die and that this moment of acceptance was actually the beginnings of death. But it did not strike me as such. What it seemed like was that Allah came to me and helped me accept His will and helped me to relax even though I was dying. At that moment, I felt myself slip into a state of Union with Him.

The next thing I remember is I was sitting up and coughing and Amun was asking me if I was ready to speak the truth.

"I'm not Muhammad," I said between coughs and completely out of breath.

Other than my coughing and violent breathing, there was silence. I took advantage of it.

"I promise you, I am not Muhammad. That's a name I made up to hide my identity from my wife. I wanted her to think I had died."

"Who are you then?"

"I am Yusuf Alsawari."

"We know that Yusuf Alsawari is dead. He died in the World Trade Center. Furthermore, we know that you are responsible, at least in part, for the deaths of a number of sailors in Yemen. What we want to know is the nature of your involvement in 9/11."

"I swear I don't know anything about Yemen and I don't know anything about 9/11. I swear this on the name of Allah the Merciful."

"He may not be so merciful if you continue to lie and take his name in vain. You need to understand that we know. Do you need more of this water treatment to convince you of what we know? It's all up to you. You decide."

"I swear to you that my name is Yusuf bin Ismail bin Ibrahim Alsawari and that I had nothing to do with the death of anyone. I promise you. Please consider what I am saying. Please let me tell you my entire story. I promise you. If you…"

"I see you have decided your fate. Strap him back down."

Amidst all of the sounds of chains and straps, I could smell that Amun was smoking a cigarette, and I wished he would give one to me. But more than anything, I wanted time before they drowned me again. "Please give me a cigarette," I shouted.

"What did you say?" said Amun.

"A cigarette. Please."

"A cigarette. He wants a cigarette. All right. I will give you a cigarette. But understand. This is going to be a very dear cigarette indeed. In return for it, I want answers. And if you make a fool of me, and do not give me answers, I will not be a happy man. And if I am not a happy man, I will see to it that you are not a happy man. Are our minds attuned?"

"Yes," I said. "Completely." I was filled with terror at what he might do to me when he heard me repeat what I had said before. But how could it be any worse? And at least it would not be happening right now.

They freed my hands and loosened the strap on my chest so that I could sit up. My legs were still chained and I was still blindfolded. Amun told me to hold out my hand. I half expected he would hit it or burn it, but I held it out anyway and he placed a cigarette between my fingers. I held it up to my mouth and he lit it.

I have never enjoyed a cigarette as much as that one, though, like the previous cigarette Amun had given me, this one was far too strong. But strangely enough, while I had been nearly choking before smoking it, the cigarette seemed to calm my cough. But I did continue to sneeze and every time I did, water gushed out of my mouth and nose. My sinuses were full and I felt as if I had a terrific head cold.

I heard the other two men say thank you, so I assumed Amun offered cigarettes to them as well. None of us spoke during this five or six minute period. We were simply four human beings enjoying a smoke. With every puff I took, I was aware of the approaching end of the cigarette, the end of this moment, the shrinking of this tiny island of peace on which I stood, the coming moment of fear and pain. I kept my cigarette going as long as I could—it was filterless and I smoked it until it was so short that it blistered my fingers. I thanked Amun when I could hold the butt no more and someone took it from me.

"Now what is it that you have to say to me," Amun said.

"I wish to tell you my story. If you will listen to it, you will understand that what I am saying is true."

"I offer you a cigarette and this is how you repay me?"

"I promise you…I am telling you the truth."

"If that is your notion of the truth, then we must try to change that. Strap him back down."

"Please, do not do this. I will do anything, but please, not this." I was whining in a way that seemed completely foreign.

"Tell me the truth, and I will not do it." Amun spoke matter of factly, as if he were reasoning with a child. As he spoke, the men continued to strap me down.

"I am telling you the truth. I promise you. In the name of Allah, I promise you."

"I'll let Allah address your blasphemy. I'll address your lies."

During the past several days, I had experienced more fear than I had ever experienced in my life. And now the thought that I was going to have to experience drowning again made me feel like a small child.

This time, when the assistant told me to open my mouth, I refused. The man started squeezing the sides of my cheeks to pry my mouth open. At that point Amun intervened.

"No, don't do that. I have a better idea. The American has told me of a different way and that is what we will now try. Go to the cafeteria and return with a roll of plastic wrap," he told an assistant.

I heard one of the men leave. At first, Amun and the other man were just standing there, but as soon as the other man returned, the three of them moved to the other side of the room and they spoke at a volume I could not understand. Now they approached me. One of them lifted my head and the other wound plastic wrap around my face and head several times, completely blocking my ability to breathe—my nose was blocked; my mouth was blocked. I worked so hard to get air that I could feel my eardrums nearly caving in. They just left me like that for over a minute.

I was sure I was going to asphyxiate and I felt the worst kind of helplessness. Then one of them poked a small hole in the plastic where my mouth was, and just as I was frantically breathing in air, someone poured water into the hole and I sucked a bunch of it into my lungs. I began coughing but the water had no place to go because the hole was too small for it to escape through and more water was pouring in. It felt as if the top of my head was going to blow off. No matter how I turned my head, the water kept coming in through the hole.

I don't think it took me half a minute before I was right back where I had been, realizing that I could not fight this, that they were going to win. I thought again on Allah and relaxed into place and again I must have passed out. When I came to, they had me sitting up, the plastic was gone, and I was coughing. I was breathing as I would have if I'd just sprinted half a mile. Before Amun had even asked me anything, I spoke.

"I promise you, I did nothing to deserve this. You must listen to me. You must hear me out. I speak the truth and that is all. Listen to me."

He was silent for a moment. I think I surprised him.

"Apparently you are not susceptible to this particular treatment. That is fine. We have other options available to us. And we will make use of those options. Just now I am feeling that it is time for my lunch. But I will call for you another time. And you will see that you cannot hide the truth from us. The truth will be exposed and then, my friend, you will understand that all of the pain that you chose for yourself was in vain. You will then see that you could have taken a much easier path."

He continued: "In a way—I will admit it—I admire you for taking such a difficult path. It is as if we are climbing a very high mountain, and what do you do? Instead of taking the proven path that has delivered numerous climbers to the summit, you choose a path that no one has ever previously mastered. If I had met you under different circumstances, I believe that you and I may have become friends. You can imagine then, how difficult it is for me to continue with this. But I will continue. This is my job, and I always do my job. Always. You see, I am very much like you."

With that he told his assistants to return me to my cell, and I heard him walk toward the door and leave.

Chapter 11

I spent the next morning, Wednesday, 9/12, holed up in a coffee shop reading every article in the *New York Times* about the hijackings and al-Qaeda. There was a heaviness in the air, not only from the smoke and the smell of the Trade Center, but they definitely contributed to it. It felt as if everything had changed and that it would always be different. Not a single article mentioned the fear in Bush's eyes. I took that particular denial to mean that the entire country was afraid.

Occasionally I'd remember the money I'd potentially blown, and I'd worry about it for a while, and I'd think about how I wanted to get out of New York as soon as possible. The longer I waited to leave, the more likely it was I'd run into someone who knew me and word would get back to Ruth.

It was that fear that prompted me to visit one of those glasses stores. I remember that on the way, I saw two women and a man standing on the street talking, and one of the women was crying and holding a tissue to her nose. This was a sight I would see repeatedly during the next week or so.

I took out my contacts and asked for an equivalent prescription in glasses. Later that afternoon I picked them up. I had ordered some large, dark frames that I believed drastically altered the way I looked. For one thing, they were far more contemporary than my usual taste. Later that day, I shaved my mustache. I felt confident not only that I was unrecognizable—I didn't even think I looked Middle Eastern.

But that evening, walking on Houston Street, I ran into some teenagers and after they had passed me, one of them yelled "fucking towel head." It took me a few seconds to register that he was referring to me. I had never experienced a comment of that sort in New York; I'd received dirty looks that I'd assumed expressed an anti-Arab sentiment, but that was the extent of it.

I spent that night in the same hotel. On television they

were still showing the Trade Center getting hit, collapsing, or collapsed and I lay there on my bed crying. Most people had someone to talk to about it, but I had no one and it built up in me and affected me all the more. Once again, I could barely resist calling Ruth.

The next morning I lay about until noon, and without showering, I bought a copy of the *Times* and went to a diner for breakfast. I overstayed my welcome reading every article about the attacks that I could find. After that I began reading other articles. But not until I sank to reading sports articles did it become clear to me how filled I was with dread. It was only Thursday, 9/13, and I didn't know what to do with myself. I had to hang around until Monday, at least, before I could pick up my new identity. I had nothing to do, nowhere to go.

I wandered over to the main branch of the New York Public Library. I hadn't been there in years, so when I couldn't find the card catalogue, I asked a librarian about it.

My death had left me vulnerable—losing Ruth and all that went with it. And the reality of the Trade Center's collapse continued to sink in. It was a landmark that had been completed while I was still a baby. It was part of what lent my world a sense of permanence. You would think that by comparison a tiny thing like finding out that the card catalogue in the New York Public Library had been closed to the public six years before would not even register in the midst of so many shocks. But it did. It was just one thing too many. It felt like everything had changed. I sat there for a while looking at a computer screen for books that were of interest, but it was difficult to feel a connection between what I saw on-screen and the books on the shelves. With the card catalogue it had been different—there was a unique correspondence between a specific card and a specific book. Not any more. Many different computers could now access a specific book simultaneously. The one card, one book, voodoo correspondence no longer existed. I'd been going to that library since I was a kid, and I'd expected that it would always remain the same.

I left and wandered around the streets. I kept obsessing about the safe deposit key. If I didn't take care of that one loose end, my entire plan could crumble and I'd be yanked back into life. At first I had thought I would pick it up during the day while Ruth was at work, but by now I had realized what it meant that her place of work had been destroyed. Morgan Stanley did have other buildings in Manhattan, but I doubted that the developing world was their top priority. They'd be far more apt to worry about finding space for the more lucrative aspects of their business. And even if they did resettle her department, it was doubtful it would happen very soon. If I were to sneak home during the day, there was a high probability I would run into her; moreover, I stood a good chance of being spotted by a neighbor. I decided my best chance of getting the key undetected would be to go there during the middle of the night while she was asleep. The thought of it scared me, but the alternative scared me more. The thing I had going for me was that she was a fairly deep sleeper.

I thought about all of this as I walked around. I couldn't bear the thought of heading out there tonight, but some night I'd have to—and soon. Just not tonight.

As I passed Brooks Brothers on 44th and Madison, I re-membered what it was I'd told myself I needed to accomplish today. This was the third day that I'd been wearing these clothes. I needed something new to wear.

I hadn't been in Brooks Brothers since I was a kid when my mother had dragged me there at the beginning of every school year. Part of her wanted us to be just like other Americans. I guess I'd wanted it in those days as well. All of that changed for me when I took a course in college titled "The Koran as Literature." It was the first time I'd ever sat down and read the Koran except when I'd been forced to. For me, my pride in my Arab roots developed as a result of my pride in Islam.

As a kid, our Islam had embarrassed me even more than being Arab had. My friends would come over and it would become time for us to perform the *salah*, the prayer toward

Mecca that Muslims do five times each day, and I would just want to disappear. My siblings all hung out exclusively with Arabs, so for them *salah* didn't matter. They all treated me like I was a traitor because I hung out with non-Arabs and I made my embarrassment clear. Moreover, for a couple of years, my best friend had been a Jew.

And yet, my siblings, who scoffed at me for being American, were in some ways far more easily embarrassed at our Arab roots than I. I've wondered about this a lot and I've come to the conclusion that being Arab didn't embarrass me as much as being Arab-American. I'm an all or nothing sort of guy. The half-this, half-that approach of my family didn't set well with me.

Here's what I mean: my father had a cousin, Umar, who occasionally visited us from Ahwaz. When he came, he always wore his *dishdasha*, the ankle-length robe, and a *keffiyeh* which he wore turban style. Ironically, he was not permitted to dress in this manner back in Ahwaz, Arab dress having been forbidden in certain places by the Iranian authorities.

When he would come, he would walk around our neighborhood proudly. During one such visit, when I was ten or eleven, it inspired me to pull out my own Arab clothes, which we normally wore only on special occasions, and I accompanied him several times on his walks. He always walked with his hands clasped behind his back, carrying his *Subha*, his Muslim prayer beads, the thumb and forefinger of his right hand moving from one bead to the next as he said the ninety-nine names of Allah and listened to me prattle on about my life.

My siblings would never have been seen walking with Umar in his Arab garb, and there's no way they would have donned such clothes themselves and walked through the neighborhood. But it made me very proud.

Anyway, for the most part he was silent on our walks. In fact, the only time I remember him actually speaking to me during those times, was when he one day said, "Always remember, Cousin Yusuf, never place your trust in a Shiite."

Now you need to understand that I made no distinctions within Islam. At the time, the only distinctions I knew were Christian and Muslim, American and Arab.

I asked him, "What is a Shiite, Cousin Umar?"

He stopped walking and looked at me. He faced me now and stooped so that his face was at my level. "Do you speak earnestly?" he asked me. "Is it true that the son of my cousin does not know what a Shiite is?"

I must have looked ashamed, because his tone softened. "The Shia are the Muslims who cannot be trusted," he said. "The Shia believe that when the Prophet (peace be upon him), that when he died, the Shia believe that the next Caliph should have been a relative of the Prophet (peace be upon him) by the name of Ali. They have not let there be peace with the Sunnis ever since."

"Who are the Sunnis?"

"We are the Sunnis. We are the majority of Muslims in the world, but not in Iran. The Shia are the majority there and they are like babies who when they did not get their own way after the death of the Prophet (peace be upon him) began making problems and they continue to do so until this day."

He said that he had met three Shia whom he could trust, but that otherwise, they were the sworn enemy of the Sunnis.

As I said, I had not been exposed to such differences. In the US, followers of the two major branches of Islam were living in relative harmony. But in Iran, a lot of resentment existed between the two groups. The Shia there were by far the majority. This was true not only of Persians but also of Arabs who lived there. All Sunnis had it difficult, even Persians. But people like my family—Sunni Arabs—had it even more difficult.

When Saddam Hussein, a Sunni Arab, attacked Iran in 1980, he was trying to annex Ahwaz, it being Iran's major oil producing area. Saddam was hated not only by the Persian Shia, but by the Arab Shia as well. Both of these groups suspected Arab Sunnis of Ahwaz of collaborating with Saddam's regime. My father's cousin and his family all suffered during this period. My family had left Ahwaz in 1969, the year before I was born, so none of that affected us. But it affected Umar profoundly. He lost his job and his life took a terrible turn during the Iran-Iraq War. I later found out that my father kept him afloat during this period.

At any rate, as I came to Brooks Brothers, I stepped inside. And I'll admit it—there was something practical in my decision. That teenager, in calling me a towelhead, had definitely left his mark. You couldn't get more American than Brooks Brothers.

Prior to this, I had for a long time been dressing casually—khakis or jeans and a polo shirt or tee and possibly a sweater. And once in a while I'd wear a button-down shirt, but that's about as dressed up as I got. That day, however, as I walked around Brooks Brothers, I felt drawn toward the suits. A blue Madison Bird's Eye Two Button caught my attention. I didn't notice the price until I was trying it on—over seven hundred dollars. I could definitely afford it, but normally my entire wardrobe wasn't worth that much. But a new identity required a new way of dressing. I definitely did not want to draw suspicion to myself now that I was assuming a fake identity. I wanted everything to appear completely trustworthy, and what could be more trustworthy than a man in a suit?

I loved the way I looked in this thing. The deep blue went well with my dark skin. Looking at myself in the mirror, I wondered why I hadn't done this years before. I looked great; my new glasses actually enhanced the effect. I told the man I'd take it. I tried on another suit, this one a taupe, two-button sharkskin. It also looked good on me and I told him I'd take it as well. The pants for both suits needed to be altered. He said I could pick them up the next day.

I looked at shirts now and found five that I liked and even picked out some underwear. The man encouraged me to look at shoes as well. I looked, but that's where I had to draw the line. All of them looked so staid that I couldn't quite believe anyone would wear them. I told him I didn't see anything I liked and he asked me if I was all set for ties. I told him I was. I would not be wearing ties. I paid him with my Caymans debit card. I took the underwear, and told him I would pick up the shirts when I returned for the suits.

I walked down Madison until it ended at Twenty-Third Street and then west to Broadway, which I followed a few more blocks south. I came to a shoe store and went in, determined to find a pair of shoes that would go with my new clothes. The only shoes I could imagine wearing were some running shoes I saw. I decided I'd keep looking and I continued my walk.

Down by Union Square I came upon another shoe store. This one too I entered and once again I realized that I couldn't imagine myself in any of the dress shoes in the store. But I did find some desert boots that I found acceptable and a pair of Wallabees. This was as dressy as I could bear and I bought them both.

I walked to Seventh Avenue where I boarded the Number One IRT to Columbus Circle. From there, I walked back to my hotel. I tried on my new shoes and realized that the Wallabees in particular were extremely quiet as I walked across the floor. They would be perfect for breaking into my home and snagging that key.

I sat at the desk in my room and pictured the entire operation. The thing that disturbed me was the lock on the front door—no matter how you turned the key, it made a fairly loud noise. The back door would have been far easier because it was farther from our bedroom and it didn't make a sound when you unlocked it. Unfortunately, I didn't have a key to the back door with me. For a while, we had kept a copy of it under a rock in the garden, but we had dispensed with that practice after we showed the hiding spot to a local boy who fed our cat while we were away. It appeared that the front door was my only option.

As I reexamined the situation, however, I remembered that there was a window in the basement that would be unlocked. The lock on that thing had been jammed since we'd bought the house, and I'd never bothered to replace it. In fact, I had once entered the house through that window when we'd been locked out. I decided I could do it without making much noise. For one thing, it was on the opposite end of our house from our bedroom. There was the problem that the cellar stairs sometimes creaked when you climbed them. But I decided that with patience, this was a job I could handle. Once I had decided that, I decided that I might as well get it over with tonight. Who knew when she would begin going through my stuff?

It was five o'clock now and I decided I should wait until two. Usually Ruth was in bed by ten thirty on weeknights. What occurred to me, however, was that on weekends she often stayed up a couple of hours later. And though this wasn't the weekend, now that she probably wasn't working, she might be staying up late every night.

I tried to picture everything the way it would be. I pictured the yard, the cement path I would take to get out back, the way I would have to crouch to get in the basement window, how hard I would have to push to get the window to open. I pictured myself climbing through the window feet first. I pictured it all so realistically that my heart was pounding. I pictured how dark it would be in the basement. And I couldn't use the basement light, I remembered. The switch made a terrible racket. Not only that, it was nowhere near the window I'd be entering. Without a light, I might step on something and wake her. I'd need a flashlight. On a piece of hotel stationery, I jotted a reminder to myself.

I pictured myself walking from the window to the basement stairs, climbing the stairs, opening the door at the top of the stairs, walking down the hall, away from our bedroom toward my study. I had stopped locking the study door a few months after our split, so there would be no problem there. I pictured myself entering the study, moving toward my desk, and there in the center drawer I would find a little wooden box in which I kept the compass my mother had given me when I was a boy so that I would always be able to find the direction of Mecca for prayers. I pictured myself lifting the box and underneath it is the key. Yes, this was definitely something I could do.

* * *

I counted meals to keep track of how long it was before they came for me. They were giving me two meals a day. I had supper that evening, breakfast the next morning, supper the following evening, and breakfast that next morning. After that, Amun's two assistants appeared at my door. Again, I could barely see because of the light.

They marched me to a door at the end of a long hallway. One of the men opened the door and I was ushered down a flight of five or six stairs into a room that was maybe six feet by six feet. It had a very high ceiling, in the center of which was a big pulley and a rope hanging from it. The walls were made of cement and I noticed a large drain in the center of the floor. And then, about a foot up the back wall there was a fire hose spigot capable of delivering huge amounts of water. The two men put on boots that went up to their knees.

They blindfolded me, but not with a hood, and they had me stand there and we waited. Finally, I heard the door open and I assumed it was Amun I heard coming down the stairs.

"Hang him by his feet," he told the men.

They had me lie on my back on the floor while they placed metal shackles around my ankles. Then I could feel them connecting something to the shackles and I felt my legs being hoisted toward the ceiling. The higher my legs got, the more weight was placed on the points where the metal shackles cut into my ankles. Soon the shackles were supporting my entire body—all of my weight was on the places where the steel met my anklebones. My ankles slipped through the shackles and for a second I thought I was going to land head first on the cement floor. But my heels and the roofs of my feet caught me, and now they were holding my entire weight as I hung there. The pain was unbelievable, and to fight it, I remember focusing on the foreign feeling of the pressure of the blood in my head.

As I hung there, Amun asked me, "So are you ready to begin talking?"

"I have been ready all along."

"As you wish," he said.

I heard someone climb the stairs and then I heard Amun's voice from above me say, "Okay." I heard water begin gushing from the spigot and soon I could feel water droplets spattering onto my head as it accumulated on the floor.

Before I felt the water itself touching the top of my head—now the lowest point of my body—I felt the cold from the water gathering below me. And then I heard the water flow change pitch, that is, as the water level rose above the level of the spigot, the sound changed.

It took less than ten minutes for the water to reach the top of my head, and two or three more for it to reach my mouth, then my nose. Seconds later, I had to raise my head to keep from drowning. At about that point, the water stopped running and I was relieved.

Relieved is a relative term. The pain of the steel digging into my feet was mind numbing. But within fifteen minutes, it was unnoticeable. The pain I now noticed was in my neck. I had to keep lifting my head to breathe.

After another ten minutes or so, I heard Amun tell his assistants to add more water. They did this and by the time they shut it off, it was above my shoulders. From that point on, to breathe, I had to pull up my torso with my stomach muscles as if I were doing a sit up—but a very difficult sit up. This tired me very quickly. I would raise myself until my mouth was above the water, breathe in, then lower myself until I was completely relaxed and my head and shoulders were submerged. I would breathe out through my mouth and when I could hold my breath no longer, I would raise myself again, take several breaths and then hold my breath again and relax. It didn't take five minutes of this before I was absolutely exhausted. At one point, I lifted my head and screamed to Amun that he please let me out of there. But I screamed in vain.

Again, I panicked and became convinced that Amun had decided to kill me. But I was saved again from my panic by my memory that Allah knew what I was going through. I felt encouraged to continue my struggle though every time I pulled myself up, my body was shaking from strain. At some point along in there, I can no longer remember what happened. My next memory is of myself being held up by the two men and I could hear the sucking sound of water draining. One of the men was removing my blindfold and shaking me and I was coughing. Amun was yelling at me from above, apparently still on the stairs to avoid getting wet. I don't know how I had the presence of mind to keep my eyes closed, but I did.

I still remember his first words to me: "I'm hoping that now, Muhammad, you are ready to talk. I'm thinking that you now understand a bit more about the situation. We obviously know at least some of what you have done, and we need to hear the rest of it. Are you ready?"

My eyes were still closed as he asked me this, and I remember thinking that if I were to simply keep my eyes closed and not speak, and not stand on my own, he would think I was still out. I decided that if I were to come to and deny what he was saying, he would simply repeat what he had done to me. I knew I was incapable of a repeat performance.

He said to me, "I know you're awake now, Muhammad. I can tell by the way your breathing shifted a couple of minutes ago. So please acknowledge that you can hear me. Otherwise, I'll be forced to hang you up again by your feet."

For an instant, the panic returned. But I immediately realized that if I were to do as he directed, he would definitely hang me up again. This was at least worth a try. I continued to play the unconscious role. Amun told the assistants to slap my face. One of them slapped me twice, but I showed no reaction. Finally Amun had his assistants take me back to my cell. They put me on a gurney of sorts and wheeled me back. I was still in my wet jumpsuit when they laid me on the nest and closed the door. I continued to lie there, afraid that one of them might have stayed inside the cell with me to see if I moved. I kept my eyes closed and lay there and finally I fell asleep. I didn't wake up until supper was served and I was freezing in my still damp jumpsuit.

Chapter 12

I didn't leave my room again until ten. Walking down Broadway, I noticed that in the southern end of Manhattan, the horizon was glowing. I was seeing the lights of the firemen and rescuers and the still burning Trade Center. The smell had become background by now—everywhere in the city it was present. Diesel fuel, plastic, cement dust and burning flesh.

I came to a bodega where I bought a flashlight and batteries. It was small enough that I could fit it into my pants pocket, yet bright enough to do the trick. After that, I stopped at a run-down pizza place and, sitting in the corner by a stack of empty pizza boxes, I gulped down a couple of slices with the help of a grape soda. When I left, it was not yet eleven. Two o'clock seemed a long way off.

I headed toward Fourteenth Street, deciding on the way that two was too late. Maybe Ruth would be so distraught about losing me that she would be going to bed early. Maybe the best way to proceed would be to go out there at once and watch the house. If the lights were on when I arrived, I'd wait until they went out and give her another half hour to fall asleep. If they were off, I'd wait half an hour in case she'd just shut them off.

I got on the Brooklyn-bound L. For a Thursday night, the train was crowded. I hadn't considered that I might see some of my neighbors on here, but sure enough, at the end of the car I spied a woman who lived on the next block over. And though I didn't truly know her, Ruth knew her and I'd met her at least twice. She would certainly have heard about my death. I was relieved that I'd shaved my mustache and had worn these glasses. I would have felt a little more at ease had I been wearing one of my new suits. And some sun glasses. I saw at once that I needed some of those.

I moved back a couple of cars to get away from her. Then when we arrived at the Bedford Avenue stop, I took my time moving toward the stairs so there would be no chance of being spotted by her.

I came above ground on the southeast corner of Bedford and North 7th only to realize the risk I was taking. Normally, Frank—the homeless man to whom I'd been giving a couple of dollars a day since we'd moved there—would have been sitting at the top of those stairs. He was the sort of guy who would have recognized me regardless of how I was dressed, and I had completely forgotten about him. Luckily, he was not there tonight. And I had not considered the Palestinians who ran one of the shops at that same intersection—they knew me well. I kept my face pointed away from their door.

With my head down, I walked down Bedford in the direction of Metropolitan Avenue. At North Fifth, I took a right and walked until I was just west of Berry Street. I stood across from the one family home we had purchased a month after our wedding. With the exception of a couple of night-lights, the house was dark. Ruth's car was parked alongside mine in our front yard. The parking situation was one of the main reasons we had bought the house. The previous owners had cemented over the two tiny front lawns, one on either side of the front stoop, and had turned them into parking spots. It was an ugly solution, but practical.

I had thought I would wait half an hour after getting there to make sure she was sleeping soundly. But as I stood out here, I grew afraid that I'd be seen by one of the neighbors. Fred, who lived next door, often came out on his stoop at night to smoke a cigarette, and I could see that his lights were still on. If he came out and recognized me, that would be it. At the very least, I had to hide in our back yard.

There was so little space separating the two houses that my shoulders nearly scraped as I walked the narrow cement walkway between them. Out back, all of our lights were also off. I walked over to the basement window with the broken lock. I pushed on it and sure enough it opened. By this point, I was so nervous, I completely forgot about waiting. I took out my flashlight and shone it into the basement to make sure my feet wouldn't land on anything noisy. Good that I checked. There were some planting tools in a metal bucket directly beneath the window. All I had to do was keep my feet back away from the wall as I lowered them and I'd be fine.

I put my flashlight in my pocket and crouched in front of the window with my back turned to it. Putting one leg over the sill, then the other, I pushed myself back through the window and lowered my legs, remembering to keep my feet away from the wall. I felt them touch the floor and I was inside the cellar.

I was getting increasingly nervous now. Turning my flashlight on, I surveyed the situation. I had an unobstructed path to the stairs and I took it. Seeing the bottom stairs, I remembered that several of them creaked. The problem was, I couldn't remember which ones. I placed one foot on the second stair and slowly shifted my weight to that foot. The stair creaked before I had even half of my weight on it. I stood there listening for a few seconds before withdrawing my weight from that foot. Now I tried the first step. This time I was met with silence. I had a mere thirteen steps to go. I tried the other side of the second step and it worked. On a hunch I skipped the third step and the fourth step was silent. I proceeded in this fashion, one step at a time until I was at the top. Now I had to open the door.

I had forgotten about this door. It was going to be a problem. It opened away from me, but to keep the knob from squeaking, I remembered that I would have to pull on it quite hard before turning it. I did this successfully. I pushed the door open and I was on the first floor, the floor where we slept.

I had also forgotten that we had a night-light in the hallway. And since the door was between that light and our bedroom door, the door's shadow had just been cast down the hallway toward our bedroom, thereby altering the amount of light entering our bedroom—I assumed our bedroom door was open. I stood there silently for as much as a minute waiting to see if Ruth made any sort of response.

When I heard nothing, I decided to leave the cellar door open so that it would block my shadow as I moved toward my study. My heart was pounding and I was breathing so loudly that I feared Ruth would hear. As I neared my study, I noticed that my Wallabees were completely quiet with their crepe soles. Not a board creaked during this part of the procedure. My breathing was still far louder than anything else, and my heart was pounding loudly.

When I got to my study door, I was surprised to find it closed. One time Ruth had told me that when I was away, she sometimes slept in my study, that it made her feel closer to me. Back then, we'd both been Muslims, and it had been my study and our *musalla*, our place of prayer. After our breakup, it remained my study and became my *musalla*. I wondered if she was sleeping in there right now. It would make sense. She would be missing me, and sleeping in there might comfort her.

I hesitated by the door, wondering what I should do. If she were in there, would I be able to open the door and look in without waking her? She was a deep sleeper, but to open a door in the same room someone was in, that seemed like a big gamble. But the idea of coming out here again was also a big gamble, equally big. For one thing, I wondered how many more times I'd find the nerve to attempt this. I was sweating now and I could not control my breathing. My heart was punching my chest.

I stood there so long trying to locate the courage to act that my legs were getting tired. Finally, I told myself I had to get the key. If I didn't, I couldn't allow myself to leave her. I couldn't risk that she would find out that I had not died, but had simply left her. It would hurt her too much.

I turned the knob slowly and pushed the door open. I looked to the back of the room toward the couch. Not enough light was entering through the window from outside to be certain. I pulled out my flashlight and with my hand over the lens, I turned it on. Pointing the flashlight up at the ceiling, I removed first one finger, then two from the lens. There was enough light now to see clearly that she was not in the room.

I pulled the rest of my body into the room and closed the door most of the way, but not so much that it latched—I didn't want to have to open the door so carefully again. With the help of my flashlight I moved toward my desk. I held the light between my teeth and looked for the letter from the bank that had worried me—it was sitting right on top of my desk under a folder. I placed it in my pocket and opened the center drawer. Slowly, carefully, I removed the wooden box from its place. Beneath it lay the key. I took it and placed it in my pocket. As I did so, the door opened and I reeled toward it, and in the process banged the wooden box against my desk.

The cat stood there and meowed. I can't tell you how scared I was and how relieved then scared again. There was no way Ruth would not have heard this. I stood completely still now. My breathing had been heavy before, but now it was insane. "I wanted to just yell out, Ruth, it's me. Don't be afraid."

The cat walked over to me and rubbed herself against my leg. I returned the box and closed the drawer. I'd never actually liked the cat, but I stooped now and petted her. She purred loudly. I scratched her back just in front of her tail and she gazed up at me appreciatively. I waited for the inevitable, listening for the sound of movement. Nothing. Upon leaving the room, I closed the door. Just as I got it latched, I realized the cat was still inside. I had to get her out or Ruth would deduce something was up. I went back into the room and couldn't find her anywhere. I shone my flashlight around and finally saw her lying by the baseboard heater.

I picked her up and carried her to the door. Before I could lower her, she jumped from my arms. I don't think any cat has ever made a louder landing. It was so loud in fact, that I stepped back into my study so that if Ruth came into the hall she wouldn't see me. I waited there with my ear by the cracked door. There was no sound at all. Strangely, by this time I'd made my peace with the fact that I was going to get caught. I wasn't even nervous. I was simply trying to plan what I was going to say when she caught me. "I've decided to come back home," sounded like the most reasonable thing. I pictured her coming to me and hugging me and crying and telling me how worried she had been and I pictured myself telling her how sorry I was for putting her through this and that I loved her and that I couldn't go through with it, that during this event I'd discovered how much I truly needed her. And as I imagined saying this, I realized it was true.

But I continued.

I moved back into the hall. I closed the study door and continued down the hall toward the basement stairs. I arrived without a sound. But as I began to close that door, I worried about the night-light and the door's shadow. Would it be better to just leave it open and make it look as if the cat had somehow opened it. Not only that, it now occurred to me, the cat may have gone into the basement. There was no way I'd be able to hunt her down and return her upstairs with anything approaching silence.

I chose to leave the door open and, using the handrail as a guide, I moved slowly down the cellar stairs. Why I didn't have my flashlight on, I don't know. My plan was to turn it on when I got to the bottom of the stairs. I felt confident with the railing in my hand. And besides, when I'd come up the stairs there had been nothing on them, so why would anything be on them now.

It was in that moment that I stepped on the cat's tail. I had been shifting my weight from one foot to the next with extreme caution. I had barely put any weight on her tail, so there was no need of such screeching.

After that, it was clear to me—the game was over. I stood there stupidly and waited for Ruth to find me. But there wasn't a single sound. Not even my breathing. That's because I was holding my breath.

When Ruth's footsteps failed to materialize, I continued down the cellar stairs. I had just placed my foot on the cellar floor when I turned around and began moving back up the stairs. What was I doing, I asked myself. Did I want to get caught?

I felt compelled to catch sight of Ruth one last time. I knew that I was going back up the stairs and over to the bedroom, knew that I had to get one last look at her as she slept. I didn't even try to talk myself out of it.

I don't know why I even bothered to be quiet at this point. She had to have heard the racket. But I attempted silence anyway. I went through the door at the top of the stairs. I closed it part way, casting my shadow on our bedroom door, which I could now see was closed. That's why she hadn't heard me. I was vaguely surprised. Now it's true that we usually kept our bedroom door closed when I was home. But when she was home alone, she usually kept it open so that the cat could sleep with her.

I moved as stealthily as I could toward our door and when I got to it, I hesitated. As I took the knob in my hand and turned it slowly and steadily, I was surprisingly unafraid. It didn't make a sound. It was completely unlatched now and I had only to push on the door. I did so enough to look in. The bed, which was just opposite the door, had a white duvet on it so, despite the lack of light, I could see it clearly. It was unmade and she was not in it.

I wondered if she had grown afraid when she'd heard the commotion. Could it be that she had sneaked over to another part of the room. I opened the door far enough to get inside, a bit nervous about poking my head around the door. I half feared she'd be standing there with a club in her hand and as soon as she saw a head, she'd let me have it. But it didn't happen. She wasn't there. Now I spotted the answering machine on the nightstand. It was blinking the number seven. Clearly she had not been home for a while. The fact that her car was outside meant that one of her sisters or her father had picked her up. That could only mean she wasn't doing well. I closed the door again and walked to the kitchen. She'd set a huge bowl of water out for the cat and a big dish of food. Both of them were nearly full, so she was obviously checking in periodically.

I considered going out the front door, but worried that I'd be seen. I returned to the basement, found the cat and shooed her upstairs. I walked back upstairs to take one last look at my study. I wondered if Ruth had even been in here. If she had, she'd left no sign. All of my papers appeared to be where I'd left them, and the filing cabinets were still stuffed

the way I had left them. I even found my life insurance papers. If she'd pulled them out, she'd returned them exactly
where she'd found them. I decided that she had not searched
my effects so I opened my center drawer again and pulled out
the wooden box. I considered taking it, but concluded it
would be too risky. She may have noticed it was there. I did,
however, open the box and take the compass. I felt strongly
that I wanted to take something my mother had given me, and
this was the item I felt most connected to. Later Ruth would
discover the compass was missing, but I suspected she
wouldn't know when I had taken it.

I returned the box to the drawer, closed my study door
and I walked to the stairs that led to the second floor bedroom
where we'd planned one day to set up a nursery. We'd never
really used the room. Since becoming a Christian, Ruth went
up there occasionally to read her Bible and pray. The upstairs
bathroom was also her domain. I maybe went in there three or
four times a year when I felt like taking a bath. The downstairs tub was far smaller. It worked fine for showers and
wudu. But when I wanted a bath, I took it up there.

I looked around our closet where we kept old photos until
I found a wallet-sized picture of Ruth and me sitting on a
beach in our bathing suits. I placed it in my wallet and went
back down stairs. Just as I was starting down the basement
stairs, I remembered a picture we had in our living room. I
walked over to it and looked at it. It was Ruth's high school
graduation picture. It was such a beautiful picture of her and I
wished I had the courage to take it. I looked at a few more
pictures. Many of them were also on my desktop computer. I
considered making a c.d. of them, but I realized I was playing
with fire. I pulled myself away and returned to the basement.
I closed the cellar door, climbed out the window and closed
it. I felt numb.

I walked between our house and Fred's, stopping just before getting by his porch to listen for him. I heard nothing. I
proceeded with caution and found that he was not there. I
moved back toward Berry Street and down toward Bedford
Avenue, where I turned left and headed up toward North 7th. I

entered the subway from the west side of Bedford in case Frank, the homeless man, had returned to his spot. When I arrived at my hotel, I felt incredibly relieved. And yet that night as I lay there trying to sleep, I pictured Ruth with a tear-stained face, and I cried myself to sleep in a way I hadn't done since childhood.

* * *

I lost count of the number of days that went by before they summoned me again. Meanwhile, there came a point when I realized that if I didn't exercise, I was going to lose all of my strength and that I would grow increasingly depressed.

I began doing push ups before every meal. At first I was quite weak and ten pushups seemed like an enormous amount. Soon I was doing thirty three times a day. Later I began doing sit-ups as well—fifty twice a day, just before breakfast and dinner.

One day, as I was doing push-ups with my head by my door, I heard what I realized was another man crying. It was very faint, but I was fairly certain of what I was hearing. I yelled to him, "Who are you?"

The crying stopped but no answer came my way. I yelled again, "What is your name."

This time I heard him say, "Ya'Sin."

I yelled back, "Hello, Ya'Sin. My name is Yusef."

"Hello, Yusef," he yelled back to me.

"Where are you?" I yelled to him.

"I don't know," he yelled. "I know only that I'm in a cell."

"Me too," I yelled. "They think I'm a terrorist."

"They think I am too," he said. "I am a good Muslim— nothing more. They do not understand."

"I did nothing," I said. "Nothing. I don't even know why they're holding me."

After that, we said nothing, and I never heard from him again, though I yelled to him several times to learn more about him.

At the time, I thought it was probably a month before they came for me. But looking back on it, I realize that it may have been two or even three months. I wondered at times if they were ever going to come again. And then one morning after breakfast, they appeared.

I know that I'll never be able to explain this, but mixed with all of the dread that I'd been feeling that they would return, there was always a disappointment when they did not. And today, when I heard them at my door, mixed with the fear I felt, I was aware of a feeling of excitement that I had not been forgotten.

They took me to the second room I'd been in, the room with the inclined table. This time they did not place me on the table. They blindfolded me and sat me in a backless stool, much like the stool I'd sat in the first day I'd arrived, and they handcuffed me to the sides of it.

I heard them walk across the room and sit at what sounded like a metal table and metal chairs. I sat where I was for half an hour or so and I tried to make out the conversation that was happening between the two of them. When the door opened, the conversation stopped and Amun approached them. I heard him say something to them and they came over to me, removed my handcuffs from the stool and stripped me completely naked. Now they placed my hands behind my back and cuffed them together. They then walked me over and had me stand on what felt like a metal plate. After that, they attached something to my genitals—at first I thought it was a clothespin or something like that, but I soon realized that it was an alligator clip that was attached to an electrical wire. I'm not quite certain about the other wire, but I assume it was attached to the metal pad I was standing on. One of the men seemed to be turning a crank of a primitive generator and I was given a series of shocks.

When I was in college, I had a friend, a physics major, who created what he called a game that tested our ability to withstand shock. I won it every time I played. People's ability to withstand electrical shock varies widely. And these shocks that Amun was administering, while they were definitely uncomfortable and even quite painful, in no way did they compare in my mind with being nearly drowned. I felt quite brave in the face of them, particularly at first. After a few minutes, however, I lost my ability to withstand them.

The first question that Amun asked me was, "Are you ready to admit that you are Muhammad Muhammad?"

"I am not Muhammad," I said. "Notice that I have been consistent in what I am saying. This is not because I am…"

At that point I heard the crank and I was jolted.

"You can drown me," I said. "You can shock me. But that does not change the fact that I am not Muhammad." The cranking started up again and a jolt of electricity went through me, but I continued speaking. "I don't know what Muhammad did, but he is not I. If I were Muhammad, I would admit it. I wish I could admit it, but I can't."

"You should understand me by now," said Amun. "You should understand that I am not going to give up. I will hear you say that you are Muhammad. You will see. I have never failed to obtain a confession."

"I concede that you may get a confession from me," I said. "But if you do, realize in advance that it will be false if it involves me as Muhammad or if it involves me as a terrorist. I promise you, if I say I am a terrorist or that I sympathize with terrorists, it is a false confession."

"Why did you move to Seattle?" he asked me.

"I moved to Seattle because I had left my wife following the World Trade Center collapse. The two of us had been having difficulties…"

I heard the cranking and I felt the shock. They had clearly changed the settings on the machine. At that point, I could barely stay on my feet.

The shock stopped and I continued. "She became a Christian and as a Muslim, I did not approve. After that…"

I heard the cranking and I felt the shock. And once again, it was extremely powerful.

When it stopped Amun said, "We know that you are not married."

"Maybe Muhammad is not married, but I am. I'm telling

you, I was simply trying to hide my identity from my wife. There was no mention of…"

The cranking. The shock. I stopped speaking and waited to be asked a question. After maybe half a minute, the cranking began—violently—and it was followed by a violent shock.

"What do you want?" I said.

"I want the truth. Admit that you are Muhammad."

"You can't have both of those things. Either I tell you the truth OR I tell you that I am Muhammad. Which do you prefer?"

The cranking.

"I take it that you want the lie. Okay, I will lie to you. My name is Muhammad. I am a dangerous terrorist, and every chance I get I…"

At this point the cranking began and after what felt like fifteen or twenty seconds of it, Amun must have nodded to his attendant to stop. They all walked out of the room and left me standing there with my hands tied behind my back and the alligator clip still attached.

A few minutes later, I heard the door open and only two sets of footsteps approached me. They undid my handcuffs and handed me my smelly jumpsuit. I put it on and they walked me back to my room. I lay on my nest and felt like things had just changed. I wasn't sure it was good change, but something had happened.

Chapter 13

I dreamt that Ruth was walking toward me on an empty street. It seemed as if we were the only two people in existence, and though she was walking toward me, she kept receding. At some point I realized she was on one of those moving walkways they have in airports. She was walking toward me, but the sidewalk was pulling her back. In the light, her brown hair had a reddish tint that surprised me.

I woke up; it was three thirty and I couldn't get back to sleep. I turned on the television and flipped channels. I watched an infomercial about a device that could help you keep track of your important papers. To me it looked like a filing cabinet, but they kept talking about it as if it were a completely new invention. I tried some other channels and found one with a naked woman who was sitting and talking to a naked man. They were acting as if their nakedness was not an issue, and she seemed to be interviewing him. They were laughing and carrying on, and even though they were naked, there seemed to be less sexual tension between them than if they'd been fully clothed.

I don't think there is a Muslim scholar anywhere who would suggest that pornography is anything other than evil. Now I'm not talking about simply to be avoided. I'm talking about evil. No doubt there are those who would quibble about whether what I was witnessing was pornography, but the Koran makes quite clear that if it's shameful and indecent, it's forbidden. To me it seemed both. And yet, as I lay there in my bed, I felt powerless to take hold of the remote to change the channel. Instead, I took hold of my penis.

Masturbation is something that is to be avoided according to most Muslim scholars. Some will say that if it prevents you from breaking a larger law, it is acceptable, e.g., if it spares you from adultery. But I was in no danger of adultery. Yet I lay there and continued. The only thing I can say in my defense is that before I reached my climax, I shut off the television and pictured not the woman on the screen, but Ruth. As soon as I finished, I felt as though I had defiled myself.

I got up and showered, ashamed of my weakness. I turned on the light by my bed and pulled out my computer. I found the file containing the Koran and I performed a search for the word "shame."

I found a few instances of the word, but the one that spoke to me most was in The Elevated Places (7.26): "O children of Adam! We have sent down garments for you to cover your shame, and for beauty. But clothing that guards against evil is best."

I then searched for "forgiveness" and found a number of instances of the word. It is difficult to compare precisely how many times each word occurs since there are synonyms for both words in Arabic which is the language in which I was reading it. But taking all of that into consideration, I believe it's safe to say that the notion of "forgiveness" occurs in the Koran more than twice as frequently as the notion of "shame." To me this was proof of Allah's mercy. There are those who speak of the Koran as a book of vengeance and hatred. Here is the proof that it is not.

I read a number of the passages about "forgiveness." But the one that spoke to me most was from The Family of Imran. (3.134-135): "Allah loves those who do good, and those who, when they act with indecency and are unjust to their souls, remember Allah and ask His forgiveness. And who will forgive their faults but Allah."

As I read, I became aware of how far I had degenerated during the past few days. I had skipped my *salah*, my five daily prayers. I decided now that even though I was late, I would perform *Ishaa*, the prayer performed at night. At first I considered performing *Witr* instead of *Ishaa*. In fact, technically, that is what I should have done since *Ishaa* is not to be performed after midnight. My problem was, however, that *Witr* is a prayer that was given to Muhammad as a way of increasing one's blessings. It is considered an additional prayer, a prayer that is over and above the five mandatory prayers.

And in my present state I did not feel that I deserved extra blessings. All I wanted was communion with Allah. I suspect that I would never be able to justify my decision to any *imam* or Muslim scholar, but that is what I felt led to do and it is what I did.

First I went into the bathroom to perform *wudu*, ablutions. I began by bringing a bit of order to the bathroom. A towel was lying on the floor, and the toothbrush and toothpaste I had purchased were lying haphazardly on the side of the sink. After that, I made *Niyyah*, or intention, trying to bring that same order within myself that I had brought to the bathroom. I brought myself to a place of purity in my heart and mind by repeating, "*Bismillahir Rahmanir Rahim*," which means, "In the Name of Allah, the Most Merciful, the Most Kind."

I stepped into the bathtub and with my right hand, followed by my left, I washed both hands up to my wrists three times, ensuring that the water ran between my fingers. I then caught water in my hand and placed it into my mouth and rinsed out my mouth three times. I took water in my hand and held it up to my nose and sniffed it into my nostrils carefully and blew it out, careful also to wash the tip of my nose. And once again, I did it three times. I then wet my hands with fresh water, and washed my face from right ear to left ear and from my forehead down to my throat. Three times. And three times I washed my right arm followed by my left from wrist to elbow. I brought my wet hands up to the top of my forehead and moved them toward the back of my head, and brought them forward again. This I did but once. I passed the wet tips of my index fingers into the holes and grooves of my ears and passed my wet thumbs behind my ears, moving them from my earlobes upward and running my wet hands back over the nape of my neck. I then washed each foot three times, beginning with the right foot, followed by the left, making sure the water touched between my toes and all parts of my feet. As I was doing all of this, I repeated—and all of this was in Arabic—"Oh, Allah! Forgive my sins, grant abundance to my home and bless my livelihood." I finished the entire procedure by saying, "I testify that there is no god but Allah and He is One and has no partner and I testify further that Muhammad is His servant and messenger."

As I was preparing to step out of the bathtub, I realized that *Wudu* was not enough since I had ejaculated. I needed to perform *Ghusl*, the ritual washing of one's entire body.

I turned on the shower and ran water over every portion of my body. And since the waste water had run over my feet as I showered, as I finished up I bathed my feet again.

I toweled myself dry and left the bathroom, ready to perform *Ishaa*. I got out the compass my mother had given to me to determine the direction of the Ka'bah, the Holy House of Allah in Mecca built by Ibrahim. I rotated the special 400-degree compass until the needle pointed to 320 degrees, which is the *Qibla* code for New York City. I faced in the same direction as the little image of the minaret on the face of the compass and prepared to pray. Standing, I raised my hands to my ears and said aloud, "Allaahu Akbar," or "Allah is the Greatest." I placed my left hand on my chest and my right hand over my left hand. I recited, again aloud, Al-Fatihah, the opening Chapter of the Koran:

"In the name of Allah, the Most Merciful, the Most Compassionate, Ruler of the Day of Judgment. You alone we serve; You alone we ask for direction. Guide us along the right path, the path of those who earn Your favor, not the path of those who draw Your anger nor of those who go astray. Amen."

After that I chose the verse from the Koran that I had just read from The Family of Imran. "Allah loves those who do good, and those who, when they act with indecency and are unjust to their souls, remember Allah and ask His forgiveness. And who will forgive their faults but Allah."

I raised my hands once again to my ears and said, "Allaahu Akbar." After that I went into the *ruku* position, that is, I bowed and placed my hands on my knees while keeping my back straight and I said silently three times, "Glory be to my Lord, the Supreme."

I stood now and said aloud, "May Allah hear the one who

praises Him." Silently I said, "Our Lord, for You is all praise." I raised my hands to my ears again and said aloud, "Allaahu Akbar."

Now I went into the *sujud* position, that is, I prostrated, touching my forehead, nose, hands, knees, and the bottoms of my toes to the floor, making sure that my forearms and elbows did not touch the floor. Three times I said silently, "Glory be to my Lord, the Most High."

Then aloud I said, "Allaahu Akbar," and I sat on my heels. I repeated "Allaahu Akbar" and prostrated again as before, saying silently, "Glory be to my Lord, the Most High." I now stood up, having finished one *rak'ah* or unit of prayer. Now I began by placing my hands on my chest, my left hand first, my right hand over it, and repeated the entire process. Ordinarily, I change some of the verses that I say after I say the Al-Fatihah, which must be said during each *rak'ah*. But today I was so moved by the verses I had chosen the first time through that I repeated everything as I had before until I got to the part where I sat on my heels. After that I said the first part of the Tashahhud: "All glory is to Allah. All good deeds and worship are for Him. Peace and mercy and blessings of Allah be with you, Oh Prophet. Peace be with us and all of Allah's righteous servants. I bear witness that there is no god but Allah, and I bear witness that Muhammad is His Servant and Messenger."

I now said the second part of the Tashahhud: "O Allah, exalt Muhammad and his family just as You exalted Ibrahim and his family. Verily You are full of praise and majesty."

At this point I had finished the second rak'ah. I had two more *raka'at* to go. The next two were done silently and consisted of the Al-Fatihah alone. After finishing them, I now said the Tasleem to close the prayer. I did this by turning my head to the right and saying aloud: "Peace be on you and the mercy of Allah." I then turned my head to the left and repeated it.

As I stood, I felt a quickening in my heart and a lightness in my body, so much so that it seemed as if I could jump right through the ceiling. I had just plugged myself back into the source of all Being and all was well.

I walked now to my computer to read once again from the Koran. I felt completely open to the will of Allah. As I read, I promised Him that I would do whatever He bade me do, even with regard to Ruth. I knew I wanted to continue along the path I had chosen, the path of separation from her. But now I promised Allah that if He had different plans for me, I would go along with them. I felt as if I harbored no dread or resentment of what His will might be.

I opened the Koran file and placed my finger on the page down button and closed my eyes. When I felt the urging of Allah, I removed my finger from the button and with my eyes still closed, I placed my finger on the screen. This is what I read (2:231): "When you divorce your wives and they have reached the end of their waiting period, either retain them in honor or let them go with kindness. But do not retain them in order to harm them or to wrong them. Whoever does this harms his own soul."

This amazed me since it was the verse I'd been looking for earlier. But wanting to be certain that I was on the right path, I scrolled the computer again and pointed to the following verse (9:51): "Nothing will befall us except that which God has ordained: He is our Guardian. In God let the faithful put their trust."

I took this to mean I had chosen the correct path. I had no business retaining Ruth. I should let her go in peace and let her get on with her life. Though I had chosen my path without the approval of Allah, that is, though I had not sought His will when I hung up the phone without leaving a message to Ruth telling her that I was safe, His will had been enacted just the same.

I consulted a website to see when prayer time would be. I had lost all sense of time, so when I found that dawn was at 5:22, it did not register that it was already 4:38. Not until I consulted my watch to set the alarm did I realize that I had half an hour to sleep. I set it for 5:10 so that I could be up and fully awake in time for *Fajr*, the morning prayer. I shut off my computer and the lights and returned to bed. I don't think

I even fell asleep, but I lay there feeling ecstatic. If Allah was with me, I had nothing to fear.

At some point I came out of a revery and I took my watch from the stand beside my bed to check the time. As I did so, the alarm went off. I stood without the slightest hesitation and I knew in my heart that this is how I should always rise for *Fajr*. As long as I did not hesitate, the will of Allah was easy to follow. It was only when I allowed time for a question to form that I had trouble.

I went into the bathroom and performed *wudu* and came out and began my morning prayer. This one is the shortest prayer of the day, consisting of only two *raka'at* and it went quite fast. When I was finished, I felt even more connected to the will of Allah, as if a beam of magnetic current flowed down from on high and I was operating within its narrow parameters. I continued to sit where I was until the sun had completely risen as, according to oral tradition, was the practice of the Prophet (p.b.u.h.).

I felt energized, but realizing that I'd only had several hours of sleep, I considered going back to bed. There are many who frown on such a practice, but there is nothing in the Koran that forbids it. And for many Muslims, the general rule is, what is not forbidden is permitted. I decided that since I had nothing to do for the rest of the day except await my passport, I would wait until this ecstatic feeling passed and then I would sleep as needed.

A few minutes later, as I stood, I nearly fell. But quickly I regained my balance and decided to pick up my things that I had left lying about. As I dressed, I paused and smelled the underarms of my shirt, which I'd been wearing since Tuesday morning—it was now Friday. I remembered now that today I could pick up my new suits and shirts at Brooks Brothers and I marveled at the coincidence: on the very same day that I was about to embark on a new identity and would be wearing a new suit of clothes, I had recommitted my life to Allah. Surely He was behind my actions, even when I failed to see it.

* * *

I began counting meals in an effort to make some sort of
order of my life. I was getting two meals a day and I counted
forty-two meals before they came for me again. Everything
went as normal—they marched me into the inclined table
room and they blindfolded me. What was different was that
they had me sit in a regular chair with a back at the table. Not
only that, when Amun entered the room, I could hear that
someone entered with him.

Amun began asking me questions in Arabic, as he usually
did, but then he would translate my answers into English for
the other person. The person would then tell him to ask me
such and such a question. I let this go on for a few minutes
before I said, "Why don't you just ask me the questions yourself. I'm an American."

"Tell him that by law we can not do the questioning," the
American said to Amun who translated it into Arabic.

"Well you are questioning me. You're simply doing so
through an interpreter."

"Please tell the prisoner that he should not address me
and that he should speak Arabic."

"But I'm an American. My English is great. I was working on my dissertation in English."

"Ask the prisoner not to address me directly and to clarify
his last remark."

Amun repeated this in Arabic.

In English I said, "How about this, Amun. Since you
speak English, is it all right if I answer your questions in English as long as I address them to you?"

Apparently the man nodded to Amun because Amun now
said in Arabic that it would work. I wanted to avoid having
Amun translate for me. His English was limited and his ver-
sion of what I had said was often out of focus.

I began addressing the American's question. This time I
was determined to include so much detailed information that
there could be no question concerning my identity. I told him
about how as Yusuf Alsawari I had been working on my dis-

sertation at CUNY and that I was writing about Averroes. I told him about how my dissertation advisor had been Professor Christopher Hancock who had written his dissertation under Professor Peter Walsh at Stanford University, the title of which had been "Duns Scotus and the Human Soul," and how I was married to Ruth Clevesy whose parents had been Nazarene missionaries and how she was born in Tanzania and moved to Sudan and later Thailand and how she had learned Swahili and Arabic and Thai and Khmer, and how that, along with her MBA, which she had earned from NYU, had helped her land her job at Morgan Stanley's Emerging Markets Index on the 72nd floor of the World Trade Center and how on 9/11, I had taken her cell phone to her and had intended afterwards to go to Windows on the World for breakfast, but at the elevator I had decided instead to return home to get to work on my dissertation because I had been putting it off for so long and how soon after I'd left the building, the first plane hit the Trade Center, and how I had tried to call Ruth to find out if she was all right, but I couldn't get through, all lines being busy, and how I had called our home phone from a phone booth on Nassau Street, just north of Fulton, and how instead of leaving a message, I had checked our messages and had heard her message saying that she was all right, and because our marriage had been so difficult since she had become a Christian, I decided not to call her and not to return home, and because she would assume I had gone to Windows on the World as planned, she would assume I had died, that it seemed a more merciful way of leaving her than simply walking out the door and I knew that she would be fine because she would have all of the money she made at her job plus all of the money in my individual account in addition to life insurance money.

After I finished, there was silence, and I hoped that the man would now know that I was telling the truth. Instead he said, "Tell the prisoner that we know we have the right man." As he said this, I realized that he was one of the men who had accompanied me on the plane from America. I knew that it was Peirce, in fact, but I couldn't remember his name. He continued: "We know that he is not Yusuf Alsawari because Yusuf Alsawari is dead, and we know that he's dead. We have spoken to Yusuf Alsawari's wife, to his family, to people he was working with at the graduate program he was part of at CUNY. Moreover, we know that Mr. Muhammad is not even a US citizen. So the question now becomes, how was the prisoner able to ascertain all of this information about Yusuf Alsawari. This should now become the focus of your interrogations, Amun. To have gathered all of this information means only one thing, namely, that Mr. Muhammad is part of a larger and more sophisticated network than we had previously believed. So please thank him for awakening us to that fact. I believe you know how to reach me." He said nothing else and I heard one person—I assumed it was he—walk toward the door, open it and leave.

I sat there wondering what was going to happen now. There was silence for at least two minutes. I pictured Amun sitting there looking at me, trying to figure me out. I pictured him trying to screw up his courage to do the job he had ahead of him. It seemed to me that he must have believed my story; otherwise, he wouldn't have called Peirce in to hear it. And if he believed it, continuing to torture me would force him to go against his conscience in a big way. In the end, I'm fairly certain that my suspicions were correct. And the reason I believe it is that following this event, his treatment of me felt far more callous than what I'd experienced before.

For many people that may not make sense. But I assure you, if it does not make sense to you, it's only because you have not carefully read *The Narrative of the Life of Frederick Douglass*. In that primer for anyone who cares to take a look into the hidden recesses of the human soul, we meet Mrs. Auld, the wife of a slave owner, a northern woman who had never been in charge of a slave before. When Douglass first met her, she was the kindest white woman he had ever met. She treated him as an equal, demanded in fact that he look her in the eye when he spoke to her. She even taught him to read and write. But soon enough her husband learned of the way she was treating him. He explained to her that slaves were not to be treated equally, that they were not to be taught how to read and write, that to do so would ruin a slave, that it would render him useless to anyone. After that, Mrs. Auld, ceased to be the kindest slaveholder, and became the cruelest. The reason for this, if I am reading Douglass correctly, was that she now had to go against her conscience and so was separated from herself. When one is separated from oneself anything is possible. Mrs. Auld ended up not only crossing the line that separated kindness from cruelty. She crossed way over it into the realm of abject cruelty. And so it seemed to me to be the case with Amun.

But obviously I'm merely speculating about what actually drove Amun. All I know for sure is that after the interview, a change in him was apparent. Something conveyed by his voice led me to understand that I was in trouble. It was clear at once that if I didn't tell him what he wanted to know, that I would not make it. I quickly pushed the thought away, but part of me had already made up my mind.

As I said, for a good two minutes, he just sat there in silence. But then he got up and walked a few paces from me. It sounded like he stopped and I pictured him looking at me. When he spoke, there was an anger in his voice that was on a different order from what I had experienced from him before.

He did not yell when he said, "You have made a fool of me." In fact, he spoke quietly. But there was far more anger in his voice. "I don't like to be made a fool. I want you to remember that you have brought me to this point." During the last few words, I could hear that he was approaching me. I don't remember what happened after that. I only remember waking up on the floor beside the chair with Amun yelling at me to get up and get back in the chair. My head felt as if a car had run over it, and I struggled to my feet and felt around for the chair, which was on its side. I figured out the way it was lying and I picked it up and set it up correctly and sat in it. Immediately, I felt the cable hit me on my left shin.

"Enough of these stories," Amun said. "You're now going to tell me the truth. Tell me about the network that made it possible for you to learn so much about the lives of this Yusuf and his wife."

"I am Yusuf Alsawari and Ruth Clevesy is my wife."

Wham. Again, it hit me directly across the left shin.

"I didn't hear you," he said. "It sounded to me like you were continuing your lies. I'm hoping I was wrong. Please tell me how it was possible for you to learn so much about Yusuf Alsawari."

I sat there and said nothing.

After a few seconds had passed, the cable came down on my head again.

"I have nothing to tell you that you want to hear," I said.

Wham—on the shin.

"Stand up," he said.

I stood.

"Move the chair over here."

I thought he was speaking to me, so I turned to move it.

"Not you," he said to me. I had thought we were alone in the room.

I heard one of his assistants pick the chair up and move it.

Now Amun said, "Get him onto the chair."

One of them took my arm and led me to the chair and told me to step up. I did so.

"Put the handcuffs back on him," Amun said.

Someone cuffed my hands behind my back.

"Place the rope around his neck."

Someone climbed onto the chair with me and placed some sort of noose around my neck. He then tightened it and jumped back down from the chair.

"I want you to spend some time thinking about what you've done and I want you to get yourself to the point where you'll answer my questions honestly."

I heard the three of them leave the room. I stood there afraid of how long they might leave me. I felt tired from all of the stress I'd been under and from being underfed. I was worried that he might leave me like that for his entire lunch, and at the moment I couldn't imagine that I'd be able to endure such a vast amount of time standing there on a small surface, having to maintain my balance without any errors. If I'd been able to see, it would have been much easier. But blindfolded, the task seemed impossible. I felt like crying.

I stood there unable to imagine that I could go on, aware of a part of me that had an urge to jump as high as I could and then relax so that my neck would snap and the cruelty would end. I couldn't imagine that they would ever let me go and I couldn't imagine living the rest of my days under these conditions.

At that moment I remembered the promise of Allah: "Are you in danger? Then you should pray, whether you be on foot or horseback." Even before I began, I felt a shift in my heart. "Dear Allah," I began. "Please come to me. Please be with me, Lord. Protect me from my enemies. Please, allow the truth to be known. Guide their eyes, Lord of the Universe, guide their eyes so that they can see that I am not the man they think I am. Restore their humanity. Forgive them and free them from their hatred, from their fear."

With every word I prayed, I felt stronger and more capable of continuing. I remember at about this point, the thought crossed my mind that even if they left me here until supper I would be able to survive this. A groan from within accompanied that thought, but it was not a groan of defeat, but of dread, dread of all of the pain I would have to endure if I were forced to be in this situation for that amount of time. But I knew I could do it.

I continued standing and was aware of my entire body, aware of my feet as they stood on the cold metal of the chair, aware of my calves and shins as I stood there, of my knees, my entire back bone, my shoulders, my arms and hands, aware of my neck and the angle of my head. I could see myself standing there as if I were viewing myself from outside myself and all of this provided me with a sense of balance that empowered me. I saw myself as a hero standing with Allah against evil, and I felt that Allah was waging most of the fight, and that the little portion that He expected of me was nothing in comparison to His portion. I thought of the Yusuf for whom I was named, the Yusuf who endured the hatred of his brothers who had sold him into slavery. He too had ended up in Egypt just as I had, and though it was my government who had sold me there, rather than my brothers, I had been equally betrayed. And just as he had made it through, I knew that Allah would see to it that I made it through. I had only to believe. Allah was in control of my fate, and the outcome depended on how well I remembered that fact.

All of this strengthened me and I felt as if I could stand there indefinitely. I continued to feel that way for what I suspect was a solid two-hours. Not long after that, my legs began shaking—my knees were vibrating back and forth and I was afraid that they were about to give out.

The back of my leg happened to press up against the back of the chair and it occurred to me that I might be able to sit on it to get some relief. Gingerly I bent my knees so that I could sit myself on the chair back, but by the time I was about two inches away from succeeding, the rope was so tight that I realized my plan wouldn't work.

I was shaking all over now. The act of standing on that small surface for so long while trying to keep my balance had completely worn me down. At about this point, I heard the door open and three men entered.

I could hear them just standing there, no doubt watching me. Amun commented on my shaking.

"Is he dancing?" he asked his assistants. They laughed at this.

Amun continued. "You know, the more I watch him, the more I believe it is a dance. It is not an Egyptian dance, this I will admit. But he claims to be American. Perhaps this is a dance they perform over there."

Now he addressed me. "Are you ready to tell me how it is that you came to know so much about this Yusuf and his wife?"

Thinking this was my chance to be freed of this rope, I said that I was ready to talk.

"Okay, then," he said. "Tell me. Where did you learn about this man?"

"Aren't you going to let me down first?"

"When you give me reason to let you down, I will let you

down. If you do not, I will not. I will leave you here all night. I do not think you will make it, but if you do, you will then be ready to talk, this I believe. You have embarrassed me, and this is something I do not savor. So, please, what is it you have to say?"

"Well, I have been acquainted with Yusuf all of my life, so I know a good deal about him, including his wife, his father and mother, his brothers and sisters, everyone that he knows, I know. So it is not a miracle that I know this man."

"How did you meet him?"

"I don't ever remember not knowing him so I couldn't possibly tell you where I met him."

"How did it happen that you were so close to him?"

"My parents and his parents were closer than brothers and sisters. His parents took care of me as if I was their son and my parents took care of Yusuf as if he was their son."

"Was this Yusuf also involved in terrorism?"

"He was never involved in any sort of terrorism, and I assure you I would know if he was."

"Did you tell him of your involvement?"

"No, I did not." I considered adding that I had no connections to terrorism either, but the thought of spending the night on this chair frightened me so much I didn't consider it for long. Instead I asked him, "Have I told you enough for you to let me down now?"

"A few more questions first. When did you first become involved in the plot to blow up the USS *Cole*?"

I knew I could not make it through the night on this chair. I made a decision at that moment to make something up—at least that would help me live to see another day.

"I was one of the first to learn about the *Cole*."

"Who told you about it?"

"I know this may make you suspicious, but I truly was never told anyone's name who was involved in bombing that ship. I don't know what other people have told you, but I promise you, there were fifteen of us who were brought together and none of us had ever seen each other before."

"And during that meeting, you learned about the *Cole*?"

"No, actually. As I remember it, I received a note that had a cell phone number on it and I was told to call that number on such and such a date from a phone booth. When I did, I was instructed that an American ship was coming into the port in Yemen and that I would be involved in a plan to sink it with fourteen other people. I was told furthermore that I should be on the lookout during the next few days for a telephone number to call and that I should call it and when I did I would receive more information about where and when we would meet."

"Did the message arrive?"

"Yes it did. I believe it was a week later."

As I spoke, it felt as if I was actually remembering the events I was relaying, and it left me with an odd feeling.

"And what did this message say?"

"It was simply a phone number. No greeting or salutation or date or anything. Just a phone number and it had appeared taped to the inside of my locked door while I was out. I called the number and was told that we would be meeting in Yemen."

"Where were you at the time?"

"I was in New York."

"New York?"

"Yes."

"In America?"

"Yes."

"What were you doing there?"

"As I told you, Yusuf and I were good friends. I grew up there."

"Are you an American citizen?"

"Yes, I am."

"How did you become involved in terrorism?"

"Before I answer that," I said, and I was stalling for time, "could you please let me down."

I couldn't think of anything that sounded remotely plausible. I was wishing I'd said I'd been in Afghanistan or something like that. That way I could have said that I'd been introduced to Osama bin Laden or one of his associates.

Amun told the assistants to bring me down. One of them started to climb onto the chair with me.

"Get another chair," Amun said to him. "We don't want to knock him off now that he has begun to cooperate. And remove his blindfold."

I heard the man walk over and grab another chair. Soon he was standing beside me and taking off my blindfold, then my noose. He guided me as I climbed down from the chair in which I now sat.

"Could I please have some water?" I asked.

"Certainly," Amun said.

One of them got me the water. Amun left the room and returned with a tape recorder and a microphone, which he set up in the corner on a coffee table. He called me over and had me sit in an upholstered chair, the first I had sat in since the airplane that carried me here.

"So," he said. "I am going to record what you have to say. First of all, what is your name?"

I nearly said, "Yusuf," but I caught myself. "Muhammad Muhammad."

"Your entire name, please."

"Muhammad al-Zadeh…al-Murad Muhammad."

"How did you become involved in terrorism?"

"My parents are from Ahwaz," I said, "I visited my uncle after my high school graduation. And while I was there, this man wanted to meet me because he had heard I was an American. I later found out that he and his group intended to kill me until they spoke to me and understood that many of my ideas about America were similar to their ideas. Over the next couple of weeks, they recruited me into a radical fundamentalist Muslim sect…"

At the time, it didn't occur to me that a member of a radical fundamentalist Muslim sect would not refer to it as a radical fundamentalist Muslim sect. This, however, escaped not only Amun, but also the CIA operatives who listened to my supposed confession. It was only when a low-level member of the American Embassy in Egypt heard it that this was noticed, and that, from what I have heard, was the beginning of their realization that they had mistaken me for someone else. This same person, upon listening to the tape again, noticed that I was older than a person who would have graduated from high school in 1997 and that it was unlikely that I would have forgotten what year I had graduated. She had been saying all along that my confession was forced and could therefore not be relied upon. But that was still several months away. Meanwhile…

"…they recruited me into a radical fundamentalist Muslim sect. At the time, no one said anything about specific terrorist acts, but over time, after they had grown to trust me, they began to speak about sympathizing with certain al-Qaeda missions. Later on, I remember they spoke with approval of the bombing of the American Embassy in Kenya."

"So when was this that you met them? Was this after the bombing in Kenya, or before?"

"I met them before the bombing."

"How long before?"

"I'd say a year."

"So what year was it then?"

I paused. Though as an Arab-American, I had more than a passing knowledge of the al-Qaeda attacks on American targets, I did not know the actual year. I knew merely that it was a few years earlier.

"I believe it was in 1996," I said.

"Oh, so you knew them way back then?"

"To tell you the truth, I don't remember. I'm a little disoriented," I said.

"Well the embassy was bombed in 1998."

"Okay, then. I guess I met these people in 1997. Yes, it was 1997. I remember now."

"So they spoke with approval about the embassy bombing in Kenya right after it happened?"

"That's right," I said.

"Did they say anything to indicate that they were involved?"

"Only after I said that I approved as well, and that I felt that the people who had done this were heroes."

"So who were these people? What were their names?"

At this point, I feared that I could not go through with this. I was so tired that I could barely speak. I didn't feel confident about my ability to make up names, and I feared I would give the names of real people, people who were completely innocent, people whose names I had at one point or another actually heard. I waited a few seconds before speaking to Amun.

"I am so exhausted. Is there any way that I could sleep if I promise you that I will come back here tomorrow and cooperate one hundred percent? Is that a possibility?"

He reached over and shut off the tape recorder and said, "I understand. You have been very helpful. Tomorrow morning, you will come back here and you will tell us more, is that correct?"

"That is correct. I promise you that is what I will do."

He allowed me to leave.

As I lay in my cell, I felt like a coward to have caved. But that evening, I changed my mind. When the man appeared at the opening with my evening meal—and by now I had learned that his name was Mahmoud—rather than a bowl of soup, which is what he had always brought me in the past, he handed me a plate of rice and a good-sized portion of lamb and some bread.

Technically, I'm sure it was not as good a piece of meat as I would have had at a bad restaurant. But never before or since has a piece of meat tasted so good to me. I could feel it energize me even as I was eating it, could feel my thoughts clearing. And as they cleared, I realized I had done the right thing. I had chosen to stay alive.

That night I slept far better than I had slept in months. The next morning, when Mahmoud came around, he gave me a large bowl of *fuul*, an Egyptian breakfast specialty composed primarily of fava beans and diced, hard-boiled eggs. I'd had it a couple of times back in the states, and I knew that when it's done well, it contains cilantro, coriander, olive oil, and cumin. The good news is it did have fava beans and it had hard-boiled eggs and olive oil. There was some seasoning, but too faint to qualify as serious *fuul*, but again, it tasted incredible to me.

After breakfast, I lay there for an hour or so dreading my meeting with Amun. I had to come up with names. I remembered the name Mohammad Atta, and I could still picture his face as it had appeared with eighteen other hijackers in the *New York Times* a couple days after 9/11. There was another one too—what was his name? He had traveled with Atta from Portland, Maine to Boston. I couldn't quite catch it.

I was taken into the same room I'd been in the day before and sat at the same table. The tape recorder was all set up and Amun came in and was very cordial to me. He offered me a cigarette, which I smoked greedily.

"Yesterday we were talking about the people involved, the people who got you involved in this group of terrorists."

"Yes. You know, there are a lot of people whose names I forgot, because I never saw them again. But there was one man whom I will never forget. His name was Muhammad Atta." I paused here, trying to decide whether I should act as if I knew he was involved in the 9/11 bombing. I decided I would not. I didn't want them to think I was involved in 9/11. If they thought that, I'd never get out of jail.

If Amun was aware of Muhammad Atta's name, he didn't let on. He simply wrote it down on his pad and I remember he looked at the tape recorder and adjusted the volume.

"I believe Atta had a brother there as well as a cousin. But I have to tell you, I can't remember their names. And I swear, I'm not trying to protect anyone's identity. I'm truly trying to remember. And also, I'm confused about the period of time. It was 1997, as I said yesterday, but during that period, I met a few people, you know? And Atta was definitely one of them—but later that same year, I was introduced to other people, and they're the ones who got me involved in blowing up the USS *Cole*."

I could see from Amun's expression that he did not like what he was hearing. I also knew that I did not want to continue being tortured. At this point, a brilliant thought occurred to me. Most Arabs in America use only two of their names, leaving out their middle names. I would simply give two names, and that would give absolutely no information whatsoever. It would be like saying Joe Jones or Steven Smith. The names would mean nothing.

"Actually, I just remembered," I said. "As I mentioned the *Cole*, I remembered the name of the man who first told me about this boat. His name was Waleed Abdul. And he told me personally about this ship and he was the one who gave me an airline ticket to Yemen so that I could meet with the other men and together we could plan this bombing."

"Muhammad Atta and Waleed Abdul? Is that all you know of these men's names?"

"Yes," I said. "See, the problem was that because I am an American, they often spoke to me in English, even though my Arabic was far better than their English. And because of this...I don't know. I guess they wanted to appear to understand American customs. At any rate, they only used their first and last names in the American way."

By now, I suspected that Amun didn't know much about the particular information he was supposed to be getting. I doubted that anyone did. How could they think I was a terrorist? It didn't make sense. The fact that Amun was taping this now seemed like a good thing. The fact that he didn't seem to know who Atta was now seemed like a good thing as well. And it occurred to me that maybe someone would hear this and realize that I was just making stuff up—maybe Atta wasn't even involved in the *Cole* bombing. On the other hand, I could imagine it hurting me—it depended on who heard it.

"So when did this Waleed give you the ticket to travel to Yemen?"

"That was in the fall of 2000," I said. I knew that was when the *Cole* bombing had occurred. It was at about that time that I had begun to take serious notice of Muslim terrorism, and had recognized that something dangerous was happening that was going to split Muslims from other Muslims.

"Okay, so you went to Yemen. What were your instructions?"

"My instructions were to go there and after I had arrived at my hotel, I was to phone a man—and I never did find out who he was. I was to phone him, identify myself—and I believe they had given me some sort of code name, which I don't remember—and I was to tell him that I was ready. So that's what I did." I paused wondering where I would take it.

"And what did he say?"

"Well, to tell you the truth, he didn't say anything except something to the effect of, 'Very well,' or something of that nature. And maybe an hour later, maybe more, maybe less—all of this is sort of foggy to me at this point—there was a knock on my door. I opened it and there was an envelope lying on the floor. The envelope contained a small piece of paper—so small I nearly thought the envelope was empty—and it had an address on it. And please don't ask me the address. I really don't remember it. That was my first and only time in Yemen. I do remember that we met at a restaurant in the old part of…of…in the old part of the city."

I couldn't think of a single name of a city in Yemen. I've never known anyone from there, and even though I'm of Arab descent—I don't know. It's just something I couldn't think of. If someone had said the names of a couple of cities, I would have known, "Oh, yeah. That's in Yemen." But as it was, I was lost.

"So where were you," came the question I'd dreaded.

"Ah, I was right there near the water."

"You mean, near the Gulf?"

"That's right."

I didn't breathe again until his next question:

"So you were in Aden?"

"Yes." I sighed.

The thing was, it didn't seem to occur to Amun that I would be lying because I was now telling him what he wanted to hear.

"Yes, and I was in the old section of the city at a traditional restaurant. A sign out front said that the restaurant was closed, which confused me. I simply stood outside and waited. Soon another man arrived and I could tell that he too was confused. He looked at me, but he went over to the door and it was unlocked. I followed him in. There was only one table that did not have the chairs on top of it, and this was a large circular table and a number of men were sitting at it, so I joined them. All of us were exceedingly quiet because a sign on the table read, "Do not speak." Soon a few more men joined us and then when there was only one seat left, a man came in from another room and sat at it.

"I remember he spoke to us and explained that the "Do not speak" sign was for our individual safety, that we were not to give our real names to one another, that this was a secret meeting and that even he did not know our identities, though he recognized us all from pictures that he had been shown. In fact, he had an envelope that contained—I think there were twelve of us all together—and the envelope contained twelve sets of pictures, one for each of us. And underneath each picture, a random name had been assigned and for the duration of the project, we were to go by those names only. This was to make sure that if any of us were arrested, we would not be able to give them any information about the other members of the party. We were each given a copy of the photographs and were told to take the time to learn the assigned names of each person on the team. We were to do this before we left the premises of the restaurant, at which time we would return the pictures so that no one would have any information about our identities."

I was vaguely aware that I was borrowing from the film *Reservoir Dogs* wherein each of the robbers' identities is hidden from the others and each is given a name like Mr. Red, Mr. White or Mr. Pink. I was incredibly pleased with myself at the way my story was coming together. Amun seemed to be enjoying it as well.

"And what name did you receive?"

"I ended up—and I'm sure you'll like this one, Amun—I ended up with the name Amun." I laughed nervously, and questioned now whether I should have actually used his name. He seemed to want to remain nameless to me. His first reaction was what I took to be a flash of anger in his eyes, but then he broke out in genuine laughter.

"Small world, no?" I said.

This led to another peal of laughter on both our parts. To me this seemed unbelievably funny, and I laughed and laughed and the more I did, the more he laughed with me.

"Now did you all plan this operation together?" he asked. "Is that how it worked?"

"No. No, not at all. This man handed each individual a sheet of paper that had that person's name—you know, his new name—and assignment on it. Mine said that I was to drive a mini-bus with half of the team up to the place from where the boat containing the bomb would be launched. There were two of us with this job. We drove there in two minibuses and they were unmatched and we got there by two different routes."

I realized at this point that I had no idea about the actual details of the bombing. I had no idea about the specifics of the type of explosive device, how it was delivered or anything like that.

"They were very careful to keep all of our individual tasks secret from each other. My assignment was obviously very simple. In driving the mini-bus, everyone could see what I was doing. But the other men who carried out the details of the blast each had very specific jobs and, when possible, they were kept secret from each other. So unfortunately, I can't give you any more information about it than that."

"What happened after that mission? Were you ever approached again to do other missions?"

I debated how to handle this question. I knew I didn't want to be tortured again, but neither did I want to make myself so involved in various activities that I would never be allowed out of custody.

"Well, I received orders several times by phone to report to such and such a place, but I never did. See, here's what happened with me. I met a woman on the way back to New York whose son had died in the blast. I felt terrible about it. It became clear to me in that moment that my activities had brought about a lot of suffering, and I promised myself never again to get involved in killing. And twice when I didn't obey the orders, I later received death threats—both times by mail. Could I have another cigarette?"

I almost called him Amun, but I didn't dare. He shut off the tape recorder and gave me one and while we were smoking it, he asked me about my Arabic. I told him that I'd been brought up speaking it, but that I'd learned English when I was very young. I told him I felt lucky to have learned both languages at an early age. He commented on the fact that mine was not Egyptian Arabic and said he could not place the accent. I told him that my parents, just as was true of Yusuf Alsawari's parents, were from Ahwaz.

As we spoke, I saw him look at his watch at one point. I took this as a hopeful sign and I was right. As he was putting out his cigarette, he told me he thought I'd given him enough information for one day, and that we would speak again the next morning.

"How are your quarters," he asked.

"Not very comfortable," I said.

"Would you like a larger cell with an actual bed?"

"Yes, sir," I said.

When his assistants arrived, he told them to give me a room with a bed.

Chapter 14

I left my hotel room at 6:30 a.m. It was Friday, September 14th. I returned to the diner where I'd eaten the morning before and I ordered three scrambled eggs, home fries and a bagel.

While I was eating, I read the articles in the *New York Times* about the attacks. After that, I could think of nothing to fill this empty day. It was too early for Brooks Brothers so I headed toward my hotel rather than wander the streets aimlessly. On the way, I ran into a prostitute who was still plying her trade at this early hour.

"Want a date, mister?" she asked.

Nearly as much as by her voice, which was coarse and gravelly—and I guess if the truth be told, it reminded me of my mother's—I was attracted by the dissolute way she wore her hair. It was as if she had no time for such mundane matters. She was older than I, probably in her mid-40s, and the way she smiled at me had a surprising effect. It was an easy smile and completely disarming. Her skin was lighter than mine, and I would say she was Puerto Rican, possibly Dominican. She had a delicate look that seemed at odds with her age and profession.

After my reconnection with Allah just hours before, I have no idea how I could have even contemplated her. I have no way to explain it, and even now as I write this, I am ashamed. But the shame I feel toward those who might read this is nothing compared to the shame I feel toward myself. And that shame is nothing when compared to the shame I feel toward Allah. But Allah knows what I have done, whether I write it or not. And since I promised Him that I would write everything that has happened to me during this past year as a way of demonstrating how easy it is to drift outside His will, and as a way of demonstrating how none of our experiences are accidents, but are Allah's way of calling us to Him, I will continue.

To tell you the truth, I don't believe the prostitute's question even registered with me on a conscious level. It registered far deeper. I only became aware of her question when I heard myself reply, "Maybe." I was far too clever to say "Yes." Had I done so, I would have shocked myself into a state of awareness. Instead I said "Maybe," thereby convincing myself that I did not quite actually intend it—I was just flirting with her. Moreover, I was in effect, inviting her to take the first move and letting myself off the hook. It worked perfectly. She put her arm through mine and said, "Where we going, then?"

I told her I had a nearby room and we walked toward the hotel together. That was the first indication to myself that some part of me had just slipped loose. But by then, or so I told myself, it was too late to change. The plans had been made.

As I walked with her, no battle raged within me such as I might have expected. There was only the merest rumor of a skirmish. Never have I demonstrated such skill in drowning out the voices of goodness. I could feel the presence of Allah, of His messengers, working in concert to awaken me, but I would not allow them to get through. As soon as one of them attempted to inject reason, I could feel myself—and this was not the devil, mind you; it was I who was responsible—I could feel myself demand that *my* will be done and no matter the arguments they mustered, I was able to drown them all out systematically with an impenetrable fortress of thoughts and excuses. I poked loopholes in every argument I encountered.

Maybe I *was* sinning, I told myself. But at least I was being honest, being who I really was instead of hiding what I was feeling and wanting. And besides, Allah loved sinners. He was the God of forgiveness. And later I would seek His forgiveness. Only first let me have this one time. Afterwards, I would belong to Allah. All would be well. Surely He would forgive me if He could forgive killers and thieves. I was hurting no one.

"But do you not see that you are toying with Allah," another part of me would warn. "You are blaspheming His Holy Name. You are blaspheming all Goodness." And then in that moment the whore would speak, and her timing was such that if I'd later been told she could read my mind, I would have not been surprised.

This woman had been in this situation before, this much was clear. How many a cash paying customer had she lost to conscience on the long walk to a hotel room. She was determined that I not be among them.

"It's so cold out this morning," she said. She drew her collar up against the cold.

"Yeah," I said. "I was surprised when I first stepped out."

"How long you been out for?" she asked.

"Just a few minutes."

"Where you been at?"

"Breakfast," I said.

I could see her watching me to see if I was safe. And maybe to see if I could pay. She was like a private eye.

"Oh yeah?" she said. "So what cha have?"

"Three coffees, scrambled eggs, home fries, and a bagel."

"No bacon?"

"I don't eat bacon?"

"No? You a Muslim?" She knew her clients well.

"Yes, I am, actually."

"Ooooh, I see," she said. "So you must be one of them bad Muslims." She was smiling.

"What do you mean, bad?" I said. "I don't eat bacon." I smiled back.

Now you'd think that hearing myself described as "a bad Muslim," and hearing myself admit that, in effect, I was, you'd think it would have filled me with shame, that it would have awakened me and that I would have stopped. The reality is it had the opposite effect. Even as I heard this, I was telling myself that soon enough I would be a good Muslim again and it would happen with a single prayer. All would be forgiven. And I know it sounds impossible, but as I was saying these things to myself, there was no scoffing within me. Within I was keeping an earnest façade—mainly for myself—so much so that I believe I would have been willing in that moment to die for Allah if the situation had demanded it. Dying for Allah was easy. Living for Him—that's where the difficulty arose.

Her next remark appalled me: "Is bacon all you don't eat?" She raised her eyebrows flirtatiously.

During the entire time I was with her, that was her one misstep. I have never felt right speaking about sexual matters. When I grew silent, she guessed this and was very quick to change the subject.

"What's your name?" she asked me.

"Yusuf. What's yours?"

"Belinda."

"That's a nice name."

"Thanks," she said. "Where you from?"

"New York."

"Yeah? So why you staying at a hotel?"

"Long story."

"It always is."

"Are you from New York?" I asked her.

"Yeah, Queens."

"So how long have you been doing…this sort of work?"

"What sort of work is that?" she asked. She kept a straight face for so long that I grew nervous. But then she laughed at the perplexed look on my face.

She said, "I'm just kidding you, Yusuf." It was only then that I realized I'd told her my real name. She laughed again. Now she softened. "I'm looking forward to being with you."

"Me too," I said, and I felt so wrong in myself at that moment that I actually shuddered. At the time, I convinced myself that it was from the cold.

As we entered the lobby of the hotel, I was ashamed to be with her. It wasn't that she was unattractive, and, in case anyone's wondering, it wasn't that she was Hispanic. Seeing her with me, many might have assumed she was Middle Eastern. What ashamed me was that it was clear that she wasn't my wife and that she wasn't my girlfriend. Of course to others this might not have been clear. It wasn't as if she was dressed as a stereotypical hooker. But it was so clear to me that I was doing wrong, I assumed it was clear to everyone. To make it worse, the man at the desk had come on after I'd left, and he'd never seen me before.

"Can I help you?" he asked.

"Yes, I'm up in 1420."

"Name?"

"Muhammad," I said.

"That's your last name or first?"

"Both."

Belinda laughed as if I were quite a card. This of course made the man at the desk suspect something was amiss. He clacked around on his keyboard for a couple of minutes before asking to see my room key.

I handed the card to him.

He did something with it and as he handed it back to me, he apologized.

During this encounter, I nearly lost my nerve, but the moment he handed the key back, all fear was forgotten. We walked to the elevator together and boarded.

At the fourteenth floor, a couple about my age was waiting. They looked at us as we got off and again I wondered what I was doing. But the event had gathered a kind of momentum by now and stopping it seemed impossible. Now I found myself asking myself the questions—Allah and the angels had stepped back. "What are you doing?" was the question that played like a soundtrack in the background. Another part of myself would say things like, "It's too late now," in the most hopeless tone imaginable.

"Maybe I could just pay her and ask her to leave," would come the thought.

"You'd hurt her feelings terribly if you were to do that. She's got pride you know. How's that going to make her feel? Don't just think about yourself."

I stuck the card in the door and opened it for her. She entered. From the way she looked around, I wondered if she'd been to this same room before under similar conditions. If not this room, maybe one in the same line.

I didn't even have the door completely closed when she began removing her clothes.

I was new to this sort of thing and wondered if there were things about the etiquette of entertaining a whore I was expected to know. Did she know she was my first prostitute? Part of me hoped she did so she would have no expectations.

By this time, there were no more concerns about staining my soul. What I now wanted to know was the price. I wished I had asked her about it out on the street when she'd first approached me. By not asking, I'd basically told her I would pay any price. Did she see all of this in my eyes? At this point it seemed rude to bring up such a thing.

"Aren't you curious about the price?" she asked as she removed her blouse.

The hotel was not exactly luxurious, but it cost two hundred twenty-five dollars a night, so she knew I wasn't a poor man. I had no doubt that she would set her price accordingly.

"Sure," I said. "What's the price?"

"Two hundred," she said. I noticed that as she said this, she kept a remarkably straight face—a little too straight.

"Works for me," I said.

She smiled a little too broadly and took off her bra. After that, all sense of struggle vanished in me. It wasn't that her breasts were perfect. The fact is they were a little too large. But they were breasts. Don't forget, I'd been tantalized the night before my death by my wife and I'd never had my second course which was always the one I truly needed. I was capable of going without the first course for months at a time, but that second course was truly indispensable. Look at me— I'm making excuses.

I stood there gazing at her. By now she was wearing nothing but sky blue panties. She looked to me for direction, her eyes open and a look of expectation on her face. I moved over toward the bed, all the while feeling like a robot, driven by something that barely resembled sexuality. Something else was at work. My mind was blank now and I felt completely unsure of myself. Who was I? I felt that I was dreaming, had that feeling that sometimes occurs in a dream of looking around for the forgotten fact, the fact of course being that this is a dream. But in this case, it was not a dream and realizing that gave it the feeling of hyper-reality.

She followed me onto the bed. I sat with my back against the headboard, wondering what I was doing. She took her cue from the fact that I remained fully clothed. She straddled my legs and unbuttoned my shirt. When she had it unbuttoned, she told me I had a very masculine chest. She took me by the shoulders and pulled me forward so that she could completely remove my shirt. Now she unbuckled my belt and undid my fly. At one point I caught the bewildered look on my face in a mirror across the room, which prompted me to close my mouth.

She removed herself from my legs and pulled the top of my pants down, encouraging me to lift my butt so she could remove them completely. I complied, thankful that she knew her trade, and soon found myself sitting in my boxers beside her.

"What would you like?" she said.

"I don't know," I said. I laughed now. "You'll have to forgive me. I'm lost." That last sentence echoed in my head so that I missed what she said to me.

"What?" I said.

"Are you married?" she asked.

"In a way," I said.

This seemed to tell her what she needed to know.

I've learned from movies and novels that prostitutes don't kiss, but in that moment, she moved herself up toward my face and she kissed me. It was a very sweet kiss and it seemed to have been delivered with a good deal of feeling. At any rate, after that, I was back on track again. We kissed for four or five minutes and then she reached down and grabbed me and we proceeded from there.

As I said, I really don't feel comfortable talking about sex, so please understand that I won't be giving you the details of our encounter. I will simply say that as we were finishing up, a deep depression set in. I have never felt so de-

filed or that I had taken such advantage of another human being. As I paid her, I told her I was terribly sorry for what I'd
just done, that I had never done anything like this before, and
I promised her that I would never do it again. I was practically crying as I told her that she should stop letting people
take advantage of her like this, that she was a beautiful
woman and that she could find someone to marry her and live
a good life and that Allah would help her if she would try—
that Allah would take two steps toward her if she took one
toward Him.

She seemed confused but also strangely touched by what
I was saying and she hugged me before she left. I lay back on
the bed after that and just moped. I was trying to find a place
in myself that would make it possible for me to cry, but I
couldn't. There was no feeling in me at all except a feeling
that all was wrong.

* * *

My new cell was a definite improvement over the old
one. Though it wasn't clean, neither was it filthy; moreover, I
could see that it wasn't filthy. A bare bulb—I'd guess it was
twenty-five watts—hung from a fixture in the center of the
ceiling. Rather than a dirty bucket for a toilet, I had a clean
one, complete with a cover and several sections of newspaper
for wiping. And in place of a nest on the floor, it had what
you'd have to call a mattress. Not very thick, but a mattress
just the same. I hadn't lain on it for five minutes before I was
sound asleep. When I woke up, I thought my sleep had been
even better than it was. This is because when I heard Mahmoud fitting my tray through the slot, I assumed it was sup-
pertime. I had assumed that my suppers from now on would
be like the one I'd received the previous night. As a result, I
was a little disappointed to discover that the meal contained
no meat.

I didn't realize my mistake until a few hours later. He
came round again, but not with breakfast, which is what I'd
predicted, but with supper, and this time there was a good-

sized chunk of meat. It was then I realized that I was now receiving three meals a day. I'd grown so accustomed to two meals that eating the bread that came with the evening meal would have been a stretch. I decided to save it in case I got hungry during the night.

A couple hours later the light went out and once again I was in darkness. But not nearly as complete as that of the first cell I'd occupied. The door of this cell was comprised of bars through which light shown from the hallway, making it easier to move around the room. That first evening as I sat with my back leaned against the bars of the door, I saw my shadow projected by the hall light onto the far wall of my cell. It reminded me of Plato's cave, wherein the people in the cave mistake shadows on the wall for reality. And it reminded me of the way I had been living my life. If I had understood the nature of reality, would I have chosen to leave my lovely wife?

As I sat there, I could hear the other prisoners in the block talking. There were six of us. We were all lined up in a row so that we could not see each other. They showed no curiosity toward me, and I wondered why this was.

I slept quite soundly that night. The next morning, after breakfast, Amun's assistants retrieved me. This time they took me to a bathroom that had a nice shower. Prior to this, my showers had been extremely infrequent, and the conditions were so appalling that I nearly dreaded the experience. The only down side of today's experience was that the bathroom came equipped with a mirror. I caught my first glimpse of myself since my captivity and I was astounded by what I saw. My beard was amazingly long and I looked wild and unkempt.

When I finished showering, clean clothes awaited me. It was still an orange jump suit, but of a far less abrasive material. After that, the men walked me up several flights of stairs to a comfortable office with upholstered chairs and a round table and a large window that looked out onto the streets of Cairo. Amun was sitting in one of the chairs and a western man whom I'd never seen before was sitting in another.

I greeted them and Amun asked me if I had had a better night.

I told him I had and that the new cell was a huge improvement over the last one.

"Good," he said. "Good."

Now he pressed the record button on the tape recorder and spoke in English to the other man. "How would you like to begin?"

"Well, tell him I have some questions for him, and that the way he answers them—in other words, whether he's truthful or not—is going to have a lot to do with what we end up doing with him. So the main thing is he's got to tell the truth."

As soon as he spoke, I recognized his voice as that of Peirce, though I still couldn't remember his name. He had bored eyes and a weak chin, and when his mouth was shut, his lips were so narrow they all but disappeared.

Amun turned on the tape recorder and I began. Remembering his little game that he'd insisted upon before, I continued it. I said to Amun in English, "Well tell him that I have every intention of answering his questions honestly."

The American spoke: "Amun, please tell him that if what he says is true, then he has no reason to fear anything."

This game seemed to confuse Amun more than it did either of us. As a Middle Easterner, he wasn't accustomed to the western style of deceit.

"So Amun," I said. "Please ask him what his first question is."

"First of all, I'd like to know his complete name."

"My name is Muhammad Muhammad."

"Ask him about his patronymics?"

I knew it was pointless to try to remember what I'd told Amun previously. So I focused on getting the name out as quickly as possible. "Muhammad al-Mahmoud al-...Jamal Muhammad."

"Where are you from?"

"I grew up in the United States."

"So, you've lived there your entire life?"

"No. I moved there from Canada when I was six. I was born in Canada. The rest of my family was born in Ahwaz."

"Ask him where that is, this Ahwaz," he said to Amun.

"Ahwaz," I said, "is in Iran."

"Iran? But aren't you an Arab? How is it that you're from Iran?"

"Ahwaz is a section of Iran on the western side of the country in which a number of Arabs live."

He was silent for an unnervingly long time. He consulted some papers he had and he was looking skeptical. At one point, he looked over at Amun—to me it looked as if he was trying to see if this made sense to Amun.

"Ahwaz is also called Khuzestan," I said. "That's the Persian name—that's what most Iranians call it."

"Okay," he said. "Yeah. I know Khuzestan." He looked at his papers some more and then said, "Ask him, Amun, if he's an American citizen."

"Yes, I am," I said.

He looked up at me from his papers for several long seconds. He clearly didn't believe me, and I grew worried.

"Ask him, if you would, Amun, about his part in the USS *Cole* bombing."

"Well, as I told you yesterday, Amun, I was…"

I couldn't remember what I'd told Amun yesterday. I knew I'd said that I'd been to Yemen and that I'd stayed in a hotel, that I'd received an envelope, etc. But as I set out to repeat the story, I lost my nerve, worrying that I wouldn't be fluent with the details during my telling. It had something to do with Peirce's attitude—he was such a cynic; moreover, the tape recorder made me nervous. I pictured the two recordings being compared. I started out again, nervously.

"So yeah, I was told to go to Yemen…"

"To what city?"

I was so relieved that Amun had jogged my memory the day before. "Aden," I said.

"Okay, so continue."

"Yeah, so anyway, I got there and as I'd been instructed before leaving for Yemen…"

"Before leaving from where?"

"Ahwaz," I said. I forgot that I'd told Amun that I'd left from New York. Today he didn't seem to notice, probably because the American and I were speaking in English.

"Yeah," I continued, "and when I got there, I called this number they'd given me and I was told that directions would arrive soon. I waited and a day later an envelope was delivered with the address of a restaurant. I went there and found a bunch of people and none of us knew each other. They had pictures of us in an envelope with fake names on them. And like I was telling Amun, the name they gave me was Amun."

I looked at Amun again, and tried to get him to join me in a laugh. But he just sat there adopting the cynical attitude of the American.

"At any rate, they assigned each of us a task; they had me drive them in a mini-bus to a place near the bay where the boat was launched and that was basically it. I stayed there for a while, and a few of them came back in less than an hour and I drove them back to the restaurant we'd started from and I parked the van where I'd been told to park it."

"What restaurant?"

"I really couldn't tell you. That was my one time in Yemen, and I don't have any frame of reference for remembering that sort of detail. I couldn't even tell you where it was, except that it was in the old section of the city."

"The old section?"

I assumed it had an old section. Most Middle Eastern cities have old sections.

"Yes," I said. "You know, the original city that was built in ancient times."

"Right. But how would you describe it?"

"Describe it?"

"Yeah. You know—what's its main feature?"

"Feature?"

"Yeah. What's the first thing that comes to mind when you picture it?"

"I don't know."

"How could you not know? It's so obvious. I was there

and it's the first thing I noticed."

"I obviously didn't notice it. I'm not a trained observer. And not only that, I was there for less than two days."

"The old section of Aden," he said, "is situated in the crater of an extinct volcano."

"Is that what that is? I definitely noticed that it was…that it was…I don't know. It looked like an odd place to put a city," I said. "I thought you were talking about the city itself, not its geology."

"Well, anyway… So, yeah. That was it, ha? You flew into Aden, you met the other people at the restaurant, you drove the men in a van to the launch site, and you drove some of those men back to the restaurant."

"That was it. And that…" I had intended to say that evening I flew home, but I wasn't sure what time of day the attack had taken place.

"And that?" he asked me.

"Yeah, and that's about it."

"Okay. Well, I'd like to move on from the Yemen situation to 9/11."

"I had nothing to do with 9/11."

"Nothing?"

"Nothing. I swear. I know nothing about it and I don't know anyone who does."

I remembered now telling Amun about having met a woman on my way back to New York whose son had died on the *Cole* and how that had made me decide I wanted nothing more to do with killing. It now occurred to me that it would be unlikely that I would have met such a woman on the way back to New York if I left Yemen right after the bombing took place. I had to correct my story.

"See, here's the thing," I said. "Later, when I was back in New York, I met a woman whose son had been killed in the *Cole* bombing—it was just a coincidence, you know?—and as I was speaking with her, I realized that my actions had caused pain to people who did not deserve pain. And I vowed to myself that I would never again be involved in taking the life of another person. Since that time, I have received orders on two different occasions to report to such and such a place. There was no mention of any sort of terrorist activities, but it was clear to me because of the similarity between that first communique to report to Yemen and those two communiques—it was clear to me that this had something to do with a terrorist action. And both times, because I haven't responded, I have afterwards received death threats in the mail."

"Did you save these death threats?"

"No. I threw them both away, and I did so in public garbage cans so that there would be nothing connecting me to them."

"So tell me about this money that you keep in your Cayman Island account." He sat there smirking.

Everything had been going so well. I had a bed, I had three meals a day, I had a light, I was not being tortured, and now he had to ask me this.

"I'm surprised you know about that," was all I could think of to say. I knew it was obvious that I looked surprised, so trying to hide it was out of the question. The main thing was, I couldn't think of how to lie my way out of this one. And if I didn't, the torture would resume. The man would accept nothing but lies.

"Yeah, we know about it," he said. "And we know that you supposedly became an American citizen shortly after 9/11."

"What are you talking about?" I said. I felt sincerely confused.

"Well, let me rephrase that. We know that during that week you received a passport. The thing is, there's no record that you ever became a citizen."

"This is all a mistake," I said.

Peirce appeared not to be listening. He was thumbing through papers in a file that he was holding.

"I'm an American citizen," I said. "I've been an American citizen since I was eleven years old."

"That's not what the records say. According to the records, prior to 9/11, you were an Egyptian citizen and that it's in Egypt that you were born and raised."

"What are you talking about?" I said. I was shocked. Then it hit me that I was supposed to have looked at information the woman at the passport office had given me about the identity they'd established for me.

"We know, furthermore," he said proudly, "that you moved to America five years before this on a student visa, where you studied engineering at Columbia School of Engineering. So what's all this about Ahwaz and growing up in Canada? Why are you mixing so many lies with the truth?"

There was no way I could account for all of the information he was telling me and make it fit into the story I had just told. Sure, he wanted lies, but he wanted the lies to make sense, and there was no way for there to be consistency between what I'd told him and what he was telling me.

I just sat there, afraid of the torture that I knew was about to resume. The only thing I could do was come clean and tell him the entire story.

"Listen," I said. "Just yesterday Amun was asking me about my accent in Arabic. He said that it's not an Egyptian accent and he wondered what it is. I speak like the people from Ahwaz, even though I've never been there. My parents are from there and they taught me Arabic. Tape me speaking and let a linguist hear it. I guarantee you he'll say that I'm from Ahwaz, not from Egypt."

"Well, he said. "I can speak like a bloody good Englishman when I've a mind and the need arises." At that point he returned to his American accent. "An accent proves nothing."

"Would you just humor me and sit there and listen to my entire story? Because unless you do that, you're making an extremely bad mistake that's not only going to hurt me, but hurt your attempts to fight terrorism."

He pressed his lips together and looked slightly amused. "And here I thought you had smartened up," he said.

"You've got this view that you believe is reality. But it's not reality. It's just a model of reality and it's false. And you're going around looking for things that confirm your model. And anything that confirms it is real, or so you would have it, and anything that disconfirms it is false, or so you would have it. Try opening your mind and listening to me. Try shutting your model off for a few minutes and just hearing me out."

"Amun," he said, "I think we're done here. You still have work to do with him." He rose.

Amun reached to shut off the tape recorder.

"Please don't do that, Amun," I said. "Please leave it on. I have more to say. Please listen to me. Humor me. As long as I was lying, you believed me."

"What do you mean? I just accused you of lying."

"But everything I told you was a lie. Just now you spoke of me mixing the truth with lies. It was all lies. The entire thing. That stuff about Yemen? That was a total lie. I've never been to Yemen. Didn't it strike you as strange that I didn't even notice that the old section of Aden was in the crater of an extinct volcano."

"Well then why were you saying all of that?"

"Because I don't like being beaten, drowned, starved, electrocuted and just generally made miserable. Isn't that obvious?"

"So what made you think of Yemen?" He sat down again.

"You know, I don't even know any more, but at some point during this whole ordeal, I was told that I had been involved in bombing the USS *Cole* in Yemen. I believe Amun was the one who told me." It occurred to me that I could get Amun into trouble, so I added, "But I may be mistaken. All I know is that someone told me that I had been involved in the *Cole* bombing and the implication was that I was involved in 9/11."

Peirce looked at Amun.

"This is true," Amun said. "I have asked to him these things."

"I promise you," I said. "I had nothing to do with the *Cole*. I've never had anything to do with any terrorist act, and to my knowledge, I've never known any terrorists. I was making it all up. That's why I told everything in such a way that I wouldn't be able to give details. Names. If I had to tell you names, I was afraid you'd know it was all false. I figure you know a lot of the names of the people involved in the *Cole*, and if I just made up names, you'd know I was lying. That's why I said Muhammad Atta yesterday. I don't know if he was involved in the *Cole* or not, but I know he was involved in 9/11. So I made a leap."

"How did you know that he was involved in 9/11?"

"Because I read about him in the newspaper."

"Yeah, well, there was also a Muhammad Muhammad who was involved in the bombing of the *Cole*."

"Well, first of all, do you have any idea how many Muhammad Muhammad's there are? There are tons."

"Why is it that you're more believable when you lie than when you're supposedly telling the truth?" he asked.

"Maybe it has less to do with me than with you. Maybe it's because when I'm lying, you're hearing what you want to hear."

With his sour look he was telling me that I needed to work harder if I was going to persuade him.

I sat there for a few seconds and decided to act while I still could. Otherwise, he was going to leave, and I was going to be left with Amun, and Amun was going to be in a worse mood than ever.

"My father was Ismail bin Ibrahim bin Jamal Alsawari. My mother was Fatima Maher al Zadah. They were both born in Ahwaz—or Khuzestan, as you call it—and they moved to Montreal in 1969, one year before I was born. My mother's birthday was October 12, 1937. My father's was August 21, 1935.

"I have two brothers, Farhad, whose birthday is October 22, 1960 and Yaseed, whose birthday is August 5, 1962. In addition, I have two sisters, Kinza, who was born on November 15, 1958, and Safia, and she was born on February 25, 1964. All of them were born in Ahwaz. Look all of this stuff up. Go look it up. Or ask them. Ask them if their brother Yusuf…"

"I don't doubt that they have a brother named Yusuf," Peirce said. "What I doubt is that you are that person."

"How would I know all of that information? Can you tell me that? Do you suspect that I could see into the future and so I knew that one day it would be handy to know the birthdays of an entire family of people? Think about it. You're being ridiculous."

"You've done your homework, there's no question."

"Listen to me. My name is Yusuf bin Ismail bin Ibrahim Alsawari and I was born on March 13, 1970 in Montreal and I moved to this country when I was six years old. What could I do to prove that I am Yusuf?"

"I'm afraid there's nothing you could do because that's not who you are."

"Have you guys bothered to look at a photograph of him slash me? That would solve the issue once and for all."

"We know who you are, so we can dispense with all of this."

"Okay, how about this? Take a photograph of me and show it to my wife. Or to my siblings. Or what if you ask my wife if the following is true. On the night I met her, the first song we danced to was 'Takin' It to the Streets' by the Doobie Brothers. Actually, she'll say it was the second song, that "Jungleland" by Springsteen was the first. Ask her about that disagreement we always had. Oh, and you know what? Ask her if I was ever impotent. I'll tell you what she'll say. She won't answer because she's incapable of lying and she is also incapable of saying anything bad about me. But if you press her and tell her what I said, she'll agree that it's true. And this is what she'll agree to. She'll agree that I was one time impotent after I had an operation on my knee. They gave me these pain killers that caused me to be impotent for one night. Ask her. I promise you, she'll respond exactly as I'm saying. I guarantee it."

"Which knee?"

"My right knee."

"Let's see it."

I pulled up my the right leg of my jump suit and showed him the scar left by the incision."

"What happened that you needed an operation on it?"

"Yeah, ask her that as well. And this is what she'll say. And remember, by the way, that's not something that I could have possibly planned in advance. She'll say that I had an operation because I tore my ACL tendon."

"How'd you tear it?"

"I was playing a game of soccer with her cousins, as a matter of fact, at a family reunion."

"When did it happen?"

"Well, it must have happened about four years ago this past June. No, excuse me. Five years ago. Five years ago this past June."

"So five years ago this past June this operation occurred?"

"That's right."

"And it was an operation on your right ACL tendon."

"That's right. And think about this. What are the chances that a person would find out about something like that about another person? And even if I had found it out, what are the chances that I would actually have a corresponding scar on my knee? And think about the impotence factor. Do you honestly think that a guy or his wife would go around telling people about that sort of thing? I've never told anyone about it until now. Do you agree with me, that if she gives you the answers I predict she'll give, isn't that proof?"

"That may be. The thing I don't know is whether the folks in Washington will allow me to talk to her. She believes that her husband is dead—they've already established that—and they're not going to be interested in getting her hopes up based on the word of someone they believe to be a terrorist, I can assure you of that."

"Okay, so what can I do?"

He sat there and shrugged. "We're convinced that we have the right man."

"How about this," I said. "How about you ask the people in Washington to let you or someone else talk to her about trying to identify her husband's corpse and ask if he had a scar on his right knee. Would that work?"

"Frankly, I doubt it. Tell me this. Why did you leave

her?"

"I left her because she became a Christian three years before 9/11. She had been a Muslim."

"Three years before 9/11? But you said you took her phone to her at the Trade Center on 9/11. Why was that, if you were already separated?"

"We continued to live in the same house even though there was next to no communication between us."

"The same house? Why was that?"

"I don't know… I still loved her. She still loved me. It's hard to explain."

"I see that."

"Ask her about it."

"For all I know, you may have read this stuff in some interview with Ruth Clevesy in a newspaper or magazine. They've done a lot of interviews with survivors and relatives of survivors, and she's both."

"Okay, but she wouldn't have told an interviewer stuff she didn't know. Like on 9/11, I used a pay phone on Nassau Street just north of Fulton to call our home phone—and I bet that's something you can check on—well, not that I made the call, but that a call was made from there to our house. And instead of leaving a message, I retrieved her message that she was fine. And it was in that moment that I decided that this was my chance to leave without hurting her feelings. And, like I said, it's not as if she would have mentioned a phone call from Nassau Street in some interview because she didn't even know about it. I didn't leave a message. I simply retrieved the message she had left."

"Well, if you retrieved a message, she would have known that, wouldn't she? I would think that only she and her husband would have known the code for retrieving messages. And on the recording, she would have definitely heard that the code had been punched in."

"She would have probably heard it, but not noticed it. It would have just sounded like some sort of…technical thing to her. And even if she'd noticed it, she wouldn't have known what it was. You don't understand. She's got this amazingly important and complicated job, but she's like a person from the stone ages when it comes to technology. And she's very proud of it and vocal about it. She grew up in Africa and Asia in some of the poorest countries on earth and she's something of a Luddite. That too is something you can check on. Please do this. I promise you—you'll see that what I'm saying is true. Ask anyone she works with."

"I don't know, Muhammad. I gotta tell you. I don't buy it."

"Listen to me," I said. "I'm not Muhammad."

He rose now and Amun shut off the tape recorder.

"We'll need to talk," he said to Amun.

Amun now opened the door and summoned his assistants. They came in and took me by the arms and walked me back down stairs. On the way, I assumed I'd be returning to my old cell, but they put me in my new cell and I was as delighted as if they'd put me up at the Ritz.

Chapter 15

I don't know how long I lay there before I fell asleep, but when I finally woke up, it was 2:00, Friday afternoon. I lay there aware that I had until 4:26 to complete *Dhuhr*, the noon prayer. But I was incapable of moving.

Finally at 4:30 I got up and dragged myself into the bathroom. Even physically I felt as bad as I had in college the several times I'd taken alcohol at parties and had gotten drunk. During my shower I pictured the way I had in effect taunted Allah and wondered at how far out of control I had spun.

* * *

A few days later, Amun's assistants came and took me for my second shower of the week. A second shower within a week was a first. Afterwards, they had me put on a clean pair of khakis and a white tee shirt. I was extremely excited, assuming that I would now be taken home.

They took me up two flights of stairs and down a corridor to a room on the door of which was written "Interrogation Room" in both Arabic and English. The fear returned and I was set for the worst. After I was ushered inside, however, I saw at once that it was not an interrogation room at all. It did have a sterile atmosphere, i.e., there was no extraneous furniture except for a table with two chairs. But there was none of the equipment that had been present during previous interrogations. I was told to sit in one of the chairs and to wait.

The two assistants left and about half an hour later, a young woman came in. She was between thirty and thirty-five and she was quite attractive even without make-up. She had large brown eyes and blond hair that was pulled back, revealing a high forehead.

She walked over to me and held out her hand.

"Hello, Mr. Muhammad. I'm Cecily Beaumont, and I'm

with the American Consulate here in Cairo. I'm told you speak English. Is that correct?"

I realized now that the sign on the door had been for PR purposes only.

"Yes, I do," I said.

"There's some question as to whether you're an American citizen. In the event that you are, I'm here to check on your treatment."

"I am definitely an American citizen," I told her. As I spoke, I was wondering how I should handle this. Should I tell her the truth? My real name? How much power did she have, anyway? Was she actually with "them" and checking to see how much I would tell if I were released?

"So how is it going for you?" she asked.

"It's not bad," I said.

"No? So you're comfortable and you're being treated well?"

"Yes. I'd rather be back home in the States, but yeah, seeing that's not possible, I guess things are going okay."

"So they haven't hurt you or anything like that?"

As she said this, something was communicated, something very human and caring and it passed through all of my defenses and tapped the feelings of vulnerability that had been building and that I'd been suppressing extremely effectively. At that moment I began crying.

Simultaneously, several other things happened. For one, my macho Arab nature was not at all pleased with me for crying in front of a strange woman and I viewed myself through eyes of contempt. This in turn made me feel even more vulnerable, divided as I was from myself, and I cried so hard that I began to hiccup the way I had as a small child when I was upset.

She spoke to me now with genuine concern in her voice. There was nothing condescending about it. It was a very human tone through which she spoke the words, "So they have hurt you?"

I couldn't answer the question. I was convinced that she was a well-meaning, caring woman. But how much power did she have? The CIA, or whatever it was, was not going to take its marching orders from the State Department. She was young and she'd go back to the Embassy and tell them I was being tortured. What would happen then? Who was I in their opinion? I was a terrorist suspect and I was not connected to any one with power or influence. They would think I'd manipulated the wide-eyed white girl. No one cared about me. My wife thought I was dead. What if I told this woman that I was not the man they thought I was? She might believe me. But would they believe her? It was a gamble I didn't dare take. All I knew was that I didn't want to make my situation worse. I was in a cell that was relatively comfortable. They were feeding me much better and I was getting three meals a day. And for the moment, I was not being tortured. I could survive like this indefinitely, and I didn't dare allow myself to believe that they were going to let me go. My best bet was caution.

She spoke again. "I hate to hurry you, but they only gave me fifteen minutes to speak with you, so if you have something to tell me, you should tell me now."

I got hold of myself and in a few seconds I said, "They haven't hurt me. But I am so sad that I can't go home. I really didn't do what they think I did and I can't make them believe me."

"What do they think you did?"

"They think I was involved in the bombing of the USS *Cole*," I said.

"And you weren't?"

"No, I wasn't. I promise you I wasn't."

"Why do they think that you were?"

"I don't know. They think I have the same name as someone who was involved in that attack. But the thing is…"

I debated getting into the name thing—Muhammad Muhammad and how without the patronymics, they couldn't be certain of who was the terrorist. The problem was, that would make her think I was Muhammad Muhammad and if she were to do some investigating, it would lead her down a wrong alley.

I said, "The thing is…"

I'd intended to tell her I was Yusuf Alsawari. But I decided against it because she would soon discover that Yusuf had died in the World Trade Center, and I didn't have enough time to tell her the entire story.

"The thing is what?" she said. "Please tell me. We don't have much time."

"Well, if you can, do this. Listen to the tapes that have been made of the interviews with me. Can you get access to the tapes?"

"I don't know if I can or not. I'll ask the ambassador. He may be able to get me a copy. He knows a lot of people."

"If you could do that, I think you'll understand the situation," I said. "There's too much to explain. It's a very long story. But please do me a favor and don't say that I've been tortured or anything. I'm being treated very well right now and I'm happy with that. I don't want anything to change. Unless, of course, it's to be sent back home."

"Where are you from?"

"I grew up in New York, and I lived there until just before I was detained. But then I moved to Seattle, and that's when all this happened."

She was taking notes as she listened. "Okay, then," she said. "Well, you hang in there and I promise you I'll try to listen to those tapes. Okay?" She put her notebook into her purse.

"Okay," I said. "Thanks for coming by."

She rose and I did too, and I put out my hand to shake. But she hugged me instead. "Good luck," she said. I could see now that her face was red and I wondered if it was because she was embarrassed that she had hugged me, or if she was angry at my situation. Either way, I decided it was a good sign.

Chapter 16

Even after my shower that I followed with the afternoon prayer, I left the hotel feeling as if I had violated everything that mattered most. Most people will not have a clue about what I am saying. For most people, especially in America, God is no more than a concept, some imaginary superhero who lives in the sky. But for people who truly believe, God is what is. God is reality and eternal and this temporary thing called life amounts to no more than a single teardrop in the ocean. Our life is our mere signature, yet this signature stands for whom we have decided to be for all eternity. Will we side with God or will we side with the Shaitan, the devil. Most people these days have lost all sense of that, just as I had that morning on the way back to the hotel. The Shaitan gets us to believe that all of this that we see before us is all that there is, that all of this is what matters. He wants us to make our decisions accordingly. But picture for a moment that the view that the Shaitan promotes is wrong. Picture for a moment that everything that happens to us in this world is a test, that we're all being tested to see what we value more—what is temporary or what is eternal. The Shaitan wants us to believe in the temporary because when we side with the temporary, we are waylaid from the pathway to Goodness, the pathway to God. When you understand the drama in those terms—not as an idea, but as a reality—you may have some understanding of how I felt as I made my way across town.

When I passed a barbershop, I didn't even think—I just walked inside and sat down. When it came my turn, I asked the barber to shave my head.

He was an older black man who himself had a shaved head. He looked as if he had learned a lot from the errors he had made in life and that he no longer owed anything to anyone. He was polite, but made clear with his bearing that he was nobody's fool.

After hearing the sort of haircut I wanted, he turned the barber chair around so that I was facing away from the mirror. He got out his clippers and clipped my hair down to the quick. I was tempted to turn and look at myself in this intermediate stage, but I decided to wait for the full effect. He stepped away from the chair for a minute and as I sat there without the distraction of his hand or clippers on my head, I caught how different was the sensation of having no hair. He returned with a handful of heated lather. As he patted it on, it hugged my head with its warmth.

The barber pulled a straight razor from a pocket and ran it across a leather strop that hung from the side of the chair. All the while the warmth of the lather worked its way through my scalp. Soon he stretched his hand across my forehead to hold my head steady, and he began running the blade across my head in long, even strokes. He worked quickly and moved around my head silently, concentrating on his work. Within ten minutes he was done and was wiping off the excess lather with a towel. He brushed some hair off my gown with a small whiskbroom and dusted my neck with talcum powder. He asked me my name.

"Yusuf," I said.

"Well," he said, "It is my pleasure to present you with the new and improved Yusuf," and with that he turned the chair so that I faced myself.

I was amazed. I looked so different from what I had expected. I had to examine my face for signs that I was even myself. While he took off my robe and swept up my hair, I studied myself for a full minute in the mirror.

"So, whatta ya think, Champ?" he asked.

"Intense," is all I said.

He laughed about that a good bit. He said, "Now let me get this straight. You thought you were going to shave your head and it was not going to be intense? Is that what you thought?" He laughed some more and I did as well.

"You've got an intense face, young man," he said. "And when you shave the head of a man with an intense face, you get a very intense face. I know all about it," he said, and he looked at himself in the mirror, pretending to fix his hair. We laughed and I asked what I owed him.

"Fifteen bucks," he said.

All I had was two hundreds and a fifty. I gave him the fifty and waved him off when he started for change. He thanked me with a sincere nod of his head, a bow of sorts, a generous bow, but proud in the best sense of the word. I liked this man and I wished I could just tell him what a fool I'd been as I looked at myself in the mirror.

My new haircut made me look ugly in a way that I couldn't quite believe, and yet I really liked it. My features were so pronounced. It was amazing the way a little hair made me look relatively civilized. With it gone, I looked like a killer. I felt like a terrorist, and the fact that I was getting myself a new identity enhanced that feeling. It seemed like this look came with a lot of power over which I wasn't quite prepared to assume responsibility. I still wanted to think of myself as part of the housebroken masses, and yet with all that had happened during the past few days, it no longer seemed possible.

* * *

I was sitting on my mattress thinking, just as I had been since my interview with Cecily three days before. I was nurturing the hope I'd felt after speaking with her. I had just eaten supper and I was waiting for Mahmoud to collect my tray. I was picturing the way my life would have been if I'd never been abducted and if I were still living in Seattle. I decided that I would probably be out for a walk—maybe smoking a cigarette, and I pictured myself in Steinbrueck Park sitting on a park bench looking out at the water. What would my life be like if Ruth had not led the tour of NYU when I had visited the graduate school as I'd tried to decide which school to attend? I would never have met her. Who would I have met instead? Or, what if Ruth had said no to her mother's final request. What then?

What if 9/11 had never happened? What would I have been doing if I'd still been living with Ruth in New York? I realized once again that I'd been an idiot to end my relationship with her when she'd returned to Christianity. We served the same God. It made no difference whether she saw Issa's role as exceeding Muhammad's (p.b.u.h.). Couldn't I allow her to see things her way and I see things mine? According to the Koran, both Issa and Muhammad (p.b.u.h.) were apostles of Allah. Why did I have to join the age-old fight between the followers of Issa and the followers of Muhammad (p.b.u.h.)? Allah sent both men. He loved them both. Surely leaving Ruth as I had and then sneaking away from her like a coward, surely sitting here in this cell was my payment. How could I have been so stubborn, so cruel?

I began sobbing as I sat there and I realized that it had been many days since I'd performed the daily prayers. This only intensified my feelings of estrangement and my sobbing continued. I felt as if I had been abandoned by Allah and I didn't blame Him a bit. I had abandoned Him so many times, and now He had abandoned me. It seemed only right.

From nowhere the promise in the Koran came to me: "If he repents of his iniquity and reclaims himself, then surely Allah will look upon him with mercy." I knew that He had not abandoned me, that all I needed to do was ask his forgiveness. I called out to Him—literally called out with a loud whisper: "Forgive me, Lord. Forgive me for losing faith in You again. How many times must I repeat this mistake before I learn?"

That was all it took. I could feel Him in my heart in the form of courage and hope and joy.

As I wondered how I could maintain my promise to stay true to Allah, another verse came to me: "Without a doubt, this Book is a guide to those who wish to guard themselves from evil." Immediately, I saw the problem. I had been living through this ordeal in the absence of the Koran. I decided that I would do everything I could to get a copy.

I could hear Mahmoud walking down the corridor, gathering the trays. He was a grizzled old man with an inadequate education and he looked like a man who had made many mistakes in his life. Yet he was the kindest man I met during my entire ordeal. I greeted him by the door as I handed him my tray.

He thanked me and looked at me through the bars of my cell door. He clearly recognized that I had something to say to him.

"Mahmoud," I began. "Do you happen to know if it's possible for me to get a copy of the Koran in here?"

"Definitely," he said. "Definitely. Many of the prisoners have them. You have but to ask and you will be given one. In the 'dark wing,' where you were before, even there they would have given you one, but you would not have been able to read it because there is no light in the cells. Yet there are prisoners even there who have a copy and feel strengthened by its presence. If you would like a Koran, I will have one for you in the morning. Nor will there be a need for you to hide it from the authorities. This is entirely allowed."

"Thank you, Mahmoud. If you could bring me one, I'd really appreciate it. Tonight I realized what was wrong. I've been without the Koran since coming here. Normally, I read it each day, but lately, because I have not, I feel as though my practice has fallen apart. Up until this evening, I didn't even realize what the problem was."

"I will gladly bring you one. I am not supposed to ask prisoners if they want the Koran brought to them—I guess they fear it would become expensive after a while. But when I am asked, I am supposed to bring one."

He seemed overjoyed to be able to do this small service for me and I realized that he had made a strong commitment to Allah. I said to him, "You do a great service to Allah with your job. I hope you know that."

"I am a simple man," he said. "But Allah can work even through the least of us."

He said this with complete conviction, and I realized he was absolutely right. He made me realize that even I, though a mere prisoner and at the lowest level of society, even I could help others to realize Muhammad's (p.b.u.h.) message.

After he had left, I performed *wudu*, and this time with water from a pitcher that was filled, each morning. After that, I performed the sunset prayer and I felt completely whole.

The next morning when Mahmoud brought my breakfast, he brought me a Koran as well. It was brand new. In fact, it was still shrink-wrapped. When I thanked him, he beamed with joy. He was clearly aware that in that moment he was playing the role of a messenger of Allah, and though his impact would not be felt as strongly as that of Muhammad (p.b.u.h.), it mattered to me a great deal.

Before eating my breakfast, I tore the plastic from the Koran and let my finger fall where it might. It fell on a verse in The Pilgrimage: "And that they to whom wisdom hath been given, may know that *the Koran* is the truth straight from the Lord and that they may believe in it, and submit their hearts to it: for those who believe are surely guided by Allah onto the straight path."

What more proof did I need that Allah was there for me, guiding my finger to a sign from Him!

Chapter 17

I arrived at Brooks Brothers at 5:45 p.m. The man who had sold me the suits was there.

"Oh, yes," he said. "I believe you have cut your hair since your last visit," he suggested.

I confirmed his memory.

I tried on my altered pants. Both pairs fit me perfectly, and I decided to wear the blue suit along with a new pale yellow shirt. I was already wearing my Wallabees and with my newly shaven head, though I may have looked like a terrorist, I looked like a well-dressed one; I had to give myself that. I felt a little better now, but only on the outermost level. Deep inside, there was a remorse for what I had done with the prostitute earlier that day, and it was percolating up through me, making it difficult for the good mood that was trying to establish itself.

What with my boxes and bags, I took a cab back to the hotel. I put things away and decided to go out to eat. At that point, I remembered that at 7:09 it would be time for sunset prayers, which gave me about ten minutes.

I performed *wudu*, hoping to cast off the feeling that was still with me. Then I said my sunset prayers. Ever since I was in college, I have sought actually to be there as I said my prayers. But tonight, I worked at this in a way I don't think I ever had before, and it paid off. It was not that my depression lifted. But I saw that if I persisted in my movements toward Allah, that it would lift. I could feel His love behind the depression and I knew that eventually He would help me. In fact, He was trying to help me now, but my guilt was so thick that it was not allowing His love to get through.

After I was finished, I found myself wondering if there

was someone I could call to eat dinner with. I abandoned that
idea as soon as I remembered my circumstances. The fact that
my first thought was not to call Ruth I took as a sign that I
would eventually get over her. I wondered if Allah had allowed me to go through my madness with the prostitute to
make it possible for me to begin breaking my bond to Ruth.

I had not eaten since breakfast, and I was extremely hungry. I ended up wandering the neighborhood until I found a
Chinese restaurant. I sat at a small round table by myself. As
I ate my vegetarian meal, I noticed that two women at a table
were looking over at me. I now wondered if my real reason
for going out was not to get food, but to be seen by the opposite sex in my new clothes and haircut. I no longer trusted my
motives.

I asked the waitress for the check and she put the rest of
my meal in a doggy bag. I headed back to my room and ate in
silence. I didn't dare watch the television at this point. For all
I knew, I would see something pornographic and not be able
to change the station.

I finished my meal just in time to perform *wudu* and say
Ishaa, the night prayers which tonight came up at 8:26. After
that, despite my extensive nap, I was tired, and after looking
up morning prayer time for the next morning, I set my alarm
for 5:10 and went to sleep.

* * *

From that point on until the end of my imprisonment, I
read the Koran several times daily and performed the five
prayers. It was extremely difficult to keep track of the time—
I had no access to time and there were no windows to help.
My only time indications were the three meals. Mahmoud
had told me the times that the three meals were served—six
a.m., noon, and six p.m. A week or so later, I asked him if he
could write down the times of *Salah* for the next few days. I
knew that I would be incapable of observing the prayer times
with any accuracy, but the meals were an indicator of sorts
and they would help.

The next morning, as Mahmoud served me my breakfast, I realized he had sneaked a sheet of paper that he had torn out of a little *Salah* calendar onto my tray. As he stood there, I asked him the date so that I could use the calendar correctly. I assumed that he was going to say that it was mid to late December. When he whispered to me that it was March 23, I asked him to repeat it. He looked around and repeated it, but this time more softly. The New Year had come and gone—it was 2002. My birthday had come and gone—I was thirty-two and Ruth was thirty-four.

After that, I attempted to say my prayers at something approaching the correct times. The morning was the most difficult to gauge, at least at that time of year in Cairo, because it came before I was normally awake. For instance, on March 24, 2002, the morning prayer was supposed to begin at 4:34. After I had slept what felt like a long time, I woke up and assumed that it was about the right time. I performed the prayer and sat there thinking it was about time to eat. Soon, I realized that no one else was even stirring, so I returned to sleep and woke up what seemed like several hours later. I rose again and repeated the process, and when I had finished I sat on my mattress again waiting. Once again, I waited for a long time, going in and out of sleep before Mahmoud's arrival. I suspect that the first time I woke up, it was shortly after midnight.

This happened on several other occasions, but I did not mind. Normally, after my light went on, I spent an hour or so reading from the Koran, falling in love with it all over again. My days passed far more quickly now and I felt that I was living in the light of the Koran.

Chapter 18

After morning prayer, I returned to bed and slept until 11:00. By now I was beginning to feel some vague connection to my former self. I put on my other new suit and a light blue shirt and went out for breakfast. I was aware of how proud I was in my new clothes and realized I had to watch this vanity, that it could trip me up. In fact, I decided that after my noon prayer, I would go out and buy some casual clothes. The only clean clothes I now owned were my new shirts and suits.

Noon prayer was to begin at 12:54 so I waited before going out. After that, I walked downtown and bought myself a pair of cord pants, two pairs of blue jeans, and some khakis. In addition, I bought four polo shirts, two sweaters and a lined windbreaker. When I got back to the hotel I reinvented myself once again with a new set of clothes. Even though they were far more similar than the suits to my former clothing, this identity too felt superimposed.

I had no idea who I was. I had no idea what to do with myself. I felt crazed. I had no place to go but I had a strong need to be elsewhere. It seemed like the real world had become just me in my hotel room. When I stepped outside that room, the world took on an unreal quality. All of it seemed as if it had been built to tempt me away from Allah. Sounds on the street seemed artificial and I had difficulty imagining that the people I saw on the sidewalk had actual existence apart from my perception of them.

Part of the problem was that by now—and I don't think it was simply my imagination—I was getting an increasing number of strange looks from my fellow citizens. I had seen news reports about how the mistrust of Middle Easterners had reached an all time high since Tuesday. Now it was Saturday, September 15th and people had changed. Though I had received no stray comments save from the kid who'd called me a Towel Head, I expected an insult at any minute.

I guess I'd have to say that by this point I was—I don't know—something wasn't just right with me. I mean, I was aware of it and everything, and it wasn't as if I was dangerous. But I felt free in a way that most people would classify as unhealthy. By free, I mean I lacked definition, lacked boundaries to keep me in check.

At one point that day, I saw a policeman and I imagined going up to him and just saying nonsensical words to him, gibberish, just to see how he would respond. After that, I actually did walk up to a distinguished looking man—he was probably in his mid-50s, the type whom no one ever approached on the street. There was something intimidating about him. Either he was a CEO of a major corporation, or that is what he wanted people to believe. Anyway, I spoke to him in Arabic, asked him if he had any idea that one day he would die.

He looked at me with feigned respect and said, "I'm sorry, but I don't speak Hebrew."

This amused me so much that I laughed out loud and sought an excuse for my laughter. I pointed at my watch now and laughed and told him, also in Arabic, "It's never too late to learn." He kept looking at my watch for the secret of my laughter. This made me wonder if the real reason I had pointed to it was that it was expensive. In pointing to it, had I been bragging to him that he wasn't the only one with money? What amazed me was that I hadn't consciously set out to do any such thing, but that's how it had ended up. Perhaps some inner urge had expressed itself without my knowledge. Whatever it was, it felt familiar.

Since my experience with the prostitute, all that I saw when I looked into myself was vanity. It felt as if the only thoughts and feelings I had that were not aimed at raising myself up in other people's eyes, were thoughts and feelings aimed at raising myself up in my own eyes. Moreover, I realized that this had always been the case. I whispered a prayer to Allah to help me over my vanity.

* * *

I filled much of my time with my prayers and reading the Koran. But there were times during which I would just sit and picture what I would do if I were ever released. Since coming there, I had fluctuated between hope and despair—hope that I would be released soon, that I would be able to get back to my life, and despair that I would die there. Now that I was reading the Koran and faithfully performing the five daily prayers, things had changed, and I was often in a state between hope and despair, a state in which I began to realize that this was my life. Like everyone else, I was on a mission from Allah and this is where He had chosen to send me. Like Jonah, when he was called by Allah to preach in Ninevah, I'd had trouble accepting my mission. Jonah had not accepted Allah's will for his life until he was inside the great fish. But as soon as he accepted the Will of Allah, he was spat out by the fish and left immediately for Ninevah. I was beginning to realize that my mission was different. My mission was to remain inside the bowels of this great Egyptian fish. If Allah wanted me elsewhere, I would be elsewhere. My job was to be content with where I was. And yet…

During those "and yet" times, I would just sit and wonder what I would do if I were told that they had made a terrible mistake, and that they were sending me home immediately. I tried to picture how I would feel, what I would say. I would picture various scenarios, and I would play with alternatives to them, as if I were word processing them and going back and reworking them.

One scenario had Amun's assistants coming to me, taking me to the shower room, and then handing me a new set of civilian clothes, similar to the way it had happened when Cecily from the American Consulate had spoken with me. Then they would take me out to Amun who would shake my hand and he would apologize to me and thank me for not hating him the way many prisoners had done, and he'd tell me that I actually had more reason than most to hate him because I'd been innocent all along.

Sometimes I would picture him coming to my cell personally and saying all of this. Or maybe the American man would be there too. He would be on the plane that took me back to America. This time they would not have me in handcuffs and blindfolded. I would be sitting there with them and we would all be playing cards together. How would I feel about playing cards with them? Would I do so, or would I play it cool? I decided I would play cards with them and let them know what it meant to be a true Muslim, able to forgive, able to show mercy just as Allah showed mercy to those who made mistakes and corrected them.

I would also wonder to myself what I would do when I returned to America. No doubt, they would return me to Seattle. What would have become of my apartment? All of my possessions would have been removed. I would go to the landlord and explain what had happened. Would she believe me? I had been detained by a government agency for months and months—or by then would it be years and years? I would explain that I had been taken to Egypt and tortured. Otherwise I would have paid my rent. The landlord would be angry with me for telling such an obvious lie. I would offer to pay all of my back rent if only she would tell me what had become of my possessions. The thing I would want would be the compass given to me by my mother, the one I had taken when I had sneaked home to pick up the safe deposit key.

And what about my watch, given to me by my father? Would I ever get it back? The men in Seattle who had first abducted me had taken it from me. The few possessions that I had in this world, would I ever see them again? What about my wallet with my credit card and banking card from the Caymans? Without them, how would I access my money? And my passport? Where had all of this stuff ended up? Would anyone know? Would they allow me my fake passport back, or would they force me to return to my real name?

A lot of this time would be spent in wondering whether it would be wise, after so much time had passed, would it be wise to put Ruth through the strain of letting her know that I had survived the Trade Center, would it be wise to tell her what her country had done to me? How would she handle this knowledge when she had such high expectations for America? My answer to that question depended on how I was feeling on a particular day. One day I would be convinced that I should just continue my life without her; the next, I would have rethought the situation. I would picture my life without her, stretching out into a bleak future versus my life with her and a future filled with hope. But what if in the meanwhile she had befriended one of the men in her church and what if they had fallen in love? Even if she had, surely by now she would not have been married. No one would get married before a year was up, would they? Then it would hit me that I didn't know if I would be released within a year. This back and forth in my head would go on for hours sometimes. And then I would remember the other attitude, the attitude of Islam, that I was where Allah wanted me. For some reason He wanted me here, and this was where I belonged. He had a plan for my life, and all I had to do was remember that fact, and allow Him to work at His own pace. For Him, a year was not even so much as the blink of an eye, and He might well keep me here for three or four of his blinks; my job was to accept it as His will.

I would stay in that perspective for perhaps as much as two or three hours. But when I would lie down for a nap, I would drift back into my future plans, back into My Will. Most of the time this would happen without me even noticing it, but there were also times when I did. During those times as I lay there, I would not allow my mind to drift in this way and I would try to hold onto the thought that this is what Allah intended for me right now—for whatever reason, this was His will. I might even fall asleep with that thought in mind. But when I'd wake up, I'd have drifted back into my own plans.

Chapter 19

I ordered take-out Chinese food and spent Saturday evening back in my room. I decided to risk television again and I flipped back and forth among news channels. They were still showing the towers being struck by the planes. On one station they were presenting middle-eastern Americans who were being discriminated against by their neighbors. In some cases they had been physically hurt because of the mistrust that had surfaced during the past few days. On another station, they were interviewing people whose husbands and wives had worked in the Trade Center and had not been heard from since. I saw a woman speak about her husband, about what a good man he had been, and how she hoped they would find him alive beneath the wreckage. At one point she said, "I miss him so much. So much…" She broke down, and when I pictured Ruth, I broke down, and I wondered if leaving her was the right thing.

After *Ishaa* I went to bed and fell immediately asleep. In the night at about two or so I woke up and I felt the weight of what I had done with the prostitute. As I lay there I had an exceptionally strong sense that I would one day die. I visualized my dead body lying in a coffin with my hands folded on my chest in that way that corpses do and I realized that I had so little time left. Even if I lived to be a hundred, it was so little time because my life was going so fast and I cried, feeling that I was just wasting it. I didn't have any children; and now I didn't even have a wife or a career. My life was just racing past, one day after another, and one day I would die and if I didn't start paying attention, my life would mean no more than the life of a dog.

* * *

Across from my cell was a stonewall that looked ancient. As I mentioned, there were five other prisoners in this cell-block. Usually I only heard them, but occasionally one of them would walk past, accompanied by Amun's assistants. I assumed they were on their way to shower or a meeting with Amun. When Amun's assistants were not in the cellblock, the six of us sometimes spoke. After I'd been there for a few weeks, the others began to be friendly with me. I soon found out that informants had been placed in these cells, and that it took a while to trust newly arrived prisoners.

We all spoke in fairly friendly terms back and forth until I mentioned one day that I was an American. I had been tempted to tell them I was from Ahwaz but I couldn't lie to them. After that, a week or so passed during which they all but ignored me. Bassam, the man next to me, had heard me performing my prayers every day, and he told the others about this.

For twenty minutes or so, they spoke openly to each other about me, argued about whether they could trust me. Finally, Bassam asked that I speak. I felt as if I was in a very ancient court of law. Though there is a lot of respect for learning within Islam, I decided against speaking about my graduate studies, mainly because I feared mentioning Averroes. Among other things, he had preached equality of the sexes and has always been considered too liberal by dogmatic Muslims. I feared that if I mentioned him, bridging the gap between us would be impossible. Instead I spoke about growing up in a home in which Islam was spoken of with great respect, but that it went no deeper than that. I told them about how as a child I had been embarrassed by Islam, and how it was not until I was in my twenties that I had truly committed my life to Islam. After that, things shifted and it was clear that I had been accepted.

None of them admitted to being terrorists or being connected to terrorism in any way. I suspect that they would never have admitted such a thing to an American. But there's a good chance that they wouldn't have admitted it to anyone. And there's a good chance that they were not involved in terrorism. Either way, all of them were what I would have then called radical fundamentalists.

When I told them how I had been abducted and brought there to Egypt, two of the others told of nearly identical experiences. Both were of Egyptian origin. One had been a student in Canada. On his way home for the summer break, he had been abducted at Heathrow Airport in London. Another had grown up in France. Following a flight to Frankfurt to visit his brother, he had been abducted and brought to Egypt. In both cases, it was Americans who had brought them here. No wonder these men had a difficult time trusting me.

Since I had recommitted myself to praying daily and reading the Koran, I had sometimes heard one or two of the others moving about in ways that sounded like they might be performing *wudu* or prayers. One day I suggested that we all perform our prayers as a group. One of us could assume the role of the *muezzin* and we could have a call to prayer, and one of us could assume the role of *imam* and at the appointed times we would pray together.

There were two *hafizes* in our midst, that is, two men who had completely memorized the Koran, which, of course, made them equal. But one of them knew more about the *Hadith*, namely, the words and deeds and recommendations of Muhammad (p.b.u.h.) that became codified after his death. So this man became the *imam*. I had originally thought we might all take turns, but that was far too radical a notion for all of them except one.

All together, there were six of us in the cellblock. The two men on the ends could not hear each other unless they yelled. It worked out well because, as it happened, the *imam* was in one of the two middle cells.

I had only one cell to my right and four to my left. The *imam* was two down from me. We all agreed that the others could take turns assuming the role of *muezzin*, but that the two on the ends would have to sing loudly.

Though Egypt is predominantly Sunni, there was one Shiite in our midst. As an American, such distinctions hardly mattered to me, though as an Islamic scholar, they were of

interest. Oddly enough, the disagreements that we had regarding format had nothing to do with the Shiite. The *hafizes*
were the problem. In the beginning they argued about everything. But after a while, things evened out and we had some
very moving prayer times together.

Right from the start, it was clear that collectively we
would have the same problem with the morning prayer that
I'd been having on my own. It was nearly impossible to guess
the right time. As I recall, this was near the beginning of
April in Cairo, so we were supposed to pray at about 4:30,
about an hour and a half before breakfast. But that was not
easy to guess. We did the best we could. That first morning,
the designated *muezzin* was the Shiite. He was three cells to
my left and he began the call to prayer, as we had agreed,
when he judged it to be the correct time. All of us were fast
asleep and I suspect that we all thought he had begun several
hours too early. I was content to let him continue. I have always loved the call to prayer—I find it to be the most beautiful moment in all of Islam, particularly that first call of the
day. This Shiite had a beautiful voice that reverberated
through the stone halls lending a majesty to the moment and I
felt at one with Allah. But two men—first one, and then another—shouted to him that it was way too early for the call. I
am certain that if he had been a Sunni, they would never have
felt they had a right to interrupt him as they did.

I was impressed with how well he took it. He stopped
singing at once, and apologized. But we had barely returned
to sleep when the lights came on and Mahmoud began his
rounds. It was clear that, if anything, the Shiite had been a little late. That led us to decide that even if we were absolutely
certain that the *muezzin* was mistaken in his estimation of the
time, we would go along with his decision, and that following
the call, we would perform *wudu*, and the *imam* would begin
the prayer.

According to Islam, praying in the mosque provides
twenty-seven times more *sawab*, blessings, for the practitio-
ner than praying at home. But all of us agreed that our services together provided the same *sawab* as if we had been in a

mosque. This was the best we could do, meaning our cell-block was our mosque.

After we had prayed together, we would go about our own private business. For me that was reading the Koran and day dreaming about the past and the future. Having some connection to other people definitely made my life more tolerable.

Chapter 20

Eventually I fell back asleep and when I woke up next time, the sun had already risen and I got up feeling guilty to have missed the morning prayer. I performed my ablutions and said the prayer anyway. As I was kneeling, I asked Allah to forgive me for over sleeping.

After that I wanted to return to sleep, but given that I had woken up late, I did not allow myself this luxury. I spent some time reading the Koran on my computer, and later I watched the Sunday morning news shows. They were interviewing people about the attacks. I must have seen the planes crash into the Trade Center another five or six times and I heard experts explain why the buildings had fallen and why the terrorists had been able to bring down those planes with box cutters. They spoke about the history of al-Qaeda and about how Osama bin Laden was an heir to a wealthy Saudi family, and how the US had helped him fight against the Russians in Afghanistan.

I went out later and bought some breakfast at a Greek diner and wandered around a little. It was a little warmer today, so I ventured over to Fifth Avenue and walked north. I entered Central Park at Fifty-Ninth Street. Thousands of people were enjoying the end of the summer in the same way I was. When I came to the Sheep Meadow, I heard a man playing an electric guitar. He had a battery-powered amplifier set up and he was playing early Beatles songs with a lot of skill. I stood for a while with a sizeable group listening to him. He had our attention, and a lot of people were throwing money into a large white bucket that stood in front of his amplifier. But then he was drowned out. His audience, still facing him, moved their raised heads uniformly as they watched two F-16s streak across the sky. With that reminder, the crowd began breaking up. Watching them, I was overcome with the understanding that all of them—all of us—were one day going to die. Then as I moved on, I took that image of death with me everywhere, and for nearly every person I saw—young, old, even a baby I saw in a stroller—it hit me that one day that person would die.

All of this depressed me in an obvious way, but there was more to it than that. In addition, there was an odd reassurance that this state of meaninglessness called life was a temporary state of affairs. So side-by-side with my depression, I experienced an elation of sorts. There were moments during which I accurately saw my bifurcated inner state and when that would happen, I felt at peace though in the midst of a war of moods.

When I got up to Strawberry Fields, I walked west on West Seventy-Second Street and over to Broadway where I walked south for nearly a mile to my hotel. I performed *wudu* and said *Dhuhr*. I lay down to take a nap, but I didn't fall asleep until much later. The strongest memory I have of that afternoon is that the sensation of not knowing what to do with myself had gotten so strong that felt I couldn't stand it. I had a moment of being tempted to call Ruth again and bring this entire show to an end. But I felt it was best to let things continue. It seemed to me that Allah was behind my decision and I decided to accept it. I lay there tossing and turning, dreading the hours that lay between the present and tomorrow when I could hopefully pick up my new passport and social security card.

What if they weren't ready? The woman had warned me that Monday would be the earliest. At that point I decided to shift my thinking to Tuesday, because as it was, I didn't think I could stand the disappointment of going there tomorrow and being told to come back the next day. I decided to accept that I would probably have to wait until Tuesday.

I lay there trying to remember what I had been thinking about earlier because whatever it had been had given me a pleasant feeling. I then remembered that it had been death, that everyone, myself included, would one day die. I laughed to realize that thinking of death had been the happiest set of thoughts I'd had all day. By thinking through the grooves once again that had been etched in my brain during my walk, I returned to that feeling of peace and it was only then that I was able to go off to sleep.

* * *

It seemed like it might have been as much as two months since my meeting with Cecily and I had given up hope that anything would come of it. I'd had no dealings with Amun whatsoever. For the most part, my relationship to the Koran and my return to praying in a community of Muslims had prevented me from launching into full-scale bouts of paranoid depression. But occasionally despair would get the better of me. And I was not alone. A number of times I heard crying sounds from the cell of one of my neighbors. None of us ever spoke of this, nor did we try to comfort each other during those moments. But the imam, whom I came to respect, often quoted passages from the Koran having to do with despair which reminded us that Allah knew all and controlled the universe and that there was nothing that escaped His notice. These verses were a comfort to us all.

Right after breakfast one day, Amun's men came for me. I had a feeling that this was it—that I was about to leave.

Normally, when they took me out of the cellblock, I passed the four cells to my left, but not the one to my right. Today I asked Amun's assistants if I could speak briefly with Bassam, the man on my right. They allowed this.

Bassam asked me if I was leaving. I told him I wasn't sure, but that it was possible. I stuck my hand through the bars of his cell door and we shook and we wished each other luck. "May the peace of Allah be with you," he said to me, and I wished him the same, and I thanked him for standing up for me when the others hadn't trusted me.

Just as I was letting go of his hand, he pulled me closer and whispered, "I believe you have committed your life to Allah. It's now time that you commit your life to Islam as well."

I wasn't quite certain what he meant; I'd never considered the two to be different. But I nodded—he was an older man and I was showing respect.

"Qutb," he said. "Sayyid Qutb."

I was fairly certain that I had heard him correctly. Nevertheless, I asked him to repeat it.

"Sayyid Qutb. Have you read his work?"

"No," I said.

I was familiar with Qutb. I had read an article about his influence on Islamic Fundamentalism in a scholarly journal about a year before 9/11, and though I had not read his writings, I was familiar with his antecedents. I knew that he had been influenced by the 18th century theologian, Muhammad ibn abd al-Wahhab and by the 13th century theologian Ahmad ibn Taymiyyah. As a result, I also knew that Qutb advocated returning Islam to its purest, original state, of getting rid of everything that would interfere with the spread of Islam throughout the world. I'd also read that he'd had a huge impact on al-Qaeda.

"Start with *Milestones*," said Bassam, still holding my hand. "It will open your eyes. Will you promise me?"

I promised him, albeit, reluctantly.

I moved on and said my potential goodbye to every man in the cellblock. I was moved by how sincerely each man bade me farewell.

Amun's assistants took me to the shower and handed me freshly pressed civilian clothes—khakis and a white, button-down shirt, both of which smelled strongly of starch and were so stiff that they resembled cardboard. I was also given a razor, which I didn't use, though I did trim my beard and hair with scissors I found near the sink.

They walked me down to Amun's office, where I had originally met him.

"You will be leaving now," he said to me. "They are returning you to the United States."

"Will I be free there?"

"This I do not know. They never tell me details of that sort. We have only to wait another five minutes, and then Mr.

Peirce will be here to escort you back home."

I looked at Amun and found it difficult to believe that months before this man had tortured me to the brink of death. At the time I felt he was happy that he wouldn't have to torture me again. But who knows what's going on in the mind of another. I have enough difficulty keeping track of my own mind.

As strange as it may sound, I bore him no hard feelings. It may be that Islam was responsible for this. I only knew that when he tortured me, he believed that I was guilty of terrorist activity. That is what he had been told. But like I said, sitting there in that office behind his desk with his warm demeanor, I had trouble seeing him as the same man who had beaten me, attached electrodes to my genitalia, and nearly drowned me.

When Mr. Peirce, the American, showed up, he ignored me. With his same detached manner he signed a few sheets of paper that Amun had for him and had Amun sign a few others.

Then Peirce turned to me and said that we were returning to the States. "I'm assuming that this is good news for you, so I'm not going to place you in handcuffs."

At that point my heart sank. It seemed to me that if he was even contemplating putting me in cuffs, it must mean that I was still a prisoner. I let him know that I would cooperate and that there was no need for handcuffs.

"Good," he said. He looked at me as if I were a worm. I was confused as to why he was still so hostile.

He walked toward the door, and though it was clear that I was supposed to follow, I turned toward Amun and shook his hand. "May the peace of Allah be with you," I said to him. He looked moved. I turned to leave and realized that I had not been able to thank Mahmoud for all he had done for me. I asked Amun if he would please thank Mahmoud for me and wish him good-bye. He said he would.

Peirce was waiting impatiently by the door looking at me as if I were some sort of freak. I walked with him down the long hall and out into the hot air of the Cairo morning.

"What were you saying to him?" he asked me.

"I was thanking him for his hospitality," I said, hoping to provoke him.

"Hospitality, ha?"

"Yeah," I said.

He grunted and walked me over to a van that was waiting. An Egyptian man was driving us. I soon found out that he was the same driver we'd had on my arrival in Egypt. Two other Americans were sitting in there. I greeted everyone cheerily. That's how I felt.

After we had been riding for about ten minutes, one of the Americans said, "You smell better than you did the last time I saw you."

The driver laughed and said, "Yes, last time you smelling very bad. Very bad smelling last time. I never smell a man that smelling."

The two unnamed Americans laughed at this and I realized it was funny, and I laughed, despite myself. Peirce just sat there with death eating him from the inside out.

Chapter 21

Monday morning I was up in time for the morning prayer and felt like the day was off to a good start. I dreaded going outside. I knew that as soon as I did, I'd be wanting to head downtown to see if my new identity had come through. I finally decided that I would permit myself to check in at the passport office, even though I knew I risked disappointment. I would check in, fully understanding that I would have to wait another day. Moreover, I would not do so until 1:00.

I permitted myself to fall back asleep after praying and I got up at 11:00. After my noon prayers, I went out and ate an early lunch. I even ate a piece of cherry pie that tasted as though it had been baked days earlier and kept warm during that entire period. What I enjoyed most about it was that eating it took time.

I started out for the passport office on foot, but after a few blocks I got impatient and grabbed a cab. Much to my surprise, the office was open. Sheila looked up and asked if she could help me. I'd forgotten that I'd shaved my head and donned glasses since the last time she'd seen me. I was pleased that she didn't recognize me. I reminded her who I was. "Oh, yes," she said. "You're in luck." She walked out from behind the counter, and locked the front door.

She went out back and returned with two large envelopes and a small one. She handed me the two larger ones and kept the smaller one which she now opened. It contained, I assumed thirty-three thousand dollars, but she explained to me that the six thousand had already gone to the people who had created the passport and social security number, which brought it down to twenty-seven thousand. And then she had taken seven thousand more—her four thousand profit for the passport and social, and three for cashing the check. She handed the envelope to me.

I looked through it, but I didn't count it. I knew only that it contained a lot of one hundred dollar bills. What I was interested in was the passport. It looked completely legit. It even had the water marks and the hologram of Ben Franklin. The Social Security Card I had to take on faith. It looked legitimate and everything, but I wouldn't know for sure until I needed it. I didn't intend to apply for a job, but I guessed that at some point I would need a driver's license. It occurred to me now to ask Sheila about one. I wasn't sure how easy it would be to find someone in Seattle who would give me a fake license. I couldn't imagine going through the hassle of a driver's exam and possibly driver's ed. After all, there would be no record of my having had a license under my new name. If I went to Seattle already in possession of a license from New York, I could probably just switch it over.

"Are your people able to get drivers' licenses," I asked.

"Of course they are."

"How much are they?"

"They're easy. Seven hundred."

"Really? So can I get one?"

"Of course. You'll have to fill out this form—it's around here someplace—and you'll probably get it on Wednesday."

"Is there some way…"

"Here it is."

"…to speed it up. I need it today. I would really like to get on with my life."

"An extra three hundred and you can get it tomorrow. That's the best I can do. If you'd come in this morning, I might have been able to get it today."

I began peeling off ten hundreds and stopped. "Can I give you a check?" I asked. I grinned.

She looked at me like I was being a pain and said, "Okay. But that's going to be an extra hundred."

"You are brutal," I said.

She tried not to laugh. "Brutal?" she said. "Damn. That's the first time anyone's ever called me that. Well, maybe not the first time, but it's the first time today."

"You just made seven thousand dollars off me. For nothing, I might add."

"Well, my goal is to make even more if I can." She was laughing now, and showing small signs of softening.

"Haven't you bled me enough?"

She smiled. "Okay," she said, like she was being taken advantage of. "Write the check. One grand it is."

I wrote the check and asked her if she could have it by tomorrow at ten. She thought she could. At that point I started to leave and she reminded me about filling out the form. Then she told me that if I just signed it, that would be enough. She said she had a copy of the form that accompanied the social security card and she could fill it out based on that information. She reminded me that I had to look at that information, the information that accompanied my social security card. She said it contained my new place of birth, my address, my parents' names, etc. She warned me that I needed to memorize it before I did any sort of travel. She also told me that her passport people had been nervous about me because of my Middle Eastern name. In the end they'd decided that the only way they would do my passport would be to make me a newly naturalized citizen.

I walked west on Delancey and uptown on Bowery to Houston where I walked west. After that, I headed over to Washington Square Park where I bought a pretzel and sat on a bench near some men playing chess. I watched as people walked past. Many were casting suspicious looks my way. This had been going on since Wednesday, September 12th, but it was getting progressively worse. I wondered how it would have been if I hadn't cut my hair. Now my Arab face was completely out in the open, naked.

After a while I worked my way up to West 14th Street and 7th Avenue where I caught the IRT Express uptown to 42nd Street. I walked from there up to my hotel. By now it was nearly six and I said my afternoon prayers, albeit, a bit late. Following that, I lay down for a nap. I was disappointed that I would have to be there another day. But at least I would have things set up fairly well for my move. As I lay there, I remembered that I needed to tell Sheila about the letter that was going to be sent to her from the bank about the safe deposit box. I simply wanted her to destroy it. I worried about the various problems all of this could lead to if she were to send it back to the bank. They knew my actual home address.

Unable to sleep, I got up, located the business card that Sheila had given me, and I called the number on it. I got a machine, and left a message asking her if she would remind me to tell her something when she saw me the next day—it concerned a letter that she would be receiving that would be addressed to my former name.

Now I began worrying about luggage. I had no luggage and I needed to carry my clothes with me to Seattle. I decided it was time I sat down and made a list of all of the things I needed to do tomorrow so that I would forget nothing. I also had to make a plane reservation. I realized I could do that right now with my computer.

I went online and found a flight to Seattle for the next day at a little after noon. Before making the final payment, however, I remembered the new security guidelines since 9/11 and realized I'd need more time. Not only that, I had to buy new luggage, so why not wait. I finally chose a flight scheduled to depart LaGuardia at 6:00 p.m. When it came time to fill out the information, I automatically wrote in my name as Yusuf Alsawari. Luckily I remembered in time and I changed it before sending it out.

That evening I watched a news report that included an interview of a Muslim husband and his Christian wife. They seemed completely happy with each other. At that moment I began to ask myself why I had made such a huge deal over Ruth's conversion. Obviously I had been hurt at first. But couldn't I have gotten over it? Plenty of people had mixed marriages. Why had I reacted as I had?

I acknowledged for the first time that it had to do with Mother. It's true—she was dead when Ruth returned to Christianity. But when it happened, it was as if Mother took charge, or rather some icon of her that had resided within me like some sort of deeply embedded sleeper cell.

And what was Mother's problem anyway? The truth was,

she didn't care about Islam. I'm over stating it, but it's true. Sure, she went through the motions, and she made sure her kids did the same. But she had no genuine understanding of Muhammad's mission (p.b.u.h.). And to tell you the truth, she didn't really care about it. I know that sounds terrible, but I fear it is true. I remember when I was in college and first felt fully drawn to Muhammad (p.b.u.h.) and his message. While home on spring break, I remember telling my mother about it and she told me that was great, and without even pausing, she asked me if I had thanked my aunt for a birthday present she'd sent me. I told her I had, and I continued with what I was saying. Within a couple more minutes she was steering the conversation in a completely different direction. I never held it against her, but it was clear to me that it wasn't Islam that she cared about. It's just that Islam was her social fabric. She had no idea of this. If I had ever mentioned this to her, she would have exploded and called me an ingrate and it would not have been pretty. I was never even tempted to do such a thing, but I knew it was true. And just as it was true of her, it was true of my siblings.

It was different for Father. I believe he had some understanding of what it meant for humanity that Muhammad (p.b.u.h.) had been sent by Allah to try to correct the misunderstandings that had occurred in the Jewish and Christian people's relationship to Allah. Father understood what it meant that the Prophet (p.b.u.h.), a mere human being, had delivered Allah's message completely undiluted and untainted for all of humanity to see and hear and believe. But in the end, Father was a practical man. The things of this world were where his heart was. If he had been asked, he certainly would have said that Allah was the most important thing in his life, followed closely by his family. The truth is, his family came first, his business came second, and Allah came a close third. But how was he to know that? He was not an introspective man. He was hearty and outgoing and he wanted to make everyone around him happy, including Mother. He gave. He was always willing to give. She knew this about him and she used this quality of his to get him to do her bidding.

She did the same with me. She made me feel so guilty with the way she criticized me for wanting to marry Ruth. Why did it matter to her so much? That night in the hotel room, I realized for the first time that it had to do with her sister. I remembered now that, before Ruth and I even met, Mother's sister's daughter had married an American, a non-Muslim American, and Mother had made such a big deal about it. She was Mother's older sister, and Mother always felt like her older sister thought she was better than she, and it's probably true—that's how her sister was. But I remembered now that when Mother heard that her sister's daughter was marrying an American, a non-Muslim to boot, Mother acted so horrified. She got on the phone to her sister and told her how sorry she was for her and she was weeping for her. But it was such an act. What she was really doing was rubbing it in that her sister was less than perfect. This was Mother's moment of glory.

Not that she ever said anything to us to let us know how happy she was for this turn of events. In fact, I bet she didn't even let herself know how happy it made her. It would have exposed her to herself. At the time I didn't know what to make of it—I just placed it aside for later viewing. But tonight, as those memories came back, I saw Mother in an entirely new light: the reason Mother had made such a huge deal when I married an American—even though Ruth was a Muslim—was that Mother knew it was payback time. And knowing her sister, I'm sure it was.

I have trouble admitting all of this. It pains me. But it is the truth, and that evening as I hung out there in my hotel room, aware that the next day I would be leaving New York for good, I faced all of this for the first time.

After this realization, why couldn't I have simply called Ruth and told her I was fine and told her that I wanted to try our marriage again, that I loved her, that I missed her, that without her I felt incomplete, that I didn't know who I was? The fact is, I got myself to the point where I felt that I was capable of making that call. But I didn't. I have no idea what stopped me. At the time, I thought it was Allah. One thing I recall from that night was thinking that I would go through with my plan to go to Seattle, and if I continued to have second thoughts, I would consider calling Ruth and trying to mend our differences. But beneath all of those thoughts was the recognition that once I left New York, there would be no turning back.

I said *Ishaa*, watched the news and went to bed. I lay there nervous about the fact that I was leaving the next day. I worried that I may have forgotten to take care of a loose end that might prove I was alive. For instance, that safe deposit box key. How many more telltale items were lying around the house that Ruth might find and thereby deduce that I was merely playing possum.

I kept going back and forth between thinking that if Seattle didn't work out, I could always return to Ruth. But just as strongly I realized that leaving New York was final. After she received insurance money, after she got used to the fact that I was really dead, after she got a Christian boyfriend, after she was remarried and had a child, after all of that, calling her would not be an option. Leaving New York made my decision seem final, and it scared me. I truly felt as if I was facing my death. And if the future was going to be full of days and nights like the ones I had experienced since I'd left home, I couldn't imagine wanting to live very long. Finally, I told myself, just as I'd told myself dozens of times during the past six days, that I would get over Ruth, and that I'd find someone and my life would begin to make sense again. Thinking this way, I lay there, and within a couple of hours, I was able to fall asleep.

* * *

There was an amazing amount of security at the Cairo airport. All cars were being stopped and policemen were speaking with each of the drivers. Some cars were being searched. But when we drove up in the van, we were waved through and then we were waved through a second gate. The man operating it opened it as soon as we drove into sight and we drove through and out into the runway area, past all of the commercial airliners and to a small building over on the side of the field. There stood a white luxury jet with black numbers painted on its vertical stabilizer. The three Americans and I got out of the van and we walked toward the jet. Peirce reached up and knocked on the door which opened. A small flight of stairs was lowered and we boarded.

The plane was exceptionally nice inside. Over the door there was a small panel that said Gulfstream V. It had large, white, leather seats, wide ones of the sort you'd have on a first class flight. I was told to sit where I wanted. They seated themselves around a small white table that was surrounded on three sides by the white leather upholstered seats. I wasn't sure that this was the same plane, but I assumed that it was. And though I wasn't sure why, I wanted to sit where I had sat last time, so I sat across from them.

They weren't particularly unfriendly to me, but they were definitely a group and I was clearly an outsider. Peirce seemed aloof even from them, but he was one of them in his own taciturn way. His colleagues seemed to find his aloofness amusing.

I sat and watched now the scenes I had only been able to hear on the previous flight. After an hour or so they talked about playing cards. One of them invited me to join them, but Peirce was not big on the idea. "He doesn't even have any money," he said.

"I would have money," I said, "if you'd give me back my wallet. I had quite a bit of money before you kidnapped me."

"Kidnapped?" Peirce said. He said it so deadpan that I thought he was really shocked.

"Well, what do you call it?"

"We arrested you," he said sanctimoniously. Again I thought he was serious.

"You call that arrest? Who arrests people by putting a bag over their heads and taking their clothes and sticking them in a diaper and on a plane and shipping them overseas to be tortured? That's not arrest." I was shaking as I spoke, I was so angry.

"You don't give a shit what happens to this country, do you?" Peirce said. From the way his sidekicks were laughing, I should have recognized that he was just trying to get me going. But I took him seriously.

"Matter of fact, I do care. I'd like it to remain free." I said it with far more feeling than I'd intended, so much that I felt like a child.

"OOOkay," said one of the other men with a look of mock seriousness.

At any rate, it got me out of playing cards, and that was fine with me. I was never much of a card player. At college I'd learned how, but it was never a game that gave me any joy, and I was certain that playing with these guys was not going to change that fact.

I just sat there, surprised at how angry I'd sounded and I was now aware that I had adrenaline flowing through my veins.

Later one of the men went up back and smoked a cigarette. I asked Peirce if it was okay to join him. I didn't know what was permitted and what was not. I didn't even know what my status was.

"Why?" Peirce asked.

"I'd like to ask him for a cigarette," I said.

He made a sour look and nodded.

I walked to the back of the plane and asked the man if he would give me a cigarette.

He pulled out a pack of an unfiltered brand and offered me one.

Though these cigarettes too were stronger than the brand I had smoked back in the States, in comparison to Amun's they seemed soothing. I inhaled deeply and felt that rush of nicotine spread through my body.

As we smoked he asked me where I was from.

"New York," I said.

"You know, don't you, that we're taking you back to Seattle."

"So what's going to happen there? Am I being released?"

"I believe so," he said. "That's the way I've been hearing

it. I'm surprised Randy didn't tell you. You'll have to excuse him. He's a little pissed off because he wasted a lot of time on you. It looks like you're not the man he thought you were. Kind of makes him look bad. He's not used to that sort of thing. He's used to getting it right. He's been a rising star in this rendition thing."

"Rendition?"

"Yeah. Extraordinary Rendition. That's when they take a terror suspect to his country of origin to be interrogated."

"So there's a name for it?"

"Sure, it's like everything else."

After that I slept for two or three hours. When I woke up the others were asleep as well, and I realized that the rumor must be true, that they must intend to free me. They would never leave me unguarded if I were still a prisoner. I returned to sleep and when I woke up we were preparing to land in Rome.

Chapter 22

I woke up early the next morning, prayed, shaved my face and head, showered and got into my blue suit. I had the television on as I organized my belongings. The plan was that when I returned with my new luggage, the packing would go smoothly.

It wasn't until I saw the news that I realized that it was Tuesday, the 18th, one week since the terrorist attacks. And once again, they kept showing the Trade Center collapsing. They kept using the word "Muslim" in these reports in such a way that it took energy to keep from feeling guilty for being one. Firemen and policemen were being interviewed from Ground Zero. Once again I realized how lucky Ruth and I had been and I said a prayer of thanks to Allah for watching over us that day.

I went out, ate breakfast and wandered around as I waited for luggage stores to open. After that, I bought a *New York Times* and sat in a coffee shop and read a new section that began that day: "A Nation Challenged." The focus was the attacks and the lives that were lost. There was a series of short articles about some of the victims. I looked to see if I was mentioned, but I was not. The goal was to include a short article about each person who had died on 9/11. But first the reporters had to come up with an accurate list of all of the names and they had to interview relatives of each of the victims. I was struck by the love that the writers of the articles put into their writing and I pictured how sad Ruth would be when she got a call asking for information about me. It made me very sad for her and for the umpteenth time I just wanted to call her and confess my stupidity and my love.

It was approaching nine. I paid my check and left. I wandered until a little after ten when I found a luggage place that was open. I settled for a mid-sized suitcase and a carry-on affair. I walked it back to the hotel, packed and left again, leaving the luggage put.

I took a cab down to the passport place where I was able to pick up my driver's license. I thanked Sheila for everything she'd done and just as I was leaving she asked about the telephone message I'd left.

I told her about the situation with the bank and how they insisted that the computer would be spitting out a letter after I closed the account and that I'd listed the address of her business as the address to which I wanted it sent. I also mentioned that it would be sent under my former name. I asked her to simply throw it away.

"So, what's the name?"

"Yusuf Alsawari."

"A mystery man," she said. "He goes by many names."

Something about the way she said this made me nervous, and I realized that if I'd said nothing to her, she would have probably been confused when she received it and would have simply thrown it away. But I went and told her, meaning that she was now the one person who could put both of my identities together, the old me and the new me. It made me uncomfortable. She promised me she would throw it away, and I had no choice but to believe her.

By the time I got back to the hotel, it was check out time. I paid with my credit card. The woman behind the desk allowed me to store my luggage in a closet near the front desk. I then took off with no idea how I would spend the next few hours. I only knew I didn't want to spend it in the hotel.

I walked down town on Broadway, and when I came to West Forty-Fourth Street, I walked east on it. I wondered what I was doing. I had been avoiding this block since 9/11, and now I was walking down it with a certain kind of arrogance. The problem was, this was the location of my father's store, now my siblings' store—and, oddly enough, my widow's store as well. One of them was always walking up or down this street to take money to a bank, to get lunch, to drop off a kid at a baby sitter's, etc. What was I doing? This was insane. I had everything worked out, and now I was risking it all. But I was also thinking about the fact that I had gone through some significant physical changes—I no longer had a mustache, I had new glasses, no hair, and I was wearing a Brooks Brothers suit. There was no way they would recognize me. I didn't turn back until I thought about how I was risking not only my situation, but Ruth's as well—she could be arrested for insurance fraud.

I felt relieved that I'd prevented a possible disaster. A few minutes later, as I was headed east on West Forty-Second Street, I passed a glasses store and went in. The sign on the window claimed they could do a prescription in an hour. I asked if their offer was true of prescription sunglasses. They said it was. I picked out a pair and ordered them and found a place to have lunch.

A little over an hour later, I returned and picked up my sunglasses. Now I headed back up to West Forty-Fourth Street, having decided that it was now safe to pass the store. The part of me that protested was told to calm down, but it wouldn't until it had extracted a promise that I would remain on the north side of the street as I passed—the store being on the south side.

When I got to Sixth Avenue, I crossed to the north side of the street and slowed down as I passed the store between Sixth and Fifth. The reflections were such that I could not see through the window from over there. So after passing it, I crossed the street amid internal protests, and headed back past. There stood Farhad, my oldest brother, showing a carpet to a couple I judged to be newly weds. His wife Aisha sat bored in front of the cash register picking at her nails. Their lives seemed to have been uninterrupted by my death. I was certain Farhad would have felt something. Though there were eight years between us, I had always felt very close to him even though he was the one who tended to torture me most when we were kids. He never thought I was tough enough and he did what he could to change that. When my mother went on her campaign against me, I knew it had hit him hard. He'd gone along with it, but only because of pressure from my sisters and our other brother. Farhad was a practical businessman, and there was no way he was going to risk his place as the future patriarch of the family. I didn't hold it against him. That was just who he was.

I was walking slowly now, more slowly than I should

have been. Seeing him made me sad, and I realized that this was probably the last time I would ever see him in my life and I actually began to cry. I sped up, worried that he would feel my gaze and look at me and recognize my walk. As I neared the end of the block, I imagined that he had sensed me and was now looking out the door to see if it was I who had passed. Rounding the corner, I looked back, frightened of what I might see, but disappointed when it wasn't so. At that moment I felt I was ready to leave New York.

* * *

We were in Rome for nearly eight hours. I spent the entire time on the airplane, much of it alone. All of them left—the pilot, the copilot and the threesome. Peirce warned me that they would be gone for a while, that I should stay put because I didn't have a passport or any sort of i.d., that if I were to leave the plane, I would be on my own.

Before leaving, Bruce, the guy who had lent me the cigarette, took me to the kitchen and showed me that there was plenty to eat. In the refrigerator, there was an assortment of soda, beer and water. I asked if he would leave me a couple of cigarettes and if he would buy me a pack while he was out. He gave me his five remaining cigarettes and said he'd bring back more.

I sat there all by myself smoking and drinking root beer. This root beer tasted so good to me that it was difficult to fathom. A couple hours into the wait, I grilled myself an extra sharp cheddar cheese sandwich, heavy on the butter, and I heated up a bowl of canned tomato soup. Before eating the sandwich, I held it up to my nose and smelled it the way a wine connoisseur might. The smells of the toast, the butter, the cheese were nearly enough to satisfy me. But when I began eating that first mouthful and topped it off with a spoonful of tomato soup, I can't even begin to describe the overwhelming joy—it still makes my mouth water just to remember it.

I smoked again, and then I tipped back my seat and covered myself with a blanket that I'd found. I noticed that there was a chill in the air as I was falling asleep. By the time I awoke, three hours later, I got up and grabbed another blanket. I wished I had found out how to control the heating system before everyone had left. I looked around for a set of controls, but had no idea what I was doing. I didn't even know if the heaters could be turned on without the engines running.

I draped the blanket over my shoulders and walked to the kitchen and made a cup of coffee. Soon after that, two of the men returned, Peirce and his sidekick, whose name turned out to be John. Peirce sounded disappointed as he said to me, "You're still here?" John laughed on cue.

They asked me why it was so cold and I told them that I didn't know how to turn on the heating system. As it turned out, neither did they. Until the pilots returned, the three of us wrapped ourselves in blankets.

When Bruce returned, I was in the kitchen. He handed me a pack of French cigarettes. We smoked together and though it was eleven p.m., he asked me if I'd like some breakfast. He began cooking a big breakfast. When I saw that he was going to cook the eggs with bacon, I asked for a separate frying pan so that I could cook my eggs separately. I scrambled my eggs, squirted them with ketchup, made some toast that I topped with butter and grape jelly, and I poured myself a glass of orange juice. I'd had none of those things since the day before I'd been abducted and I was overwhelmed by how good they tasted.

After that the two of us smoked cigarettes to the chagrin of Peirce and John, who entered the kitchen during our second round. An interesting dynamic had become apparent among the three of them. No one said anything about how Bruce and I were more or less hanging out. They didn't have to. I'm sure Bruce felt it too. I say this, because a few minutes after that, he left the kitchen and I was left out there with Peirce and John. Peirce ignored me, but John kept watching me as if he thought it would intimidate me. I felt as if I was back in high school.

Chapter 23

I had seen news reports about how difficult it had become for people to get onto airplanes. I wondered whether to show my passport or my new license. I went with the license. It seemed less defensive. Moreover, if there was a chance of there being a mistake in one of them, the license would be the less likely candidate, it being a simpler document. But that thinking was purely academic. I hadn't really looked at either of them other than to verify that they had my name and picture on them.

The woman at the airline desk was fine with my license, but when I got to the metal detector, one of the henchmen there stopped me.

"Do you have your passport with you today, Sir?" He managed to say the word "sir" as if it were an obscenity.

"I'm an American," I said.

"Ah, Sir, I'm very happy for you. But that's not what I asked you, Sir."

I stood there for a second deliberating about how to answer. If I said no and they searched me—which according to news shows was happening with increasing frequency, especially for people with middle eastern names—and if they found my passport, they might then look at the thing with more scrutiny than they would if I simply cooperated.

"Yes, Sir, I do," I said. "Would you like to see it?"

"Sir, you just read my mind." Despite what he'd said, his face and voice were devoid of irony. He just looked at me with eyes vacant as those of a gull.

I pulled my passport from the breast pocket of my jacket. And here I had thought a Brooks Brothers suit would make a difference. It obviously took more than that to join the club. Among other things, it took lighter skin and a European name.

He looked at it closely and asked me if I would come with him. "Bring your carry-on items with you, if you would, Sir."

We went into a little room and he asked me to lay my bags on a table. With his finger poised on the latch, he asked, "May I?"

"Certainly," I said.

As he looked through my items, he asked me where I was going?"

"Seattle," I said.

"And the purpose of your visit?"

I nearly told him I was moving there, but I vetoed that response. "Pleasure. I've been there before and I really liked the place." I was trying to look pleasant.

He was a tall weight-lifter type with closely cropped blond hair, blue eyes and in place of a neck, he had a pyramid. He seemed fairly intelligent, but it was intelligence that had been twisted by a desire to be part of this world. He had no idea that one day he was going to die, and as I watched him, I decided I would not be the one to break the news.

"What is it about Seattle you like, Sir?" he asked. "Is it the rain?"

I smiled at his joke. "Yeah, I noticed it rains there a lot. To tell you the truth," I said, but I had nothing to add to it. My mind was racing and I was looking for the perfect detail to make myself sound believable. I decided to start again— "To tell you the truth, Sir…"

"Yeah, I'd kind of hoped you would do that for me…"

"…Well, my girlfriend and I just broke up and I'm not so much going to Seattle as leaving New York. I want to get as far away as I can without leaving America." I hoped he'd notice my patriotism.

"When are you returning?"

I realized that if he wanted, he could ask to see my ticket, so lying was out of the question. "For the time being, sir, I don't know. I bought a one-way ticket, but I suspect I'll be heading back in a couple of weeks."

"You live in White Plains?"

"No," I said. I wondered where he got that idea.

"No? So why's it say you do on your passport?"

Now I remembered. I was supposed to memorize all of the information that Sheila had given me about my new date of birth and address, etc. I hadn't done any of that. What a fool. What if he asked me my birthday to see if I knew it?

"That's where I used to live," I said. "With my girlfriend. I'm basically homeless now. I've been living in a hotel for the past week."

"Oh yeah? Which hotel?"

"The Douglass Hotel on West Fifty-Sixth Street. I have a receipt here if you'd like to see it."

"Sure."

As I searched for the credit card receipt in my wallet, I saw my old driver's license and realized I'd have to destroy it immediately. I handed the receipt to him. As he was looking it over, he began writing something on a pad of paper he was holding and he said something that I didn't quite catch.

"Pardon me," I asked.

"Nothing," he said. "I was just talking to myself."

I played back what I'd heard a couple of times and realized he'd said, "Muhammad's Books." I could see that he was copying down the last four digits of my debit card number, which along with a row of asterisks, were on the receipt.

I didn't say anything to him until he handed the receipt back to me, and I thanked him.

He told me I was free to go, and as I was gathering up my things, he asked how much money I had with me.

If I told him how much I had, I figured he'd be suspicious. "I have twenty-two hundred dollars—actually a bit more than that. I had twenty-three hundred and then I broke a hundred to take a cab here. The cab cost me thirty-five dollars. So I guess I have twenty-two hundred and…sixty-five dollars."

"Okay. Thank you, Sir."

I went to my gate and waited to board the plane.

* * *

By now we were back in the air. Bruce had told me we would be landing in Johnston County Airport, North Carolina where we would refuel and head immediately for Seattle. I had asked him why we'd stopped in Rome. He simply said that Peirce had wanted some R & R.

I did Bruce the favor of steering clear of him. When he went up back to smoke, I stayed seated. We didn't talk again after that except briefly in the van that picked us up in Seattle. The van stopped for fifteen or twenty minutes at a non-descript looking office building that had the name of some sort of communications firm housed in a business park on the outskirts of town. The three of them went into the building and I stayed in the van with the driver. Bruce was the first one to return to the van and during that time he yawned and told me he was tired. It felt as if this was his way of apologizing to me for what had happened between us and I told him I was tired as well.

After that, the van took us to the place of my abduction in the police car. But this time, when the garage door opened, it was not dark inside. We got out of the van and they took me into a large office. Peirce sat at a desk and invited me to sit across from him. "Okay, then," he said. "I'm assuming you want your possessions back?"

"Correct," I said.

"Sign this," he said, "and I will get them for you."

I read the three-page document. The gist of it was that I had voluntarily traveled to Egypt in an all-expense trip paid for by the United States government and that I had been treated well during my stay there. It also said that I agreed not to talk about my experience to anyone, as it was a matter of the highest government security.

After reading it, I looked up at Peirce. I wasn't sure what I was going to do. He was sitting there looking bored.

"You don't have to sign it," he said through a yawn.

"And if I don't, I don't get my possessions back, is that what you're saying?"

"Bingo," he said. "It all depends on what you want." He

was leaned back in his chair now with his foot resting on his knee.

I sat there and thought about what had happened to me, thought about the way I'd been abducted, about the treatment I'd received on the way to Egypt, the torture I'd endured under Amun, the way they had let me languish in prison for months on end. But I also thought about my social security card, my license, and most importantly, my Caymans credit and debit cards. Without them, I'd have no access to money, and without money, I would be unable to do anything.

There was a moment when I remembered the fishing jobs in Seattle that I had heard about. It then occurred to me, however, that without a social security number, I wouldn't even be able to get a job. And I couldn't remember my new social security number since I'd only looked at the thing a couple of times. I also considered that I could go to the social security office and pick up a new social security card, but I had no identification. Who knew what had become of my passport— I hadn't had it with me on the morning of my abduction, and who knew what had become of my apartment. And getting a new passport would also require identification. Unless, of course, I was able to get another fake passport. But that would require money. It felt to me like I had no choice. So I finally relented and signed the document.

True to his word, Peirce went to a safe and pulled out a large shopping bag on which was printed in large block letters, "MUHAMMAD." It contained everything I'd had that morning—the clothing I'd been wearing and which had been cut from my body, the wallet that contained my license and social security card as well as a little over three hundred dollars.

When he handed the bag to me, some polite portion of myself wanted to thank him, but I insisted to myself that thanking him was out of the question. I looked through the bag and removed the cell phone from the little holster still attached to the belt of the pants that had been cut from me. I dug my wallet from the pocket of those pants, checking to see that my Cayman cards were still in it, and I placed it in the pocket of the pants I was now wearing. I looked up and asked if I could go. He said I could. He walked with me out to the garage and pushed a button that opened the garage door. I emerged from the darkness of the tunnel that had swallowed me half a year earlier. It was May 15, 2002, six thirty a.m. and I was a new man.

Chapter 24

There was someone on the plane I knew or maybe just recognized. I couldn't remember the connection, but I knew I'd met him, or at the very least, had seen him. Luckily I still had on my new sunglasses and he didn't seem to notice me. The problem was, he was sitting two rows ahead of me on the opposite side, and like me, he had an aisle seat. I was worried that eventually he'd see me.

Was he someone I knew through Ruth? Was he one of the church people who had come to visit her? Did I know him through CUNY? It then struck me that I had seen him when I'd stopped in Washington Square Park to watch the men play chess. He'd walked past the players a couple of times—he seemed to be interested in their game. That's what it was. No reason for suspicion.

I relaxed now and read the new *Time* I'd purchased at the airport. There was an article about the Taliban and their relation to Osama bin Laden. I read until we had been flying for about an hour, and then I took a nap. I woke up forty or fifty minutes later, troubled about the guy I'd recognized. There was something I couldn't figure out. Now as I sat there and watched him, from time to time catching him in full profile, I realized I'd seen him today as well. Yes, as I'd walked toward my father's store that first time, when I'd had my change of heart, I'd turned around and as I'd retraced my steps, that's when I'd seen him, this same man, and he'd been walking toward me. I wondered now if he'd been following me. I couldn't imagine why he would be. It did, however, strike me as odd. And now, here on the plane—this made the third time I'd seen this guy. And in three separate places. It's true that there had been lots of times when I'd seen people in New York in different locations. But three times in three places within several days—it didn't make sense.

I wondered if I was mistaken. After all, he was not an unusual looking man. He was a white guy, about six two, in
fairly good shape—he might have weighed one eighty-five,
one ninety. He had brown hair, white at the temples, brown
eyes, and he was maybe forty, forty-five. There was nothing
unusual about his looks. How did I know this was the same
guy? I began examining everything about him. Soon he
walked past me—I assumed he was headed for the bathroom—and I looked at him to remember everything I could
about his face. One thing was certain. If he was the same
man, he didn't seem to remember me at all. I couldn't even
get him to glance my way. I decided that in a court of law, I
would be unable to say with assurance that he was the guy. I
let it go.

I read another couple of articles in the magazine, took
another nap, and the flight was over. When I picked up my
checked luggage, there was a note attached saying that it had
been randomly selected to be opened and inspected.

I got on a shuttle that took me to a motel right outside the
airport. It was two thirty when I checked in, and after un-
packing and saying *Ishaa*, I went to sleep.

* * *

Walking by myself on the street felt like a brand new experience—I was surprised by the overwhelming feeling of
freedom. I didn't know Seattle well enough to know quite
where I was, but I knew I was south of where I wanted to be
and west.

I was walking toward the building in which I had formerly lived. I knew it would be a long walk, and though it
was a little chilly, I was not tempted to hail a cab. First of all,
I didn't want to arrive there so early. But more importantly,
this was the first walk I had taken in months. I didn't have to
hurry and it took me over an hour to reach it. I stood outside
the building and looked up at the windows of my old apartment. I could see that there were curtains on them, and when

I'd lived there I'd simply used the venetian blinds that had come with the place. Clearly I was homeless.

As I walked over to ring the super's bell, I could see what looked like my lamp through his ground floor window. He did not answer by intercom. Instead, he walked out his door and over to the glass door. He stood there for a few seconds unable to recognize me through my beard. He looked at me as if I were trying to sell him something.

He opened the door. "May I help you?" he asked.

"Hey, Jasper," I said.

He must have recognized my voice. "Where have you been?" he asked. "What happened to you?"

"That's a state secret," I said. I laughed at this for reasons not apparent to him. He looked at me as if I were an alien.

"I take it that my apartment has been rented," I said.

"Yeah, well, you know—you were three months late on your rent, and Mrs. Hutchens was..."

"I understand," I said. "I was just wondering. Do you know what happened to my stuff?"

"Mrs. Hutchens asked me to sell it off," he said. "You know, to help pay your back rent. We didn't know what else to do."

"What about a little compass. Did you happen to find a little compass?" I asked.

"I don't know. There was a lot of little things that didn't sell. All of the furniture sold except one rocking chair and a lamp. The chair's in the basement, but I don't know what happened to the lamp. Someone must have taken it."

"And the little things."

"Yeah, they're in a box," he said. "I don't know—there was an alarm clock in there and there was a set of knives, and a few books—we sold most of them to a used book store."

"Well, could I look through the box?"

"Sure," he said. He was speaking to me as if he were nervous that I was angry. "Just a minute. Let me get the key." He closed the glass door now and entered his apartment. A few seconds later he came out again and opened the glass door for me.

"Here, come in," he said as if closing the glass door had been an oversight—and it may have been.

He walked me down the stairs to the basement and into a small, dark room where a lot of different articles of furniture and boxes were stored. I saw my rocking chair piled on top of a desk and in the seat of the chair was a cardboard box that had Muhammad written on it in red marker. A light blue, vinyl garment protector hung on the back of the chair.

"Here's the box," he said, and he pointed to it.

I carried it over to the light so that I could see. Inside there was a bunch of stuff I felt no connection to except the Koran. I picked it up and placed it in the shopping bag that Peirce had given me. I looked some more for the compass, but I didn't spot it until I began removing items from the box. And there it was at the bottom. I picked it up and placed it in my pocket.

I now remembered my watch. I pawed through the bag given me by Peirce and found it and put it on. I now felt complete and I stood up and thanked Jasper.

"What do you want me to do with the rest of this stuff?" he said.

"I guess I'll take the garment bag," I said. "You can have the rest of it."

"So I can throw it out?"

"Yeah, that's fine," I said. "Hey, Jasper. Thanks again."

With that, I picked up the shopping bag and the garment protector and I walked up the stairs and out of the building. He came running up the stairs after me.

"By the way," he said. "I almost forgot. Mrs. Hutchens has your passport. Yeah, when I told her I'd found it in the apartment, she said she'd take it for safe keeping."

"That's great," I said. "Thanks for telling me that." I took a twenty-dollar bill from my wallet and handed it to him and he thanked me.

I now walked to the apartment agency and asked to speak to Mrs. Hutchens. The secretary was new and she asked who I was. I told her and it looked to me as if she recognized my name. Rather than convey the message over the intercom, she walked into the back office and returned with a concerned looking Mrs. Hutchens, a short blond woman who tended toward high-strung. She looked at me as if I were going to be a problem.

"Are you all right?" she asked me.

"Yes, I'm fine," I said. "I already spoke with Jasper. I understand your reasons for what you did. It's fine."

"You were gone for so long," she said. "Is everything all right?"

"Yes, everything's fine," I said. "Unfortunately, I can't talk about where I was, but what I was wondering is—Jasper said you have my passport?"

"Yes," she said. "It's right in here." She walked over to a bank of four filing cabinets and put on her glasses. She ran her fingers over the files and chose one, which she pulled out. She leafed through it and there it was in her hands—my passport.

"Here it is," she said. She opened it to be certain it was mine and handed it to me.

"Thank you," I said. "I really appreciate the fact that you took the time to safeguard this for me. It means a lot to me. Now let me ask you. Did you raise enough money to pay my back rent?"

She looked a little defensive, as if she thought I was being sarcastic. She sounded tentative. "It came close."

"Well how much do I owe you?"

"You don't owe me anything," she said. "I'm sorry I had to do what I did, but I didn't know what else to do. So I'm sorry. It's not like I didn't try other avenues."

"No, that's fine. Seriously. It's fine."

"Where are you living now?"

"I don't know," I said. "I just got back."

"Where were you?"

"I actually can't tell you. I know this sounds crazy, but it's a state secret?"

"I didn't know Washington had secrets."

I thought she was being funny. But then I realized she meant Washington State.

"No, not 'state' in that sense," I said. "I mean it's a government secret."

"Oh," she said, and she looked concerned for my mental health.

"Well, anyway," I said. "Thanks again."

At that, I rose and held out my hand. We shook and I left.

Chapter 25

The next morning, Wednesday, I slept late. Just before noon I took a cab from the hotel into Seattle. It turned out the driver was from Yemen. He was a talker, a fairly engaging one at that. He asked me a ton of questions. I later found out that back home he'd been a lawyer and though he'd been in this country for ten years, he still hadn't managed to get his law credentials squared away.

At one point in the conversation, he asked me how I felt about 9/11. I was a little nervous opening up to a complete stranger about my feelings. Furthermore, I realized that prior to 9/11 I'd never questioned my feelings about this country. So that is what I said: "Tough question," I said. "Prior to 9/11, I wouldn't have minded answering your question frankly. Now, I guess it makes me nervous."

He said, "I know exactly what you mean. And I have to say, you're wise to answer it that way."

Then I mentioned how lately I felt like people mistrusted me, my Arab face. "And it's not only on the street. It's in the airport. It's everywhere." I told him about my airport security encounter in New York.

He said that kind of prejudice toward Muslims had always existed in America, "But it used to be they could keep it hidden, you know? But now," he said, "everything will change. Now it will all be out in the open." He said that to his way of thinking, "All of this is the will of Allah." He added that this was "the beginning of Allah paying America back for their sins of greed and selfishness and gluttony and materialism—it's just the beginning."

I can't say I disagreed with him that this was a materialistic land. But at the time I really didn't believe that Allah was out to pay us back. However, what he said sparked an association with a verse from the Koran, which I now quoted. Looking back on it, I'm surprised that the verse even occurred to me at that time. I was so moderate back then. Though I don't remember the particulars of what I was feeling right then, I suspect that, more than anything, I was trying to impress him in some way. After all, other than Sheila and the prostitute, I'd had no conversations in over a week, and I'd had none in Arabic for several months. It wasn't as if I was angry at America; nevertheless, as I said it, I noticed that it rang particularly true. What I said was, "Allah will not change the fate of a people until they change the condition of their hearts."

"Precisely," he said. "Precisely," and he turned around and shook my hand. "Did you hear," he said, "how Bush referred to this war he's planning? He called it a 'Crusade.' Everyone's busy saying he misspoke. He didn't misspeak. It's the first time he said what he meant."

After that, he said something that struck me as extremely true: "You wait," he said. "If America goes ahead with this 'Crusade,' it's only going to get worse. It will create an entirely new batch of terrorists."

Again I quoted from the Koran: "And indeed, We will force them to endure the Penalty of this life that they might repent and return and avoid thereby the Supreme Penalty."

"That's it exactly," he said.

I enjoyed talking to him though he was a complete stranger. In fact, I liked him so much that when he asked my name, it troubled me to lie and give him my new name. He told me his name was Jamal. Later when he asked why I'd come to Seattle, I wanted to tell him the entire story. But of course I couldn't do that. As it was, I told him I was moving here, that I'd broken up with my wife, that my parents were both dead. I kept as close to the truth as I could. I even told him my siblings were upset with me and weren't speaking to me, but I said it was because I'd ended my relationship with my wife.

When he learned that my family was from Ahwaz, he told me he had a cousin in Chicago who was married to a woman from there. He complimented me on my Arabic, seeing I'd never lived in an Arab country. As he dropped me off at the hotel, he gave me his card and told me to give him a call sometime. He claimed to know a lot of good Arab people. I actually put the card in my wallet. I had some misgivings, but he was the closest thing I had to a friend in the entire world.

After getting settled in my hotel room, I walked down to look out at the Sound. Jamal had told me that each year thousands of men come to Seattle to get jobs on fishing boats headed to Alaska. I was half tempted to see if I could land such a job myself. I obviously didn't need the money, but I felt restless, and what better cure was there for restlessness than going to sea. But even as I yearned, I knew it would never happen. I needed to combat this restlessness. I was practically in a liquid state. I had a new name, a new haircut, a new way of dressing, a new marital status, and I was in a new city. What I needed was to form a new life, and the only way to do that would be to stay put for a while.

* * *

I walked back up to the hotel where I'd stayed when Jamal had brought me from the airport that first day. As I registered now, I was completely confused when I came to the box that asked for my address. I went with my Williamsburg address, thinking it possible that I would return to Ruth. I asked the clerk for the same room I'd had the first time I'd been there. It wasn't available, but he was able to give me a room in the same line, two floors above my first room with the identical layout. It was furnished precisely the same as the other room had been and when I walked into it, I had the most bizarre sense that no time had passed since my first visit there. It also felt completely foreign to me.

I just sat there on the bed for a few minutes and took in all of the strange things I was feeling. Then I began crying when I realized I didn't have a clue what I was going to do, where I was going to go or anything else. And more than anything, I cried because I could now afford to. I was free.

I lay down after a while. I couldn't get over how comfortable the bed felt. I woke up at about two that afternoon. I undressed and got under the covers. As I did this, I was half asleep, but the feeling and the smell of the clean sheets were so powerful that I noted them before returning to sleep. The next time I woke up, it was dark outside. The clock beside the bed glowed three thirteen. I lay there a few minutes wondering whether to get up and what I would do with myself if I did. At some point I fell back asleep, and at about eight, a garbage truck's back-up beeper awakened me.

I got up and after saying my prayers, I walked to the diner where I'd been heading the day I'd been abducted. Everything seemed so strange to me. The sights, the sounds, the light, the smells. The feeling of being on my own. I have never noticed so much as I did during that first week of being free. Nor have I ever noticed the beauty of the world and of all people. Wherever I looked, I saw goodness. For the next few days, I would cry when I saw simple things that I ordinarily wouldn't have noticed. I saw a father bend over to tie his toddler's shoes and I began crying at the beauty of it. I saw a car stop to let another car out of a parking spot and I teared up. All over the city, people were being kind to one another, and even when they weren't, it was understandable. I saw two drunk men yelling at one another on the street, and it seemed so sad to me that they didn't see how beautiful everything was and how good everyone was and I cried. I felt as if my skin had been removed and I was an exposed nerve ending and that I could feel every sound hitting me, and every photon hitting me and I felt energized as if every perception that struck me generated a kind of energy within me, as if my senses were tiny turbines being driven by the things I perceived.

That first day, I headed to a book store and found a large, hard cover journal with unlined pages, and I went to a coffee shop and began writing down everything that had happened to me.

During that week, I have never felt so close to Allah. Every day I arose early to pray and after spending an hour or so reading the Koran, I would write of my experiences until noon.

One day that first week as I was writing, I remembered

my promise to Bassam that I would read Sayyid Qutb's book, *Milestones*. The fact is, I sort of dreaded reading it, but I had promised him I would.

The dread concerned the amount of anger I assumed I would find in the book. I was in such a vulnerable state that I wanted no part of anger.

Finding the book proved more difficult than I had anticipated. In fact, I was on the verge of quitting my search when a young clerk in the fifth bookstore I entered said she could order it for me. An older woman, probably the owner of the store, had been standing near the young woman, working with another customer. She now took over and asked that I come with her. She took me over to the spiritual book collection and as she pretended to look for the book, she said to me, "I wouldn't order that book, if I were you. They've started to keep track of those sorts of things." She looked at me over the tops of her glasses and she cast me a very grim look.

"Keep track of?" I asked.

"Yes," she said. She then told me of a Muslim bookstore near the airport, a combination grocery store and bookstore, that more than likely carried the book. She warned me that I should not order it or any similar book under my real name or pay for it with a credit card.

I asked her again for an explanation. I couldn't imagine what she was talking about.

She told me about the Patriot Act, a new set of laws that had apparently passed during my incarceration. She suggested that I look it up on the internet. I decided she was some sort of conspiracy theorist.

I took a cab to the Muslim bookstore she had mentioned. Sure enough they had my book—in fact, they had it in Arabic. Probably because I was the only customer in the store, I got into a conversation with the Jordanian owner. I mentioned the conversation I'd had in the previous bookstore. He told me I was lucky the woman had warned me. He said the Patriot Act had a provision that allowed the FBI to check into the library records of suspected terrorists, and that in certain cases bookstores had been ordered to hand their records over to the FBI.

I was horrified to learn of all of these changes that had occurred here in America during my absence. How could a country like America that claimed to love freedom, that bragged about its Bill of Rights, how could it allow itself to undo it all on such short notice? It seemed to me that the terrorists had won.

Before I explain my reaction to the writings of Sayyid Qutb, please try to place yourself in my situation. I had just been set free after months and months of torture and deprivation, during which I didn't know whether I would be freed or whether I would even survive. Upon my release from those circumstances, I was filled with joy and appreciation for everything. And during that period of emotional release, I learned that my treatment by this country—which I had assumed to be a mistake, an aberration—I learned that it was in fact part and parcel of this country's new vision of itself. It was in the midst of the feelings engendered by those two extremely opposite emotional states that I picked up *Milestones.*

Before reading Sayyid Qutb's actual words, I read a brief summary of his life. He was born in 1906 in Egypt, which was ruled at that time by the British. By the time Qutb was ten he had memorized the entire Koran. In spite of his early religious fervor, he attended a secular university and became an inspector of schools. He wrote poetry and short stories and even a novel. His life seemed to be following a secular trajectory until 1948 when he spent two and a half years in the United States studying education.

The place sickened him. He felt that the women displayed their sexuality with abandon. Even in churches, men and women were thrown in together and there was always a hint of sexuality in the air. And the racism was rampant, and not only against African Americans, but against Arabs and everyone not of northern European ancestry. But the worst thing about the place was the unbridled materialism, the way that capitalism separated people from their dignity. America provided Qutb with an understanding of life in the absence of Allah, of *Jahiliyyah*, ignorance of the Divine Law. Upon his return to Egypt, he completely immersed himself in the fundamentalist Muslim cause.

He joined the Muslim Brotherhood and began writing on their behalf. There had been division among the group's adherents—those who advocated a gradual change in Egypt versus those who advocated violent transformation of Egypt into an Islamic state. Qutb sided with the latter group. His writings gathered considerable attention and in 1953 Nasser's regime rounded up and imprisoned Qutb along with some other members of the Muslim Brotherhood.

During his first three years in prison, he had been subjected to torture techniques very similar to those that I had endured. As I read about this, I wondered if he had been in my same prison. Had he been in the dark wing? In my cell? Had he lain on the waterboard on which I had lain? Had he screamed out in agony? Had he been braver than I? Had he refused to bend during those three years? I knew I couldn't have made it three years, and I marveled that he had.

He remained incarcerated for seven more years, during which he wrote *In the Shade of the Koran*, a thirty-volume commentary on the Koran, as well as *Milestones*, primarily a political work advocating *jihad* on a global scale. Though he was critical of the West, he was far more critical of countries such as Egypt and Saudi Arabia, countries in which a majority of the citizens were Muslims, but which had not adopted *Sharia*, the religious laws.

In 1964, Qutb was released from prison. But a few months later when the Muslim Brotherhood made an attempt on Nasser's life, Qutb was once again arrested and in 1966 he was hanged. This, of course, made him a martyr for fundamentalism. His younger brother Muhammad Qutb took up the cause. He moved to Saudi Arabia and published Sayyid's books and became a professor of Islamic Studies, exerting a major influence on Osama bin Laden and other high-ranking members of al-Qaeda.

I was fascinated by Qutb's dedication to his cause. But I suspect I would not have continued reading had it not been for my promise to Bassam.

I had expected a mad man in both senses. Right from the start, I was surprised not only at the logical way he proceeded, but by the absence of anger. He begins by speaking about how the world is on a precipice, not only because of nuclear proliferation, but because the West, clearly the world's leader, lacks true values. As a result of these missing values, he continues, the world is in need of new leadership. The new leadership, he suggests, should come from Islam because Islam offers a connection to Allah through His communications to mankind in the Koran, and Allah is the source of all values.

Qutb goes on to say that one need only look around to see that modern life has been completely corrupted by *Jahiliyyah*. It is this ignorance of the Divine Law that has allowed Man to assume the role of God on earth. Man has become the ruler of other men. Qutb claimed that we see this not only in capitalism but in communism as well. In both systems we see the tendency to steal the dignity of man that God gave to every one of his human creations. Under a nation ruled by *Sharia*, no one would worship any one but Allah. Only under *Sharia* is each individual free from servitude to other men. Only under *Sharia* does each individual worship God alone.

Sharia is not something that can be replicated, according to Qutb, because it is a system that was created by God. But currently, no one can appreciate it because there is no nation in which Islam is present in its purest form. For that reason, the first step must be to bring about an Islamic revival in a particular Muslim country. After that, it will be apparent to everyone how beautiful such a nation could be. This will be the first step by which Islam will gain world leadership.

I had no sense as I read of being changed by what I was reading. Qutb struck me as over-stating his case. But I had to admit that he helped me to make sense of the new, post-9/11 America and of my experience in Egypt. Only in a world ruled by *Jahiliyyah* would it be possible to treat a human being as I had been treated.

Chapter 26

I went to a coffee shop that evening and took an early dinner. There was a newspaper lying around in which I found some classified ads for apartments. I copied several phone numbers onto a paper placemat. The next morning I found it in my pocket as I was reaching for money to pay for my breakfast. After that, I made some calls from a nearby phone booth.

Most of the apartments were listed with agencies. I'd call and they'd tell me that the particular apartment I was inquiring about had just been rented. They'd go on to say that another one had just opened up in the same building, albeit, it was slightly more expensive.

That afternoon, I looked at a two bedroom that was going for two thousand dollars a month. It was nice, but it didn't have a doorman. It was near the fish market and about five hundred dollars more than it should have been. But it was easy to get around from there, and the price included a parking spot.

With my rental agreement in hand, I was able to get a cell phone. The irony was, now that I had an apartment, I no longer needed a cell phone. After all, whom do the dead have to call, and who calls the dead? Just the same—I felt better having it. It made me feel like a member of society.

That evening, while my phone was still charging, it rang. I wondered who it could be. I picked it up and cautiously asked, "Hello?"

"Hello," a woman said back. "Are you there yet?"

"Where?" I said. I was overcome with panic and I didn't know why.

She sucked her teeth and in a tone of exasperation she

said, "The store."

"I think you have the wrong number," I said.

"Oh," she said. "You aren't Steve?"

"No," I said.

"Well, who are you then?"

"Yusuf." Even as I said it, I saw my mistake, but I obviously couldn't add, "Ah, I mean Muhammad."

"Oh, dear. Okay, then. Sorry. Good bye."

This was the first of only two calls I would receive on that phone.

* * *

I'd been back in Seattle for two weeks and I had been slowly working my way through *Milestones*. Though I had spent hours with the book, and it was a mere 150 pages, I was still only two thirds of the way through it. I had been taking notes and rereading passages from the Koran. I'd even gone out and purchased the first two volumes of *In the Shade of the Koran*. Slowly I had begun to realize that Qutb's way of interpreting the Koran was viable. This not only surprised me, but scared me as well.

Before reading him, as I said, I had expected an angry diatribe. Accordingly, I'd expected that his message would be easy to refute. What I found instead was a man whose dedication to the cause of Islam was far stronger than any other modern writer I'd encountered. In terms of his undaunted and pure faith, it was like listening to an Islamic scholar from the 12th or 13th century who had found his way into the 20th century.

It was at about that time that I decided to look up Jamal. A couple of times I walked past the taxi stand that he frequented and I finally saw him.

"Where have you been?" he asked me. "I've looked all over for you."

I laughed. "It's a government secret," I said.

He looked puzzled.

"All I can tell you," I said, "is be careful. Don't talk politics to anyone you don't know really well. Everything has changed."

"I know everything has changed," he said. "But what are you saying?"

"I'm saying be careful. You cannot imagine how screwed up everything is. *Jahiliyyah* is not just an idea."

"I know that. I tell people that every day."

"But unless you have been taken away and tortured, you will never know just how true it is," I said.

"What are you saying?"

"I can't tell you the specifics," I said. "I signed a paper saying I wouldn't."

"Why'd you do that?"

"Because I wanted my life back."

He just stood there leaned against his cab looking at me.

"I've heard rumors," he said, "about them taking people to other countries and torturing them. Is that what you're saying?"

"It is."

He looked skeptical. He pushed himself away from his cab and straightened up. "You know," he said, and as he said it, he opened the door of his cab, "I thought I trusted you."

"You *should* trust me, Jamal. I'm not making this stuff up."

He said the next sentence in English: "Something smells fishy." In Arabic, he then said, "You were not even radical. And now you're talking about *Jahiliyyah*?" Back to English: "I don't buy it."

With that, the only person in this country who came close to qualifying as my friend, got into his cab and drove off. After that, I never saw him again.

Chapter 27

During my first week in Seattle, I spent a lot of time looking out the window of my fourth floor apartment at the Sound. My living room faced west and it gave me a great view of the water. Everything had fallen into place and I had what I wanted. Despite this, I couldn't say I felt happy, though I did feel relieved. I was free of a painful marriage, free of my Ph.D. program, free of concerns about the judgment of my siblings. In essence, I was free of all responsibilities of the living.

Already I had the feeling, just as I'd predicted, that there was no turning back. At this point, I couldn't imagine calling Ruth and telling her I was fine. Added to the pain of losing me, would be the hurt that I'd deserted her, that I'd been willing to cause her such pain. I'd chosen my path and now I had to follow it.

I kept thinking about how I wanted to proceed. I thought about just going out and leasing a space and setting up my bookstore. The problem was I didn't know Seattle, and it was possible that I would make a costly mistake. I decided I should get to know a few people first, not only because I wanted friends, but through them I could learn the way things worked in this city.

One person I considered calling was Jamal. In the end I didn't because he had an edge I didn't feel comfortable with and I worried that his friends would be as strident as he. I guess when I'm honest, I have to admit that I was just being practical at this point. It was already clear that Arabs would be going through a difficult time. I didn't need to make matters worse by hanging out with people who were going to make being Arab even more difficult. That was the state of mind I was in at the time.

But just the same, I thought that I would call him as a last resort. Another option I considered was getting a job as a way to make friends. Or maybe I could take some classes at the University of Washington. It was within walking distance from my apartment and they had all sorts of courses. A course in business would probably be a smart move, since I had no idea how to run a business and I was planning to start one.

That first week passed slowly. I found a diner I liked near the fish market and after that I ate breakfast and lunch there nearly every day. I'd been eating dinner at various spots in the area. One evening as I was returning to my apartment I passed an ice-cream stand that I'd seen mentioned in a travel brochure as having dozens of strange-flavored ice creams. I passed it then changed my mind and turned back.

About forty feet behind me I saw the man I'd seen on the plane. He didn't seem to see me. He was looking at something across the street. My heart was pounding as if I'd just realized a murderer was on my tail. There was no way this guy could just happen to be walking down the street behind me after sitting on the same plane as me, after walking through Washington Square Park when I was in it, after walking behind me in Midtown Manhattan. And yet, here he came, apparently unaware that I even existed.

I considered going up to him and asking him for an explanation. But it made no sense to me that anyone would want to follow me. I'd never drawn any legal attention to myself in my entire life. I'd had maybe three traffic tickets. Otherwise, the law and I had been strangers. And I'd never been active in politics of any sort. I'd considered philosophy far more important than politics. Not only that, the philosopher I concerned myself with was a moderate from the 12th Century. Politically, I was a danger to no one.

I wondered if it could be someone from the insurance

company—maybe a detective had been assigned to see if I was truly dead. But that couldn't be. Just a few days before when I'd broken into my former home to get my safe deposit box key, it hadn't looked as if Ruth had even begun to look at my insurance policies. Moreover, even if she'd turned in the claims on 9/11, there's no way they would have been processed yet. And even if by some miracle they had been, there's no way that the claims guys would have already been able to determine that I was alive and figure out where I was. It was ridiculous.

But what other reason would anyone have to follow me? Could it be that Ruth was having me followed? I doubted it. What reason would she have to suspect I was alive? In the end, I assumed the coincidence of running into this guy so many times was some sort of statistical fluke.

Just the same—I took my eyes off him before we passed each other. In the off chance that he was actually following me, I didn't want him to know I knew. I'd act like I hadn't noticed him, and then I'd have a better chance of figuring out what was going on.

Even though I occasionally worried about being followed, and though I'd had no luck finding a good spot for a bookstore, coming to Seattle had helped me rid myself of some of the sense of emptiness and dread that I'd felt in New York following 9/11. I still missed Ruth, but I didn't feel crippled by it.

As I was walking down Pike Street one day, I passed a taxi stand near a hotel and saw Jamal standing there smoking a cigarette and talking to another driver. "Muhammad," he called out merrily when he saw me, as if we were old friends. He introduced me to the other driver whose name was Faruq and the three of us spoke about life in Seattle. I told them that I was considering setting up a Muslim bookstore in the downtown area, and asked them if they had a sense of a good location.

Both of them thought my best bet would be to find a place near the University of Washington, up around Campus Parkway. They told me the school boasted a fairly large number of Muslim students as well as programs in both Middle Eastern Languages and Islamic Studies.

At that moment I saw the problem with my dream of a Muslim bookstore. Even though I didn't think I knew anyone in Seattle, there was a good chance that someone I had studied with had landed a job out here or soon would. If I were to start a bookstore that focused on Islam, it would be like a filter for people I knew. Eventually someone would come by the store and recognize me. At that point I decided that I would wait a while and see how things went.

The three of us spoke for half an hour or so. Faruq kept bringing the conversation around to politics, made statements that sounded fairly radical, but Jamal kept quiet. The third time this happened, Jamal asked me where I was going. I told him that I was on my way home. He said, "Come, I'll give you a ride. It's on me."

He had me sit in front with him and told me that it was good that I hadn't bitten for Faruq's "political bullshit"—that phrase he spoke in English. According to Jamal, Faruq was an FBI informant. When I asked him how he knew, he said he knew because of the way Faruq always wanted to talk politics and how he was always encouraging Jamal to act on his beliefs; meanwhile, Faruq never acted on his. Not only that, one time Faruq recommended that Jamal join a group that Jamal knew for a fact contained an informant.

I had my doubts and decided Jamal was being paranoid. For that reason I didn't invite him up to my apartment though he made several hints that he wanted to come up. Then, as I was exiting his cab, he suggested that we grab an early dinner together. In the end, I said okay, mostly because I hadn't eaten meat in a while and he claimed to know of a great *halal* restaurant.

I closed the door and Jamal drove off and told me he'd show me the only good Arab restaurant in Seattle. After that he said that the only good Arab restaurant in Seattle was not in Seattle, but in Renton.

As we drove, he went on about how Faruq could not be trusted and how since 9/11 it was becoming clear that the

Arab community had been inundated with informants all along, but that now it was obvious. These guys were so desperate to get information they weren't showing any sort of caution. I started to tell him about my experience of running into the man who'd been on the plane with me.

"Yeah," I said. "I saw this man…" and as I said those words, I had this very strong feeling that I should keep that information to myself, that I didn't know whether I could trust Jamal.

I paused, unclear how to continue.

"You saw this man?" he said.

"Yeah," I said. "I saw this Arab man—from his accent I'd say he's Syrian—and he walked up to me and started talking to me and…I don't know. I guess he was talking about 9/11. I just didn't trust him, that's all, so I told him in English I didn't speak Arabic, and I walked away."

"Good instincts," said Jamal. "Trust your instincts. That's why we have them and we have to trust them, especially during times like these."

After that, we got off politics. He told me about his family, how he'd come here without them and how it had taken him five years before they could finally join him. He thanked Allah for His wisdom and mercy and said that during the time he was away from his wife, she had matured and was now ready to take her place as his wife without complaint.

We arrived at the restaurant and ate. Something seemed to be bothering him as we waited for our food to arrive. But when I asked him about it, he said he was simply tired. Maybe it was true. I never did figure out what was going on with him. I simply knew I didn't completely trust him. It could be that he didn't trust me.

I hadn't had Arab food since my father's death, and hadn't had such good Arab food since my mother's death. I decided that I would come back here once a week at the very least. We started with *mezze* and then I moved on to lamb and rice. They included a generous vat of garlic paste that I spread over the lamb.

During the meal Jamal "came back" when I began speaking about how much I liked this restaurant. After that he continued speaking about his family and neither of us mentioned politics again.

As we rode home, I asked him if I could smoke one of his cigarettes. He'd been smoking non-stop since we'd left the restaurant and smoking seemed the only way to defend myself. Before I got out of the car, I asked him if I could have just one more. He said I could and he shut off his engine and got out with me and we stood together smoking.

Now he asked me about my family. I told him again that I was separated from my wife, that we had no children, and that I had come here to Seattle to get away from her. I also mentioned that my parents were both dead. I was fairly certain that he remembered these details from our first conversation, that he was testing me to see if my story had changed.

He asked where my wife was from and again, I felt a kind of danger in telling him too much. I said, "I would rather not speak about her if it's all the same to you."

"I understand," he said. "My brother has also separated from his wife, and he too prefers not to speak of her."

Before he got back into his cab, I shook his hand and he hugged me. I wasn't sure how I felt about hugging him, but I went along with it and he got into his car and drove off. I walked toward the door of my building, but while reaching for my key, I had an urge to go to a nearby store and buy a bottle of water. I took a bottle from the cooler and as I stood at the counter preparing to pay, the cashier asked if there was anything else. I surprised myself by asking for a pack of the cigarettes I had formerly smoked.

Though I'd smoked the cigarettes of friends from time to time over the years, this was the first time I'd bought my own cigarettes since I was an undergraduate in college. I was mildly worried as I placed the pack into my pocket. I felt a bit like a liar. I wanted to confess to the cashier that I wasn't really a smoker. But I could see from the boredom in her eyes that she didn't care whether I killed myself or not.

When I got out on the street, I removed the wrapper from the cigarettes and lit one. As the smoke filled my lungs, the sting felt strangely reassuring to me and I held it there for several seconds. All the way back to my apartment, I marveled at how strange it felt to be smoking and I wondered that at thirty-one I would return to such a stupid habit.

The next morning, I saw the man again. He was in the diner I'd been eating breakfast in, sitting in the booth in which I usually sat. What was I to think? How could I ignore such a thing? I knew nothing about probability theory, but it seemed to me that this was a near impossibility. My understanding of probability became, the less likely it is that he would just sit in my seat, the more I have to ignore the fact that he is doing so. "They're trying to make me afraid," I said to myself. And "I can't let them know they've succeeded."

The next question, of course, was "Who are they?" It made no sense to me. Once again I tried on the insurance scenario. It seemed unlikely. The most likely explanation was that I had just got through changing my name and my social security number: maybe I had stumbled into the wrong place at the wrong time. Maybe the Feds had been watching the passport office I had entered because they suspected that these guys were selling fake passports and social security numbers. Maybe they were following me because I had changed my identity.

The reason I tended to discount my various theories was that this guy was not paying any attention to me at all. He sat with his back to the entrance reading the newspaper as though there was nothing else on earth that even mildly interested him. I sat at the counter and I kept shifting back and forth between thinking he was following me to realizing that he wasn't even looking my way. Not only that, he'd been there first. Who was following whom?

I even left the restaurant for a bit and stood out on the sidewalk away from his view smoking a cigarette. I wanted to see if he would follow me outside. But he didn't. When I went back inside he was still reading the paper with his back to me. It would seem that he had no sense that I even existed.

Later that afternoon I wandered down past the fish market and over to the Steinbrueck Park where I sat on a bench and watched boats move out into the Sound. At one point I looked up, and there, standing dead ahead of me by the railing and looking toward Mt. Ranier was the man in question. Once again he seemed to have no clue that I was there or that I was watching him. I looked around to see if I was being watched by anyone else, but as far as I could tell, no one was paying any attention to me. I got up and walked back up toward my apartment, and on the way I passed the taxi stand where I'd seen Jamal waiting a couple of times.

I rapped on his window and he got out and offered me a cigarette. Rather than admit that I'd bought a pack of my own, I accepted his offer. We stood smoking together and he said, "I've been thinking a lot about what you said about the man approaching you and speaking to you in Arabic. I'm very impressed with your instincts. Very impressed."

At that moment it seemed as if I was being pulled in a couple of different directions. Jamal might be connected to this guy who was following me and if I admitted seeing him or being affected by him, they'd know they were making me nervous. On the other hand, if Jamal was connected to this guy and I didn't admit that I was being followed, they'd assume I was keeping information from Jamal. Because by now it would certainly be obvious that I was being followed. I decided the second assumption made sense. If Jamal was working with this guy, I wanted them to think I trusted Jamal. If they didn't think that, they would find some other way to get to me and I might not recognize what was up. Not only that, there was a chance that Jamal was not one of them and that he could shed some light on the situation.

"Well, there's something I've been meaning to tell you," I said. "I just wanted to see if I trusted you first. I saw a man a couple of times in New York—in fact, he seemed to be following me. Several times, I saw him. Then he was on the plane I was on as I flew out here. And since I've been out here in Seattle, I've seen him at least four times. It would seem impossible that I'd just run into someone that many times just by coincidence. It seems to me that he must be following me, but he sure doesn't act like it."

"What do you mean, he doesn't act like it?"

"Well, every time I spot him, he's never looking at me," I said.

"That just means he's good at his job."

"Yeah, you might be right."

Jamal was watching me closely. "Are you afraid of this man?"

"No. I just think it's strange," I said. "Why would he be following me? It couldn't be the law. I've done nothing wrong. And I can't imagine who else it could be. I feel like I must be imagining all of this."

"Remember who you're dealing with. They consider us all wrong. We're Arabs. We're Muslims. And for most Americans, each of those is a crime in itself. That's what you have to keep in mind. So you're not afraid of this man? You don't fear that he might be intending to kill you?"

"No. Well, to tell you the truth, that hadn't occurred to me. Why would he want to kill me?"

"Why would he want to follow you?"

"I don't know," I said. "None of it makes sense."

As we left each other, I was uncertain where he stood. My sense was that he was incorruptible and that he couldn't be bought, but I had no idea if I could trust that sense.

That evening as I sat in a diner eating, I decided that I *could* rely on Jamal. This is why: a very attractive, tall, blond woman entered the restaurant just after I did. The place was not full, but it was busy. I was seated by myself at a table for two. There were other empty tables, but the woman came and asked if she could sit opposite me at my table. She said she didn't want to take up an entire table by herself.

I told her she was welcome to sit. I had been reading the newspaper, waiting for my meal when she approached me. I now folded the paper as well as my hands. I felt a little shy and I remember looking down at the table between us, wondering whether to talk to her, or whether she wanted to keep her distance. A few seconds later she asked me where I was from.

"New York," I told her.

"New York, ha? What brings you out here," she asked.

"I've decided to move out here," I said.

"Great. And why's that?"

"Long story," I said. "How about you? Are you from around here?"

"I'm from Philadelphia," she said.

"So what brings you to out here?" I asked.

"I'm actually moving out here as well," she said.

That's when I decided that Jamal was okay. If Jamal had been with them, they'd have had no reason to bring this woman into the picture, and I did feel that she was part of them. Of course, I didn't know for sure, but that's what my gut told me. Her story sounded too coincidental to be true.

After that, my meal came and I ate in near silence. I answered her questions, but coolly. And I sought to make as much distance as possible. As I left, I said to her, "Nice try."

She looked predictably surprised, and for all I know, she was. I only know that at the time I felt she knew what I was talking about.

That night I didn't sleep very well. I kept wondering why I was being followed and who it was who was following me. And then I'd wonder if I was even being followed at all. I would wake up and my heart would be pounding and I had so much adrenaline flowing through me that it felt as if I'd been injected with speed. My stomach was entirely twisted and I got up twice with diarrhea.

* * *

As I finished reading *Milestones*, I felt like a stranger to myself—it was the degree to which I felt tempted by Qutb's call to action. How could this be? I had always believed that *jihad*—and I'm referring here to "lesser *jihad*," or war against an external enemy—was only to be undertaken as a defensive measure. How was it possible that Qutb had shaken that belief in me? You've got to realize that my view of *jihad* had been part of my core beliefs. It's the view I was raised with. In fact, a good deal of my attraction to Averroes concerned his commitment to that ideal.

What I was in fact beginning to realize was that Qutb did not advocate *jihad* as an offensive practice. It only sounded that way until you understood what he was getting at. He actually had a rather sophisticated understanding of *jihad* as a series of steps by which Allah guided Muhammad (p.b.u.h.) in the Koran. A simpler way of thinking of it would be to say that Qutb opened up the notion of "defending Islam." For him, anything that stood in the way of the spread of Islam was an offense, not only to Islam, but also to each individual who was being deprived of the opportunity to be brought into Union with God. Accordingly, any person or nation that prevented the spread of Islam needed to be dealt with to defend Islam's right to exist. The more I thought about it, the more I could see what he was getting at.

No doubt as a reaction to all of that, I was aware of a certain restlessness that was setting in. I had no idea that I wanted to return to New York until I saw myself get on the internet and schedule a flight.

I took a cab into midtown to the Douglass, the hotel in the west fifties where I had stayed after 9/11. Again I wasn't able to get the same room I'd previously stayed in, but I got one in the same line, five floors lower. Once again I couldn't get over the feelings of sameness and difference—mostly difference.

After an evening nap, I walked down to West Fourteenth Street and got on the L Train for Williamsburg. I got off at Bedford Avenue at the very back of the train so that I actually came above ground on Driggs Avenue. I did this to avoid being seen by Frank, the homeless man. I walked down Driggs to North Fifth Street where I turned right and walked past Bedford and over a bit beyond Berry Street where I stood outside the house that, before my death, had belonged to Ruth and me and presumably still did belong to her. The lights were on in our bedroom and the shades were drawn. I didn't know what I was going to do. Was I going to go over to the door and knock? Or was I going to turn and leave?

I pulled my cell phone from my pocket and dialed our

number.

"Hello." It was Ruth. She sounded older.

I didn't say anything.

"Hello," she said again. I could hear a different tone in her voice, a tone that sounded harder than I remembered her.

One more time she said it, and after pausing she said, "I'm sorry. We have a bad connection." At that she hung up.

I waited out there a few more seconds before I turned and walked toward the Bedford Avenue stop. On the way my phone rang. I nearly answered. But first I looked to see who it was. It was Ruth. Apparently, in the meanwhile she'd gotten caller i.d. Only a small part of me was disappointed that I'd stuck with the default message that had come with the phone. She wouldn't be able to identify me by my message.

I silenced the phone and continued to the subway.

The next day I had my number changed. There was no point in turning back. Too much had changed. I was a different man now. She was a different woman. We lived in a different country. Turning back would solve nothing. And besides—there was work to be done.

Jason Trask lives in Western Maine in the foothills of the White Mountains. He teaches in an alternative education program, working with high school students who have been traumatized by seeing through the system. He is married and has three sons. *I'm Not Muhammad* is his first novel.

2118